One Hell of a Victim

Also by Harry Senthill

Dying For Justice

ONE HELL OF A VICTIM

A CULT THRILLER

Harry Senthill

QUODLIBET ROCK

Published 2018 by Quodlibet Rock

e-mail: quodrock@gmail.com

ISBN 978-1-9997097-5-4 (hardback)
ISBN 978-1-9997097-6-1 (paperback)
ISBN 978-1-9997097-7-8 (e-book)

CONTENTS

PROLOGUE

Most people remember Colwick Hall, as well they should. It was the scene of the worst atrocity committed in Britain in the twentieth century. Fewer remember the exact date. It's not a date I personally will ever forget: June 29th, 1998. And why do I remember that date? It's because I was, shall we say, 'involved'.

My home is on Scotsmans Moor, eight miles from Colwick Hall. The moor is a popular destination for holidaymakers, especially walkers enjoying the scenery. If you're ever one of them, there's a good chance you will see me — for a few years yet anyway — somewhere in the distance. Even if you don't, I will almost certainly see you. I like to keep a close eye on the moor; it's where I was born, where I grew up, where I lived and worked, and eventually where I'll die. So that shambling old gentleman in the distance, with his camouflage clothing, his limp, and the binoculars hanging on a strap round his neck: that'll be me.

Although walkers and hiking parties are welcome on my land, I prefer to avoid them. I'm not a naturally sociable person. But I'm not rude either, so an exchanged wave from a distance or a close-up hello are fine by me. Nor do I object when people stop me to ask the way to Lowhope Crag, which is our local beauty spot with magnificent views across the surrounding countryside. But when they ask about Colwick Hall, yes, I'll provide directions, but without a smile on my face. Mostly these people — ghouls in my opinion — sense that further questioning is a bad idea, but the occasional one, unable to read body language, or simply plain intrepid, asks if I knew the Mad Minister (as he came to be known). At that, I resort to a half-truth and say I only knew him by sight. Then comes the question I hate more than anything else: did I also know George Radman, the murderer? No more half-truths, just a plain old-fashioned lie: no, I never met the man. And then, rude or not, I walk away.

You may gather I'm touchy about the subject of Colwick Hall, the Mad Minister and George Radman. There has been a lot of speculative nonsense written about the dreadful events of that day in 1998 when seventy-five residents of Colwick Hall and their young children met their deaths, and I'm about the only person still living who knows what really happened. But I've always kept my mouth shut. I genuinely don't care what people think. As long as they leave me alone, let them believe what they like.

All that changed in March this year. My dear wife developed a bad cold in February which quickly went down on her chest, and then became pneumonia, and then a job for the undertaker. Her death left me bereft.

But it turned out my wife still had one last role to play in my life. Shortly after the funeral our solicitor called round and handed me a letter. Unknown to me, my wife had written it some years before. It began as expected, saying that since I was reading it, I must have outlived her. She said things that brought more than a few tears to my eyes, but the part of relevance here was that she had intended, if she became a widow, to tell my story — to 'set the record straight' as she put it. And she appealed to me, in her stead, to do it myself.

Initially I dismissed the idea outright. But I mentioned the possibility to my cousin Peter and he changed my mind. He said it would give me something to keep me occupied while I was coming to terms with my bereavement. And he thought I owed it, if not to myself, then to the Radman family. It was that last consideration which decided me.

The problem is, I'm not a writer. However, Peter had an answer for that. His son Thomas knows about the internet (the internet is a complete mystery to me), and Thomas came up with Harry Senthill, an author who would ghost-write the book. I duly met Mr Senthill, liked him, and the agreement was signed.

Now, six months later, the tale is ready to be told. As the words are mostly Mr Senthill's I insisted the book be published under his name rather than mine. Nevertheless, though the words may be his, the story is entirely my own.

You may not yet have guessed who I am. So I'll tell you before we go any further.

I am George Radman.

The murderer.

Paradise Lost

May 11 - May 12, 1998

1

I'm a heavy sleeper — the sort who doesn't get woken up even by thunderstorms — but I woke up that night. Something was wrong; I just didn't know what.

I quickly made out the sound of movement downstairs. My first thought was it must be Peter, the only person familiar enough with me to enter my house without knocking. But it couldn't be him. Firstly he'd have called out; and secondly, judging by how dark it was, it must have been close to midnight. He wouldn't be out on the moor at that time of night. So I moved on to considering the possibility it was a hiker who'd got lost and was seeking shelter.

And then I heard voices; the sound of things being moved; and footsteps on the stairs.

I got out of bed and started to pull on a pair of underpants. They were up to my knees when the bedroom door opened and I was caught in the beam of a torch.

"Well, what have we here?" the man said. Deep, resonant, authoritative voice, American accent.

I wasn't inclined to answer him. Not verbally. Anyone who enters my house in the middle of the night without an invitation or a very good reason deserves an altogether more physical response — a seriously painful one. I finished pulling up my underpants and said: "Who the hell are you?"

The man must have detected belligerence in my stance, for the torch in his left hand shifted slightly so as to illuminate the revolver in his right. That gave me pause to reconsider.

The thing is, this is England — Northumberland to be precise. Two years previously, a gunman in Scotland had opened fire on a class of young children and their teacher. In the shocked aftermath of this appalling crime, the government had called in all handguns throughout Great Britain. No private citizen could possess a handgun any more on pain of lengthy imprisonment. So what, therefore, was I to make of this ostentatiously displayed piece of hardware? Probably it was a replica. Probably. Unfortunately there was only one way to find out and I hesitated to avail myself of it. I wasn't about to gamble with my life.

A second person entered the bedroom. I squinted against the torch beam but could make out nothing behind it. I was literally being blinded by the light.

"Doesn't seem to be anyone here," this second person reported. Another American accent.

"Where's your visitor?" the deep voice with the revolver asked me.

I didn't respond. I hadn't the faintest idea what he was talking about.

"Somebody paid you a call, maybe four, five minutes back. Where's he hiding?"

I still said nothing.

"Mister, you got some kind of hearing problem? This in my hand ain't a water pistol; it's a forty-five. Have you any idea what a slug that size would do to your foot?"

He angled the gun down slightly.

More outraged than scared as yet, I replied in the

manner I usually reserve for idiots. "Look," I said, "this house is three miles from the nearest road. You may have noticed the front door wasn't locked. That's because I have nothing worth stealing. Nobody has been stupid enough to break in here in living memory. I really can't imagine what you think you're doing. And as for visitors, on the rare occasions I receive one of those they invariably call during the daytime, not at an hour when any normal person is asleep. So why don't you go away and be a nuisance somewhere else."

There was a short silence while he considered the information.

"The Great Serpent has seized control of your tongue," he announced at length. "Your mouth pours forth slanders and insolence. But you shall not prevail. I have fought all my life for Almighty God, and He strengthens my arm with the shield of his grace."

He stopped abruptly as if he'd become aware he was getting off the point. "Kneel," he resumed ominously, "facing the bed, with your hands behind your head."

I was beginning to feel afraid. This intruder appeared to be mentally unbalanced. How else could you regard a potentially homicidal Bible-bashing burglar? What kind of split personality...?

"Mister," he said, swiftly interrupting my train of thought, "you've definitely got a problem with your ears. Either you kneel out of choice or because you've nothing below your knees left to stand on."

Split personality or not, he just couldn't be that good at maintaining a pretence; the gun had to be real. I knelt as instructed.

"I'll keep him covered," Deep Voice informed his accomplice. "Search the room."

"Light switches?" asked the other man.

"Where are the light switches?" Deep Voice said to me.

"There aren't any lights," I answered. "The house hasn't got electricity."

"Use his flashlight," said Deep Voice, referring to the torch I keep by the bed.

Intruder number two picked it up and began directing it around the room: under the bed, in the cupboard, on top of the wardrobe — what size of visitor was I supposed to have had who could fit into the six inch gap between wardrobe and ceiling? Then he pulled off the bedclothes, checked under the mattress, and finally tipped onto the floor the contents of the two drawers from the small chest where I keep various personal items.

"Nothing here," said intruder number two, stating the obvious.

"God tells me this is where we should be looking," said Deep Voice. "Go help the boy downstairs. And be thorough."

"God is mighty displeased with you," said Deep Voice to me when we were alone again.

Under Deep Voice's scrutiny, real fear had taken hold of me. And here, with hindsight, I must confess to a failing. It was such a ridiculous notion anyone would want to burgle my house I'd not made any preparations for the eventuality. None. I had no means of summoning help or raising the alarm. I didn't even have anything handy which could be used in self-defence. There was nothing in my bedroom with weapon potential. The firearms — my certainly real firearms — I realized with a surge in my pulse rate, were downstairs.

Presently, another intruder entered my bedroom: the 'boy' presumably.

"Look what I've found," he said to Deep Voice. This third voice was young, English, but not local: someone from down south at a guess.

I turned my head to see what he was referring to. Despite the light in my eyes I could just make out my shotgun.

"That ain't what we're after," said Deep Voice.

"No, but that's not here, so I thought we could add this to the collection instead. And his rifle too."

"God commands me through the words of the young," said Deep Voice. "You find any shells for this?"

"Yep."

"Go tell Jed to load it and bring it back here."

"The rifle too?"

"No. You keep that for the collection. And then go search the garage and the jeep."

The boy went off to obey the orders he'd been given, and a minute or two later the other American re-entered the bedroom with my shotgun — presumably now loaded.

"I figure we could have made a mistake," he suggested.

"I had him in the night-scope, clear as day, Jed. When he dropped out of sight he was heading this way. And this is the only place for miles around. Nowhere else he could have gone."

"Well, he's not here now, that's for sure."

"The wrath of God is truly upon us. We must offer up a sacrifice."

"What? This guy?" said Jed, apparently meaning me.

"I don't see anyone else. Unless you're planning to volunteer."

"Ah, come on. Think of the heat."

"God must be appeased. And He tells me if I use this shotgun the cops will put it down to suicide. There'll be no heat."

"What about the mess we've made everywhere?"

"So he freaked out. Happens all the time."

"It strikes me we'd be pushing our luck."

"Have faith, Jed," said Deep Voice. "Hey, you with your hands behind your head. Say your prayers."

Was I understanding this right? If I'd interpreted the weird conversation correctly, Deep Voice was about to blast me with my own shotgun. For no reason.

In that case there was nothing left to lose. I shifted my weight from my knees back towards my toes as a first step to launching an attack. Not that I thought I had any chance of surviving.

"One thing before you go ahead, boss," I heard Jed remark. "God ain't gonna be much appeased by him. He ain't been cleaned."

"Cleaned?" exclaimed Deep Voice.

"It's your own rules. Unclean sacrifice ain't worth two cents on the dollar. More than likely it'll make God against us even more than He already is."

"God is not against us. This is the work of the Great Serpent."

"I humbly submit to your guiding correction. But even so...."

As the seconds ticked by, it occurred to me, not surprisingly, to wonder how I might make a self-serving contribution to this unusual theological debate. Doing that might prove less hazardous and more productive than launching an attack. Unfortunately I found it impossible to predict the effect of anything I might suggest. These people weren't burglars at all; they were lunatics.

"You clear out," said Deep Voice eventually. "Wait for me by the jeep. I'll follow momentarily."

"Are you going to...." Jed began.

"Get out of here," snapped Deep Voice.

I heard Jed going downstairs. The odds were improving. Only one adversary to contend with now. I tensed.

"Unclean sacrifice!" I heard Deep Voice mutter to himself. "Unclean sacrifice! Out of the mouth of an ignorant sinner comes forth guidance. It is the way of corrupted flesh.

"Well, mister," said Deep Voice to me rather more loudly. "No hard feelings, huh?"

I didn't answer. Just give me the chance, I thought, and I'll show you what hard feelings are.

"You should have finished your prayers by now. Time you were gathered to your people."

I turned, half rising to my feet. The shotgun — my shotgun — was pointed straight at my head. Involuntarily I closed my eyes, put my arms up to protect my face and tried to duck away. All quite futile.

I heard the bang, heard the fiend laugh, and then it felt

as though the ceiling had fallen in on me. There was a blinding pain in my head and the night became dark and silent, as before the intruders had arrived.

2

I was flat on my back on the carpet — all of me, that is, except my head, which had struck the wall. It was not at all clear to me why I wasn't dead. I waited for my brain to tell me what damage had been done, and when it couldn't detect any I disbelieved it.

I heard a couple of blasts from a shotgun somewhere outside.

Eventually I got shakily to my feet. Bits of something fell off me onto the floor. Whatever the stuff was it was in my hair too. The carpet felt gritty under foot and seemed to have acquired a number of small, sharp stones. Making sense of these discoveries was beyond me, almost as much as explaining how Deep Voice had missed me with a shotgun at a range of less than a metre.

They'd taken my torch with them, so I had to get dressed by touch. Downstairs, the living room had been ransacked, a fact I established mainly by treading on things accidentally. My gun cabinet was empty. In the hallway were strewn the contents of the cupboard beneath the stairs. The kitchen — the other ground floor room — was just as chaotic.

A strong desire to obtain a means of self-defence led me outside to the tool-shed behind the latrine. They'd left their calling card there as well, but my axe was still in its bracket on the wall. I took it down and brandished it the way one does when contemplating hacking someone to death. It made me feel better.

Thus armed, I went round to the opposite side of the building and the garage where Blue Beauty was housed. Mostly by touch I verified the old girl was not obviously damaged, and then surveyed the terrain round about.

Overhead was a full moon, but it was completely obscured by cloud, which gave a dull near-blackness to the scene. Of man-made lights there were none. My eyes could tell me nothing about the whereabouts of the three intruders. Provided they were lying low and keeping still, it was so dark they could have been within a few tens of metres of me and I'd not have spotted them.

There was no more to be done usefully before daybreak, so I re-entered the house, returned to the bedroom and re-made the bed as best I could. Snuggled down between the still-warm sheets I reached out and touched the axe which I'd placed on the floor conveniently within reach. Just you come back now, I thought. Just you come back now.

They didn't, of course. Probably they were too busy fighting the good fight against the Great Serpent.

*

I rose with the sun, as was my long-established habit during the lighter months. The first thing I noticed was the hole above my head. Deep Voice had obviously changed his mind at the last instant about 'gathering me to my people', elevating the barrel and firing straight up instead. A part of the ceiling really had fallen in on me. There were bits of plasterboard and loft insulation and shotgun pellets all over the floor.

The house was in a mess. Whatever they'd been searching for, they'd looked everywhere, not just places where a supposed visitor could have been hiding, but places so small a domestic cat would have got stuck in them. Nothing had been left where it belonged. Equally, nothing, apart from my firearms and a torch, appeared to have been stolen. It didn't make sense.

I couldn't face tidying up there and then, and also it struck me as likely the police would want everything uninterfered with, so I decided to get on with my normal daily chores, beginning with fetching the water. Typically I leave that till mid morning but on this occasion it seemed a good idea to do it straightaway. I wanted to inspect my territory in case those three maniacs were still in the vicinity or had done anything else I ought to know about.

The stream is roughly fifty metres from the house and babbles along the bottom of a twenty-metre wide and ten-metre deep V-shaped valley. I didn't go directly down to the water but turned left and followed it upstream to where a waterfall has excavated a deep bowl in the rock. The attraction of the location on this occasion was not the usual one of wanting to take an open-air bath. I had something more unsettling in mind. Because this bathing pool of mine is enclosed on three sides, and is thereby well protected from gales, woody vegetation grows around it. Various bushes, most of them prickly, have anchored themselves in the thin soil and in crevices in the steep rock faces. In consequence, the place provides cover — the only cover for miles, in fact — where someone with hostile intent might lie unnoticed at quite close quarters. I felt impelled to check out the possibility.

As I walked to my destination, axe in one hand, ten-litre can in the other, I scanned the landscape carefully. There was no sign of anyone on the open moor. Just the occasional bird flying by, and white woolly mounds dotted here and there that were my cousin Peter's sheep with their recently born lambs. In the far distance, where the forest began, I fancied I could make out a few deer: brown dots which must have been alive because they moved perceptibly if you stood still long enough and watched them. Half past five on a beautiful, mostly cloudy morning in mid May and all was well with my small part of Northumberland. Last night's events felt like they must have happened on another planet.

I entered the foliage around the bathing pool and advanced cautiously to the water, scrutinizing the area thoroughly as I went. It certainly appeared deserted. I began to wonder if my worries weren't a little excessive. Deep Voice and his accomplices were surely long gone.

Filling a can is not something that requires attention, so as gravity and hydraulics got on with the job I continued to look about me. My eyes were caught by a light-coloured plastic comb floating on the other side of the pool. It had been trapped by an eddy and was going round and round in circles. It wasn't a comb of mine.

Ordinarily I'd have attached no significance to such a thing, but this didn't feel like an ordinary morning. Having filled the can, I left it on a bit of level ground and clambered over some rocks, axe in hand, to take a closer look.

The comb was mixed up with twigs and bits of plant

matter all describing the same circles, and I permitted myself a brief self-congratulation for spotting it. Probably it had entered the pool via the waterfall, so I glanced over in that direction, not expecting to see anything noteworthy. My self-congratulation promptly took a hard knock; in a bush, partly over the water and about a metre above the surface, was a dead body. It was badly tangled up and the face was staring straight at me through a scanty vale of leaf buds.

I wasn't unduly shocked. Occasionally someone manages to die accidentally on the moor and I get called in to help with recovering the remains. It desensitizes you.

Approaching the corpse wasn't easy and I needed to use the axe to clear a path (which was a better employment for the implement than the potentially homicidal one I'd had in mind when deciding to bring it with me from the house!). I soon reached a location where I could touch the man's legs. A glance at his face revealed he was still looking at me. A body it might have been, but dead he was not.

For a few seconds we gazed blankly at each other. There was nothing for it but to go into action again with the axe, hacking at the twigs and branches until it was possible, without impaling myself on thorns, to seize his wrists and pull him into a sitting position and thence out. As I accomplished this feat, I confirmed I was in no danger from him. His hands were icy cold, as was the rest of him. He was pretty far gone.

It was impractical to retrace my steps over the rocks while carrying him, so I dragged him instead until I came to a patch of ground which was flat enough that he wouldn't be unduly uncomfortable lying on it. There I left him while I went to collect my axe and the ten-litre can. After that I explained I'd be back as quickly as possible, and set off for the house at a trot.

I'd intended to load him into Blue Beauty, my 1978 Series III short-wheelbase Land Rover — 'jeep', indeed! — but I found the two front tyres were flat. My nocturnal visitors had blasted them with shotgun pellets.

Alternative plan. I picked up a couple of spare blankets and carried them back to the man. He had revived slightly and so was able to cooperate while I got one blanket underneath him and the other on top. The underneath one I intended to use as a sort of sledge-without-runners, dragging him thereby back to the house. (I ruled out carrying him because he must have weighed at least eighty kilograms. I'm pretty strong — a few times in my past I've had to pick up a sheep and you wouldn't believe how heavy they are — but eighty kilograms was more than my own weight, and at fifty-five years old I needed to think of my back!)

So the poor man had to suffer the indignity and the discomfort of being dragged from the bathing pool over what was mostly boggy grass to the house.

Once inside, I got him into the kitchen and somehow seated him in a chair. He was soon drinking a cup of warm water heated up on the stove. That was the limit of what I could do for him and I hoped it would be enough.

While I waited for him to either revive or die I tidied up the room, thinking the police would still have the other three rooms and the hallway to examine for evidence. As soon as everything was back where it belonged I made myself some breakfast, glancing frequently at my unexpected guest.

"Thanks," he said at last. "I thought I'd had it."

A mere six words, but they reassured me a thousand times better than the axe propped up by the door. Partly that was due to my preferring it if hill-walkers don't decease on my real estate, and this fellow clearly didn't consider his own death to be imminent, and he should know. But mainly my relief arose because naturally it had occurred to me I might be playing host to one of last night's intruders. His voice was as plain proof of innocence as anything I could have asked for. Not American and not southern English. His accent conveyed the unmistakable tones of a Yorkshireman.

"I'm George Radman," I said.

He hesitated as if his name embarrassed him, introducing himself, seemingly reluctantly, as Clifford Hanworth.

"I suppose," he continued, looking even more embarrassed, "you must think I'm a bit of an idiot, getting myself stuck like that."

"That wasn't what I was thinking," I said, "though I'll admit I'm curious how you came to be in that predicament."

"I was out on the moor after dark. Talk about stupid! I got lost. I was following that stream, hoping it would lead somewhere. And didn't it just. Over a ruddy waterfall!"

"I guessed you must have fallen into that bush."

"Yes, and I think I broke my ankle on the way down. If you hadn't come along when you did...."

"Which foot?"

"The left one."

He made no objection while I carried out a first-aid examination. There was significant swelling but the joint was functional and the bones felt okay. "I'm fairly sure it's only a sprain," I informed him. "You just need to rest it for a few days."

Transiently there was panic in his eyes. "I can't stay here," he exclaimed.

I replied that I wasn't suggesting he did.

Mr Hanworth was beginning to worry me. He was about thirty years old, obviously in good health, of average build, not noticeably lacking mental capacity and.... nervous. Not only that. His clothing didn't fit with his being a hill-walker. He was wearing thin-soled city shoes, stylish, elegant even, fine for strolling to and from your car in the concrete jungle, but a waste of space on the moors. And there were the jeans; another no-no in the big wide wilderness. His zip-up well-padded jacket was the only sensible piece of attire he had on; it had almost certainly saved his life.

His lack of equipment also puzzled me. I ventured a question about where it was.

"Equipment?" he said.

"Yes. Tent, sleeping bag, maps, compass, that sort of thing. You wouldn't go out on the moors at night without those."

"I got lost," he repeated vaguely. "Look, I must have bothered you a lot already but I wonder if I could use your phone."

"You could if I had one."

"Damn," he cursed, visibly agitated. "I really do have to get away from here. Perhaps you could drive me to the nearest town. I'll see you're well recompensed."

"I don't want payment," I said, trying not to be offended. "That's not the way we do things up here. Anyway, my Land Rover has one spare wheel and two flat tyres. It's not going anywhere today."

"Christ!" he said.

I don't think the expletive was directed at me, so much as at the situation he found himself in. There was plainly more to Mr Hanworth than I could tell by sight, and it was wearing my patience rather thin. In addition, I was beginning to wonder if he was connected to what had happened last night.

"Did you notice when I first brought you in here that the kitchen had been trashed?" I asked.

He didn't answer.

"Three men forced their way in last night, searching for someone. It wouldn't have been you they were after by any chance?"

He gazed through the window at the moors and uttered not a sound.

"Two Americans and an English lad," I added by way of enlargement. "They weren't overly polite."

"They're no friends of mine," he commented eventually.

"Do you want to tell me about it?"

"No. It's not something I'm at liberty to talk about. Honestly though, Mr Radman, you'd be doing us both a favour if you got me away from here."

"You think last night's visitors might return?"

"It'd be a disaster if they did."

I could see the fear inside my mysterious guest. His hands were constantly in motion while nonetheless not actually doing anything. If it wasn't for his sprained ankle, I think he'd have bolted for the door and made a run for it.

Fear is a transmissible state of mind. I began to experience a compelling desire to look behind me or to position my back against a solid wall. That was no good at all. I decided to take a look around outside. And to do it from under cover.

I collected my binoculars and went upstairs to the bedroom. The fraught atmosphere had really got to me, because when I looked out of the front window I did so crouched down, peering over the window sill. As a vantage point it gave me a clear view towards the stream and across the hills on the far side. I was very thorough. If there was anyone out there they could only be concealed if they were at the bathing pool or in the water-cut valley. I had only recently come from those places and they'd been deserted (Clifford Hanworth excepted). It followed there was no one lurking on that side of the house.

From the back window much the same panorama presented itself: similar bare moorland hills. There were sheep scattered about but no people.

"See anything?" Hanworth called up to me.

"No."

I went out of the house in order to double-check the valley, as I hadn't looked downstream on my way to the bathing pool. But there was nothing unusual to see.

As I turned back towards the house I casually scanned the ground around the bathing pool with the binoculars. That was when I realized I'd made a mistake. Yes, I had checked the bathing pool earlier. But not the ground at the top of the waterfall, ground which was not visible from the pool area.

I didn't pause or let on in any way that I'd seen something, but returned calmly indoors.

"Somebody's up there," I reported to Hanworth. "Just above the waterfall. The bush you fell into would have been invisible from where they're positioned. The trouble is, if they've been watching since dawn, they're going to know you're here now. What do you think we should do?"

"Can you get me down to the road if I lean on you all the way?"

"No. It's three miles in the first place and, in the second, if anyone wanted to catch us, they wouldn't even have to run. With a sprained ankle you'd slow us down so much we'd be out in the open and vulnerable for at least ninety minutes."

"This is a nightmare," Hanworth said. He was a very scared man.

I, in contrast, was a very angry one. My privacy had been brutally violated in the middle of the night, and now it was possible someone was spying on me. I wasn't about to flee from my own home. Whoever that was above the waterfall, I wanted a word with him.

"You stay put," I said to Hanworth. "Keep the axe, but please don't use it unless you have to. I don't want to find dismembered bodies decorating the place when I return. The house is in enough of a mess as it is." I didn't tell him about my missing shotgun and rifle. He was twitchy enough already.

I went out of the front door and had a careful look down the track which led to the road, and also in the opposite direction towards Lowhope Crag. These were blind spots from indoors as neither of my end walls had windows. Close at hand the track was empty. Further away much of it was out of sight due to the unevenness of the terrain. A similar situation existed facing the other way, towards Lowhope. There could be unfriendly people within half a mile in either direction; it was impossible to tell.

Before going further, I immobilized Blue Beauty in order to pre-empt the possibility that my frightened guest might give in to the temptation in my absence to attempt driving the old girl on her two flat tyres. Then I walked openly to the valley and descended to its floor.

Down here I could not be seen by the supposed watcher; there was bushy vegetation between his vantage point and my position. Keeping low I made my way stealthily up to the entrance to the bathing pool. Crossing the stream by jumping from rock to rock, I tracked to the right, not entering the pool area but skirting the bushes along its border until I was out on the moor again. The lie of the ground here dipped slightly, continuing to conceal me from the watcher. Ascending to near the top of the waterfall I reached a point where there was no alternative but to come into the open. I ran.

Haste proved to be unnecessary. The watcher was looking intently at the house. I noticed he had a better pair of binoculars than mine, but they weren't being pointed in the right direction to tell him I was closing fast.

The sound of the nearby waterfall was loud enough here that it effectively masked my footsteps, enabling me to manoeuvre unheard and approach obliquely from behind. Still he didn't see me. I stopped.

It was an infernally difficult situation. The climb had calmed me down, and being away from Hanworth's paranoid atmosphere it had also eased my mind somewhat, and I began to wonder if I hadn't got this completely wrong. The watcher was sitting on a low rock, a young blond-haired man with a green scarf covering most of his face, and a black cape wrapped around him from his shoulders downward. Suppose he was wholly innocent: a birdwatcher or a naturalist, for example? Then again, I know such people can be dedicated, but at a remote place like this at six o'clock on a cold morning? Was that likely?

Innocent or not, doing nothing wasn't an option. At the least I had to question him. Before I could speak, his shoulders straightened in a meaningful sort of way. Something had caught his attention.

At first I couldn't see what. And then, there was Clifford Hanworth limping from my house towards the latrine. The young man watched through his binoculars.

Something made him look over his shoulder and he suddenly became aware of my presence. He got quickly to his feet, making me think of a child caught with his hand in a sweet jar.

"Are you looking for me?" I said. It wasn't a

particularly sensible question but I hadn't thought out in advance what to say.

"No," he said.

"Then what are you doing here?"

"Nothing."

"That's not what it looks like to me."

"All right then. I'm minding my own business. That's what *I'm* doing."

I noted his southern English accent. "Oh really? It looks to me like you're spying on my house. That's minding my business, not yours."

"So what."

"If you can't convince me you've got a good reason to be here, I'm going to escort you to the nearest police station and you can explain to them what you're doing."

"Oh, piss off, grandad."

How sure do you have to be before taking action? From his age and accent I had a fair degree of confidence in my identification of burglar number three, but a 'fair degree' didn't feel like sufficient. Consequently I must have been creating an impression of being irresolute and it was that, I think, which was emboldening him.

"Let me tell you something, sonny," I said. "You talk to me like that again and I'll teach you some manners. Now, it happens you're trespassing. This is private land. I want to know what you're here for."

"It's not private. It's National Trust."

"Wrong. It belongs to me. And there are some rules. Walkers are welcome to go where they please on my property so long as they don't disturb the peace, drop litter, upset my cousin's sheep, or invade my privacy.

You, unfortunately, are invading my privacy, which means you're breaking the rules and aren't welcome. So I'll ask you for the last time: why are you here?"

"Abraham was right. You're nothing but an agent of the devil. You'll burn in hell for what you've done."

"For crying out loud! What's your name?"

"What's yours?"

I was getting dangerously angry and he'd have been blind not to realize it. I noticed a slight movement of his right arm beneath his cape.

"I'm reporting you to the police," I informed him. "You'll have to come down to the house."

"I'd like to see you make me."

"Okay." I took a step towards him. He responded by showing me his right hand clutching a six-inch knife.

"You're making this worse, lad. Trespass is a civil offence. Carrying a knife is a criminal one." I took another step towards him.

"Keep away from me," he snarled.

I was furious now. I turned and walked away down the hill towards the vegetation, the sound of the boy's jeers in my ears.

The first bush I came to, I broke off an old dead branch and went back towards the insulting little prick. He saw me coming and took up a defensive posture. I think he expected me to at least pause. But I didn't hesitate. Just out of range of the knife, I clouted the side of his head with the branch, which snapped in two. He was still on his feet, if dazed. Knowing the branch would snap again if used side-on, I thrust the stump into his face. That felled him, splitting the skin on his cheek.

He should have surrendered then but his brain hadn't received the message and he was still clutching the knife. I towered over him and ordered him to let go of it. When he didn't, I cold-bloodedly stamped on his hand. He screamed.

I acquired the knife and put it in one of my pockets. Then, while waiting for my over-matched foe to get himself together, I examined a notepad which was lying on the ground alongside where he'd been sitting. It dispelled any lingering doubts; he'd kept a log of my movements. Everything had been noted down since my first appearance after dawn up until I'd disappeared into the valley below the bathing pool. There were also references to 'Isaac', which I took to be a code-word for Clifford Hanworth. The notepad went into another of my pockets.

The lad — he was a lad now, not a man with a knife — was sobbing and clearly in a lot of pain. I'd obviously broken his thumb, and maybe other bones in his hand. The cut on his cheek didn't look too good either. He got back on his feet and a trickle of blood ran from the cut to his chin and dripped onto his cape. I hadn't realized how badly I'd wanted a return match for last night, and now it was plain to me I was beginning to think I'd overdone it.

"Let's go down to the house," I said, not angry any more.

"I'm not going down there," he said. "My hand's broken."

"Look, I'm sorry I hurt you, but you shouldn't have threatened me with a knife. Now come with me to the house. Your hand isn't going to get fixed out here."

That seemed to make sense to him and we set off. I kept slightly behind him in case he had any more tricks up his sleeve but really that was guarding against a million-to-one possibility. All the fight was knocked out of him. As we walked, he demonstrated that fact by continuing to sob. His distress hurt me more than his insults ever had. I felt like an evil bully.

My conscience suffered another blow when we were about half way to the house; the lad stopped crying and fainted. Since he was quite a lot lighter than Hanworth, I was able to carry him over my shoulder the rest of the way.

Calling out in advance so Hanworth wouldn't let fly with the axe, I entered the house, went into the kitchen and laid the lad on the floor with his feet on a chair.

"Do you know this kid?" I asked Hanworth.

He looked at the unconscious face and said: "Christ! Remind me not to argue with you."

"He had a knife."

"Right. And he was watching this house?"

"No doubt about it."

Hanworth studied the lad more closely. "I think I recognize him."

"You *think*!"

"I've seen a lot of people recently. This boy could be one of them. The way you've altered his appearance doesn't help."

With a growing feeling my behaviour was going to have to be accounted for in a magistrate's court, I said we'd better get the lad to hospital, adding: "And then we go to the police."

"The police?" Hanworth queried.

"Yes, the police."

"I suppose you couldn't keep me out of that?"

"No, I couldn't."

"Okay, okay. As long as we don't hang around in these parts."

He was back on that line of thought. Hanworth was a man with a one-track mind.

I told the lad, who was pretending to still be unconscious, to stop faking and get up. He obeyed slowly, pointedly ignoring Hanworth (or Isaac?) as he did so.

Then the problem. With Blue Beauty out of action, I'd have to walk to the road. After that, there was a further half a mile to get to an isolated no-other-houses-in-sight inn with a public payphone alongside. I estimated it would take me nearly an hour to get to the phone and another quarter of an hour before an ambulance or a police car would arrive which I could accompany back to the house.

Hanworth was extremely unhappy about the turn of events. However, as walking was very painful to him, he agreed he had no choice but to remain where he was. To bolster his courage I gave him the lad's knife, and to stop the lad from absconding I tied the boy to a chair with a length of rope from the garage.

Then I set off at a brisk stride, glad, frankly, to get away from the two people I'd left behind. Mr Frightened and Mr Sullen. I hadn't asked for either of them and could hardly wait to get them off my property and out of my hands.

I arrived at the road quicker than I'd expected and reached the payphone within fifty minutes. I won't deny I was hurrying, trotting on the downhill sections of the route. I kept thinking of a wasps' nest I'd once disturbed accidentally. I only survived that encounter by running like hell. Perhaps that's what I should have been doing now.

As a concession to my forebodings I dialled 999 rather than called the local police station. The telephonist told me to wait where I was. Then I summoned an ambulance.

The patrol car got to me first and we drove bumpily towards my house while I explained the situation: that I had been burgled in the night, had found a mysterious fellow half dead at my bathing pool in the early morning, and had caught one of the burglars a short while later apparently keeping my property under surveillance. It struck me as I was telling the tale that it sounded rather improbable. And if that's how it struck me, how would it be striking the two police officers? Hopefully it didn't matter. The police would sort it out. That's what they're paid for.

As we pulled up at the house, I noticed my front door was ajar, which isn't how I'd left it. Only slightly perturbed I led the two constables into the hall and thence into the kitchen. The sight which confronted me literally took my breath away. I froze. One of the policemen pushed past me and went through the motions, checking for a pulse. Obviously an optimist.

The kitchen had been in a bad enough state when I'd got up this morning, but that was nothing compared to the state it was in now. I couldn't help wondering how on earth I was going to clean up all the blood.

3

The circus arrived with all the predictability of a textbook military operation. Uniformed officers hammered long metal staves into the ground and ran blue and white tape from one to the next till my house was completely cordoned off; a police cameraman took photographs; two smartly dressed characters donned white gowns and surgical gloves like doctors preparing to operate and then marched boldly into my kitchen and the scene of the bloodbath; several plainclothes detectives stood about in the open air talking together grimly, and casting occasional glances through the kitchen window. I watched it all from the back seat of the patrol car that had brought me up the track. People pointed me out to each other but nobody seemed particularly interested. Not yet.

I was taken eventually — my permission was never sought — to the local police station. Not permanently manned, it was now designated 'The Murder HQ'. This was the first time I'd ever been inside the place.

They showed me into an interview room and I found myself being questioned by a young fresh-faced detective sergeant. Understandably enough, he conducted himself with gravity commensurate with the horrible crime that had been committed, but was still able to lighten up sufficiently to show a degree of sympathy for my plight. For example, he supplied me with tea and biscuits. Thus it was that the homely chink of teacups and the snap of digestives accompanied the relating of my story.

At the back of my mind was an uncomfortable feeling of misgivings about the whole affair, so I told the sergeant everything, even the way I had ill-treated the lad, despite its reflecting badly on me. And I theatrically handed over the lad's notepad with its handwritten record of my movements; it was the one piece of hard evidence in my possession.

The sergeant was a good listener. I was gratified he appeared to believe my implausible tale. Every word was noted down; somebody typed it up; I signed it and dated it: 11.00 a.m. on Monday May 11th, 1998; an account of seven very peculiar hours in the life of George Radman.

As far as I was concerned that was my duty discharged. There was nothing further I could productively do at the police station, so I asked if I could leave. The sergeant remarked it was likely to be as much as a week before forensics would be finished with my house. I assured him I had family who'd help out regarding accommodation.

At which point the sergeant said: "I'd be grateful if you wouldn't mind hanging on for a little longer, sir. My boss would like to speak to you."

With the request couched politely in those terms, what would any law-abiding citizen say? I agreed to wait and be patient.

My fingerprints were taken. I was told this was so that any non-Radman fingerprints in my house could be picked out.

Hours passed. They brought me a midday meal, a substantial and well-cooked one, but beyond that I seemed to be disregarded, if not actually forgotten about.

I had the run of the building as far as I could tell, and nobody appeared to be watching me.

Around four in the afternoon I was joined in the interview room by three detectives. Two of them were physically substantial men who had a hard look about them, as if they'd seen so much human depravity it had made them unsmiling and always thinking the worst of everybody. They presented quite a contrast to the senior detective. This third man, who introduced himself as Detective Superintendent Adcock, was six feet tall, no more than a few years younger than me and utterly nondescript in appearance. Mr Average. Place him in a crowd and he'd be the one nobody would notice and nobody would remember. In any other circumstances, I'd have dismissed him as being of no account. Regrettably his role in my life made him anything but of no account.

Adcock started a portable tape-recorder.

"Thank you for waiting, Mr Radman," he began. "There are a few questions I'd like to ask you. Just completing the picture, you understand?"

"By all means."

"Perhaps you'd care to begin by telling me what happened."

"You want me to repeat what's in the statement I gave to your sergeant?"

"Not necessarily. Now you've had most of the day to clarify things in your mind, you'll probably wish to change some of the details. On reflection."

"I can't think of anything I could possibly want to change. I told the sergeant the truth. But I'll willingly go through my account again anyway. This is how it was...."

And I told him. And he listened without interruption.

*

"I congratulate you," Superintendent Adcock said when I finished telling him and his two colleagues my story. "What you've just recounted fits exactly with the statement you made earlier. Almost word for word, in fact."

I think I must have visibly relaxed. It looked like these senior, hard-bitten detectives were going to believe me, just as the sergeant I'd spoken to initially had. The misgivings I'd harboured had clearly been groundless. Whatever doubts these policemen may have countenanced about me, my upright nature and innate honesty had banished them. What's more, the consistency between the two separate accounts I had provided was surely convincing evidence in my favour. It didn't occur to me until later that a suspiciously-minded person might regard word-for-word correspondence as smacking of a carefully rehearsed fabrication.

"Unfortunately," the superintendent continued, using such a pleasant manner I felt more reassured than ever, "some of what you've said doesn't quite tie up with what we've found at the crime scene."

"Doesn't it?" I said. "Oh."

"The black cape, for example. You say the boy was wearing it when you left the house. Would it surprise you to learn we can't find it?"

"Yes, it would."

"And there's your rifle. You assert it was stolen. Why

would you say that when it's in your firearms cabinet where it's supposed to be?"

"It wasn't there when I got up this morning. They must have put it back."

"They? Is that 'they' in the sense of 'he or she', or 'they' as in 'more than one'?"

" 'They' as in 'one or more people'."

"I see. And then there's the six-inch knife. Would you like to hazard a guess as to whose fingerprints we found on it?"

"Well, I did handle the knife. But mine couldn't have been the only prints."

"Actually, Mr Radman, we found no prints at all. The knife had been wiped clean. Are you going to tell me 'they' did it?"

"I suppose," I said, and shrugged.

"Why would they do that?"

"If you'd just killed someone, I'd have thought it was an obvious thing to do."

"If it had been me, I'd have lost the knife somewhere out on the moor. Why didn't they do that?"

"Why? How should I know. Find them and maybe they'll explain."

"Good advice, doubtless. But it does rather beg the question we know who we're looking for."

"I've told you. Two Americans."

"Ah, yes, the two Americans. That's where I have the most difficulty with your statement. You point the finger very firmly in their direction, and then tell us next to nothing about them. Not a word about their ages, heights, weights, appearance. All they are are disembodied voices who come out of thin air and go back into thin air. A couple of convenient nonentities. You know what I'm wondering? I'm wondering if you invented them."

"It was dark and they were shining a light in my eyes," I retorted as the first twinge of unease struck me over the direction this interview was beginning to take. "How do you expect me to see them? Are you calling me a liar?"

The superintendent didn't reply to that. Instead he took some glossy photographs out of his briefcase. He showed me the top one: my kitchen in gory panoramic detail.

"Yes, study it closely," he said. "Especially this object just there." He pointed to a particular place in the picture. "What would you say that is?"

"It looks like my shotgun."

"Guess whose fingerprints were on it."

I breathed out heavily and shook my head. "It had been wiped clean," I said.

"Spot on. But before it was wiped clean it did this."

Adcock slammed another photograph down in front of me: a close-up of the top half of what used to be Clifford Hanworth. "Look at it," he shouted.

The lower jaw and the upper chest were a bloody mess but the neck was almost indescribably worse. It had been laid open by the shot. Pieces of vasculature and bone and god knows what else were visible.

"Who was he?" asked the superintendent, apparently in great anger.

"I've told you."

"No, Radman, you haven't. All you've given us is a

40

name. The other information we need isn't there, not from you and not on his person. No address, no phone number, no driving licence, no credit cards. No anything. And don't tell me that's 'their' doing."

"What am I supposed to tell you? Do you want me to make things up?"

"I want the truth."

"I'm telling you the truth. Why are you being so aggressive? I'm just another victim in all of this."

"One hell of a victim! You're alive. But this young man.... No one deserves that."

He thrust another picture under my nose: the second of the bodies in my kitchen. The upper right quadrant of his head had been on the receiving end of a shotgun blast. His throat had been cut for good measure. What with that and my earlier effort above the bathing pool, the blond hair was the English lad's only recognizable feature.

"Have a good look," said Adcock. "I'm going outside for a fag."

"Yes," I said, "and I'm going home. I've had enough of this farce."

"That's the last place you're going."

"You have no right to keep me here."

"No? You're providing us with vital assistance with our enquiries." He told his two colleagues to see I stayed put, and left the room.

So much for my plan to pass the evening with my mother or Peter. Before this interrogation had started I'd spent several hours fretting about the inactivity and the waste of an entire day. I was now rapidly concluding I had far worse things to fret about than that.

Adcock wasn't gone for long. The questioning resumed, mainly from him, with occasional inputs from the other two detectives. I lost track of how long we spent going over my statement again and again.

Communication breakdown became just about total. They kept asking me why other people had done things. Why had the two Americans — if they existed — murdered the English lad? Why had neither Hanworth nor the English lad been carrying any form of identification? Why this, why that, why the other? My reply was always the same. What had happened made no more sense to me than it did to them. And I could only tell them what *I* had done. They simply didn't hear.

In the end I forced the issue. I told Adcock I was leaving and if he attempted to stop me I would see him in court for assault, unlawful detention, and anything else I could think of. I was tired, confused, emotionally overwrought and furious. I wanted to break heads, and I'd have done it too if they'd laid a finger on me.

But they didn't. Adcock merely told me that as of that instant I was under arrest on suspicion of having murdered the two unidentified people found in my kitchen.

How easy it is for the police to transform a situation! By uttering the magic words, Adcock put me in a position where if I struck out it would be I who would be guilty of assault — not to mention resisting arrest. I shook my head and stayed my hand.

They transported me south to a bigger, permanently staffed police station. There, in another interview room, the questioning continued.

Again Adcock took the lead. One last time I made an effort to convince them of my innocence, but they were like a pack of foxhounds which has got its teeth into the wrong animal — completely unresponsive to restraint. They had the taste of my blood in their mouths and they were going to tear me to pieces. Tough luck, Radman.

Once the conclusion became inescapable that it was hopeless, I stopped talking. Totally. They shouted, thumped the desk, crowded me. The threat of physical violence was ever-present (though never implemented). I was silent. Not a word.

My silence was the result of a sudden insight into what they were aiming to do. The idea seemed to be to try different angles to muddle me. My answers would inevitably contain apparent — if not genuine — inconsistencies which they could throw back at me, getting me to tie myself in knots trying to say nothing harmful. Eventually I'd end up sounding so self-contradictory, so evasive, that the presenting of the interview transcript to a jury would damn me.

I concluded silence had to be the safest response in this situation. Say nothing. Don't even think answers in your head, because if you do, the temptation to give voice to those answers eventually becomes overwhelming. Make yourself deaf and mindless. Switch off. It was a great consolation — and believe me, 'great' is not an exaggeration — that my silence appeared to strike a blow at them which was more painful in its way than a well-aimed fist.

For two hours they kept up a one-sided dialogue. By the end Adcock had it all worked out. There had been no

Americans, no midnight burglary. The blond lad had been watching my house. The notepad proved that and they'd found his pen above the bathing pool, which provided added confirmation. The lad had seen me go to the bathing pool and had taken the opportunity to enter my premises, perhaps out of nothing more than curiosity. I'd then caught him and beaten him up before tying him to a chair. Shortly afterwards I'd unexpectedly found a second intruder trying to release him. In a rage I'd fired my shotgun, killing the intruder outright and injuring the lad. The latter needed to be silenced so I'd mercilessly cut his throat with the six-inch knife. To hamper the police investigation I'd burnt my victims' identification documents. (While I was being browbeaten, forensics had reported finding traces of them in the ash in my stove.) Then I had calmly sat down and concocted a lie and fabricated the evidence needed to support it. First, I had used my shotgun to blast a hole in my bedroom ceiling. Second, I had ransacked my house to simulate a burglary, leaving the kitchen tidy because the blood everywhere made it impossible for me to disturb that room. Third, I had shot out the tyres on my Land Rover in order to explain my failure to drive to the payphone, thereby giving myself time to check my story in my mind. Finally, before setting off I had wiped the knife and the shotgun clean because my fingerprints would otherwise have been the only ones on either weapon.

But I'd made a big mistake. On the way to the payphone I'd over-elaborated the account, putting in various details — the black cape, the missing rifle — which revealed me to be a liar. I should have kept it simple. By my own admission I'd been angry, and I'd gone too far. Way too far. I was, in short, the most cold-blooded, psychopathic murderer Adcock had ever encountered.

I said nothing.

They escorted me to the basement cell block and locked me in, leaving me for a time alone with my thoughts. There was a solitary flash of humanity from them in that they brought me a light meal, but it was wasted. Perfectly palatable though it was, I was in such a state the smell nauseated me and I couldn't eat it.

The food was the only kindness. After that I suffered the indignity of a supervised visit to the toilet. And then they excelled themselves. A police officer came into my cell and told me my clothes were wanted for forensic examination — looking for specks of blood presumably. I thought I was past caring. Except for my underpants I took my things off and handed them over.

"All your clothes," said the officer.

I stared at him bleakly. He was only doing his job, but to me he suddenly became the embodiment of the treatment I had endured at the hands of Adcock and his mates.

"You want my underpants, you come and get them," I stated bluntly.

He declined to take me up on the proposal, of course. Instead he called for assistance. I didn't give it time to arrive. Taking him off-guard I punched him in the groin with all the force I could muster, and as he went down I smashed the top of his nose with the side of my fist. I heard the bone break.

There was pandemonium. Another police officer tried to pinion me and made a mess of it. I twisted away from him and he toppled over, dragging me with him. My left forearm hit the corner of something hard — a chair, the frame of the bed, I don't know.

The next thing I was aware of was being laid on by a third policeman. My hands were cuffed behind my back and I was hauled up and sat in a chair. Thereafter things calmed down. The man I'd felled was helped out of the cell, his nose streaming with blood, and a doctor was summoned to sort out my forearm.

I couldn't see what damage had been done until the handcuffs were removed at the doctor's insistence. Then it became apparent a lump of skin several inches long had been gouged out just below my elbow. It was essential the injury be cleaned, so the doctor numbed the area with a spray of some kind, and set about the task as rapidly as possible. Following that he disinfected, stitched and bandaged the wound and confirmed with me that my anti-tetanus inoculation was up to date.

"You'll have a permanent scar there, I'm afraid," the doctor said before he left. "Do you want to tell me how it happened?"

"They attacked me," I said. "Two of them."

"That's a serious allegation."

I shrugged.

"I shall have to file a report," the doctor informed the two constables who'd been standing guard by the entrance to the cell.

"You do that," said one.

Once the doctor was out of sight, the constable who'd

spoken clenched his fist with the obvious intention of punching me. His colleague restrained him, saying: "It's what the bastard wants," which wasn't true at all.

"Not nice being accused of something you didn't do, is it?" I said to them.

They told me that by the time they'd finished I'd not get out of prison in less than forty years.

Alone and locked up once more I mused sadly on how quickly things can change. That morning I'd been a staunch supporter of law and order, the policeman's friend. In a mere twelve hours I had come to hate them and they hated me. I can only say the fault wasn't mine.

Something amused me eventually, though I was too miserable for it to produce even the flicker of a smile. I was still wearing my underpants.

*

I slept very little that night. My arm thawed out and throbbed relentlessly, making it impossible to relax and get comfortable. And the events of the past twenty-four hours replayed over and over in my mind, keeping me awake for mental as well as physical reasons.

A lot of the time during the small hours was taken up with self-pity. My life had been proceeding placidly, calmly, not a hint of trouble from any direction. Yet now it was teetering on the edge of ruin. I suppose some people do have that kind of bad luck, all smiles one minute and disaster the next, but I had never expected to become one of them.

What made it worse was knowing I'd contributed to

my own downfall. If only I'd not gone after the blond lad when he was watching my house from above the bathing pool. I shouldn't even have looked to see if he was there. Or given that I had gone after him, I should never have left him and Hanworth alone. The trouble was, though, that nothing I'd done was irrational. I could see my errors of judgement with hindsight. But how could I have known beforehand? Nobody, when they leave two people alone in their house, expects to find them decapitated on their return.

Eventually, in an effort to get free of the dejected state of mind these thoughts had got me into, I turned my attention to what I was going to do next. But there I was up against an impenetrable barrier. The key to establishing my innocence had to be the identity of Hanworth and the young lad. Find out who they were and with luck you'd also locate the two Americans. The problem was, if I was to discover anything useful about Hanworth and the lad I had first to be released, while to be released I had first to discover something useful about Hanworth and the lad. I couldn't win.

On a different tack I tried to think of some fact — any fact — which would give the police cause to doubt my guilt: some trivial observation, some overlooked piece of evidence, some passing remark, some move I'd made that an innocent man would have made and a guilty one would not have. I could come up with nothing. And wasn't that inevitable when I knew so little of what had been going on? Who was after Clifford Hanworth? Why were they after him? Who had murdered him? If it was the two Americans who'd done it, why had they killed the lad as well? Wasn't the latter supposed to be on their side? Why had they ransacked my house in the middle of the night? Questions, questions, questions, and not the faintest hint of an answer to any of them.

I was still thinking round and round in fruitless circles when the new day began. Breakfast was served. Then came a supervised wash and shave, and an examination by a civilian doctor doing duty as a police surgeon. Samples of blood, hair and fingernails were taken. The dirt from beneath my fingernails was also removed for analysis.

Throughout these proceedings I was wearing nothing but underpants and a blanket. To rectify this deficiency some second-hand garments were fetched from somewhere and given to me to put on. They were not a good fit and made me look sartorially incompetent (putting it politely).

These various formalities concluded, the real business of the morning got under way in the shape of several more rounds with Detective Superintendent Adcock and his team. More browbeating from him; more Big Silence from me. It was clear they'd been making great efforts to identify the two murder victims and had so far failed totally. That was bad news, given how important their identity was to my case. The most the police enquiries had revealed, in fact, was that there was no one called Clifford Hanworth. Naturally, they didn't think he'd made up the name; they thought I had.

The background of their prime suspect — or should I say their only suspect — had also come under scrutiny. How come I lived alone on the moor? Was I a homosexual? Was I hiding from something? What did I do for money? Why would a fifty-five year old man, at the end of the twentieth century, live in a place with no electricity and mains water? And no telephone? And, ultimate, incredible perversion, no television, not even a battery powered one? Did I hate civilization? Did I hate people? There was obviously something wrong with me. Was I a mental case? Why won't I answer their questions? Why don't I get it off my chest and tell them why I killed two strangers? Open that mouth of yours and confess, damn you.

I said nothing. Absolutely nothing.

The afternoon saw me back in the basement cell, dejected and shocked. The unaccustomed police food and the immense stress I was under disordered my bowels and compelled several supervised trips to the toilet, but otherwise there was nothing to report.

Around six in the evening Adcock summoned me to an upstairs room. He looked tired but determined, not angry now, merely pitiless.

"Your keeping silent has done you no good at all," he said. "You know that, don't you?"

No response.

"We've found traces of the young man's blood on your clothing." (Hardly surprising since I'd carried him to the house after he fainted.) "And your fingerprints are on the other victim's shoes." (Ditto, since I'd examined his sprained ankle.) "Do you have anything to say?"

When it became clear I didn't, he formally charged me with the two murders and asked if I had a solicitor.

I didn't reply.

He took a deep breath and said: "Find him one off the legal-aid list. And get him out of my sight before I do something unprofessional."

They returned me to my cell to pass another night. I slept better. You can get used to anything, no matter how dire, with practice.

At Bay

May 13 - June 21, 1998

4

Since being arrested I had seen quite a number of new faces, all of them authority figures, and all of them of a cold disposition. It was consequently a relief to encounter someone who didn't know me and who was prepared to be pleasant nonetheless. His name was Mr Smith, a bald, chubby man in his sixties, and he was my legal-aid solicitor.

I met him, following the ritual post-breakfast ablutions, in an interview room at the police station. It surprised me, considering I was rated as some kind of homicidal maniac, that we were left alone together.

He started out by explaining that everyone in police custody is entitled to legal aid, but once I was placed on remand legal aid would be means-tested. I told him how much money I had. His mouth gaped briefly and he said that was well above the limit. Would I agree to him representing me? I didn't ask him about cost; I asked if he was competent to handle a murder case.

"It's pretty much the same whatever crime you're accused of," he said. "Just formalities at this stage."

"Can you get me out of here?"

"On bail?"

"On anything."

"Bail is most unlikely to be granted in this case."

"How about habeas corpus?"

He smiled. "That's only applicable if your detention may be unlawful. There are no grounds for that here."

"So I'm well and truly in the mire?"

"Your situation is rather devoid of negotiational potentiality, I'm afraid." A verbose way of saying yes!

"In that case I would like you to contact my cousin, Peter Radman. As soon as he's allowed near my place I want him to board it up and make it secure. Do you know if anything's been done about my Land Rover?"

"Not off hand."

"Ask him to look after that too."

He wrote down some notes.

"And," I continued reluctantly, "you'd better inform my mother." She'd be distressed by the news, but she was bound to find out very soon anyway. Being charged with murder isn't something you can keep secret.

He was seriously keen on forms and documents was Mr Solicitor Smith. He possessed a lot of them, including the statement I'd made before my mouth shut down for the duration. He said he'd review the position and speak to me again tomorrow. Sign here. Sign there.

It turned out though that I saw him sooner than tomorrow. In the afternoon I was conveyed to the nearby courthouse for the purpose of confirming who I was, what I'd been charged with, and that I wasn't admitting the offences. Mr Smith was there but said almost nothing. No one mentioned bail.

I was surprised to discover, on this brief foray into the public arena, that my case had attracted a lot of media attention. Even national television was there, filming my arrival at court. I was offered a blanket to cover my head with but I refused it. I wasn't ashamed, which is what one normally hides one's face for, and I hoped I didn't look remotely like the butcher I was accused of being. Unfortunately, my ill-fitting police-issue clothes probably did create an impression of a mentally unbalanced person. So, I don't doubt, did the angry expression on my face.

Court appearance over, my mother was allowed to visit me. She came accompanied by her partner Malcolm — a second husband in all but name — and we talked through the bars of my cell under police supervision. She of course knew me well enough to have no doubt of my innocence, and Malcolm, a retired stockbroker and genuinely nice old boy, took his lead from her. I led her to believe the situation was a lot better than it actually was. Malcolm proved invaluable as far as backing me up and giving her support and comfort were concerned. Even so, tears were shed. I was very worried for her; she was over eighty and emotional shocks can kill at that age.

As promised, Mr Smith had a second interview with me the following morning. He went over my statement in a neutral sort of way, contrasting it with the police account of events. Then he floored me.

"You may be better off pleading manslaughter, Mr Radman," he said. "Admit you killed these people but insist you were unaware of what you were doing. There's a tolerable chance, taking into account your hitherto good character, that the prosecution would drop the murder charges in that case. If you express remorse into the bargain you'd be unlikely to spend more than seven years in prison. After that you'd be released on parole and could, if you pardon the expression, live happily ever after."

"But I'm innocent!"

"I'll be frank. The case against you is very strong. We have to start thinking in terms of damage limitation. If you're found guilty as charged and you continue to protest your non-involvement — which I assure you will be taken by the court as an aggravating factor — the judge is unlikely to set a life sentence tariff of less than twenty years, given the brutal nature of the crime. You...."

"Let me get this straight," I interrupted. "Are you saying *you* think I'm guilty?"

"What I believe is irrelevant. My job is to give you my best advice and to take your instructions."

"In that case my instructions are for you to find some other mug to keep you in the manner to which you've become accustomed."

"Am I to understand you are dismissing me?"

"Correct. I see it this way. If the truth can get me out of this mess I don't need you and your defeatism. If the truth can't get me out of it, the only difference your involvement will make will be to reduce me to penury by the end."

"That's a very short-sighted attitude if I may say so."

"I can only retain you if I have your whole-hearted belief in my cause."

"I'll do my best for you, Mr Radman, rest assured."

"Convince me. How about I don't pay you unless I'm acquitted?"

"That would be most irregular."

"You aren't convincing me."

"I can only give you my assurance...."

"In your opinion am I innocent or not?"

"My opinion isn't an issue."

The only positive thing I could say about this solicitor was that he wasn't prepared to lie to me. But if he thought me guilty, as was obviously the case, how could he ever hope to persuade anyone else to the opposite conclusion? Answer: he couldn't. To hell with him. "Goodbye, Mr Smith," I said.

He didn't seem to realize the conversation was over, so to dispel any doubt I turned my back. He blustered indignation and left.

I returned to my cell full of very dark thoughts. Family aside, no one believed in my innocence. Unless some new piece of evidence came to light I stood no chance. I was facing life imprisonment. For the first time since I was a child, my fate depended totally on forces outside my control. I was at the mercy of events. I hated it.

*

For two days nothing happened beyond that Peter was allowed to bring clothes from my house for me to wear in place of the absurd garments the police had provided me with. He told me I was now described by the media as 'George Radman, the alleged murderer'. But, hey, everyone knows the police don't accuse anyone of murder unless they're sure they've got the right man, so in the mind of the public — that is, away from Scotsmans Moor where I was known — the word 'alleged' was largely discounted. To avoid depressing me further, Peter promised to look after my mother and pledged that he and my nephew Thomas stood ready to render any assistance I needed. He had also heard from his brother Richard, my other Radman cousin who lived in Berwick, that he too was at my service. "Useful if you ever need any fish delivered to the prison!" Peter jested. (Richard owned a trawler and earned his living from the sea.) "But seriously," he said, ignoring the listening police officer, "I had a word with Dad. He just wished he was well enough to leave the care home. Other than that, he reminded me of what they say about the Radmans. I think he's got a point. Don't you?"

"Yes."

"Great. Oh, and Tupper's been at it again." Peter then managed to lighten my black mood by expounding loudly that Tupper, his prize ram, an amazingly stupid animal whose most demented recent exploit he graphically described, had more brains than all the detectives on my case put together.

Before he left, I mentioned the two Americans and suggested he enquire around. He promised he would. If there was an American within ten miles of Scotsmans Moor, somebody in our circle would know.

After Peter had gone I didn't feel so isolated any more. It meant a lot to me that the family was prepared to back me. I was especially heartened by Uncle Percy's mentioning 'what they say about the Radmans'. The saying is virtually a clan motto: *a Radman makes a good friend — and a bloody awful enemy*. The catch in this case, though, was that the identity of my — our — enemy was unknown.

Family solidarity notwithstanding, the wheels of so-called justice ground inexorably onwards. I was taken before the court for a second time and remanded in custody to the nearest prison which had facilities for remand prisoners: Durham. Not even in Northumberland! I was signed over to a private security firm who drove me there in handcuffs.

And I thought being in a police station cell had been awful! At least there I'd been *the* prisoner. My basic identity, despised though it was, had remained intact. But in prison you leave the ethos of civilization behind. It's as if you've mutated into some entirely different species.

The place filled me with horror. You're given orders. Nobody wants to know what you think or what you'd like. The only decision you're called on to make is whether to resist and be crushed, or to submit quietly. And the sick joke was I was supposed to be innocent until proved guilty. You could have fooled me. As legal maxims go, this one scaled such heights of judicial hypocrisy as to be nauseating. The police had treated me as guilty. The prison officers treated me as guilty. Even the convicts treated me as guilty. The only difference between me and those who'd already been tried and sentenced was that I had certain privileges — I could wear my own clothes, for example — but such privileges failed completely to mitigate the enormity of being locked up without trial.

Outwardly I played it tough, which was essential considering some of the thugs I was incarcerated with, but inwardly I cowered. The prospect of spending much of the rest of my life in this hideous, claustrophobic environment was so horrible I decided that if I was convicted I'd have to think seriously about suicide.

For the immediate future though I settled on the less drastic option of giving no one any trouble. I obeyed the rules, including the pointless ones, without dissent.

Only once did I risk defiance. It happened I had to endure the humiliation of being investigated by a psychiatrist. This arose because everyone on a murder charge is required to have a medical report on his mental state presented to the court. (Note again the implied presumption that I actually am a murderer.) I cooperated with this mind doctor until he started calling me a loner. He seemed to think being a loner was an abnormality, if not a downright disease. I let him use the word three times and then I gave him the Big Silence. Not another sound. He got irate, which pleased me no end, telling me I wasn't doing myself any favours. He was so obviously convinced I was a murderer — why should he be any different? — that whatever I said to him would be a complete waste of breath. I don't approve of waste.

There is, I suppose, a natural resilience in my nature, though it seemed to me that every time it showed itself somebody came along to beat it back down. My spirits had been reviving when Mr Solicitor Smith put the boot in; that was the first instance. The second instance was thanks to the psychiatrist; just as I was beginning to feel I could cope with the situation, my non-discussion with him plunged me into misery once more. It was enough to make me despair, and for a time I did.

I found myself seeking solace in dreaming of escape — a fantasy to make the unbearable bearable. Except why should it stay a fantasy? Why not just do it? I ought to be able to come up with something if I put my mind to the problem. The worst that could happen would be to get killed in the attempt, and that was preferable to suicide. With a challenge to focus my attention on, my spirits once more began their long climb out of the abyss.

Curiously, mental recovery had barely got under way when I received an entirely unexpected visit from a complete stranger — a visit which reduced the urgency of my need to escape so much that I suspended work on the project.

The woman was about my age, nice looking in a rugged sort of way, and had a wedding ring on the fourth finger of her left hand. Her accent was unmistakably American.

Naturally, this last aspect of her persona aroused my curiosity. There is nothing remotely sinister about being an American, but in the north-eastern corner of England Americans are rather rare. Meeting two together might be chance, but meeting a third smacked of conspiracy.

Fortunately she didn't come across as the conspiratorial type and quickly put me at my ease, opening the interview with a friendly: "Hi, Mr Radman." As women go she had a low-pitched voice and spoke my name in a way which struck me as strangely sexy.

Her own name she gave as Deborah Czerny. She explained she was a journalist working for the New England Sentinel, and she occasionally wrote freelance pieces for the national papers on this side of the Atlantic in addition. She wanted me to tell her my story.

I didn't ask why she was interested. Frankly I didn't

care. She was prepared to listen quietly while I recounted my experiences, something no one else had done recently, and I blessed her for it. I opened up to her like a daisy to the sun, telling her everything that had happened from the nocturnal break-in to the discovery of the double murder. It was profoundly liberating mentally being able to unburden myself like that.

"That's it," I said when I'd finished. "Nobody believes a word of it."

I waited patiently while she read through the notes she'd been taking.

"These two Americans?" she said. "You've met them before?"

"Not that I'm aware of."

"You've honestly no idea who they are?"

"Not a clue."

"But you think they were after this Clifford Hanworth guy. Are you sure about that? I mean, can you state it as a fact?"

I considered the question carefully before I replied. "I can't be completely sure. The Americans were after someone, albeit they failed to use his name. And Hanworth didn't deny knowing who I was talking about when I described the Americans to him; but that's as far as he'd go. I presume...."

"No," she interrupted. "Sorry if I sound like a lawyer, but I don't want to know what you presume at the moment. Let me ask about the English lad. Are you one hundred per cent certain that the kid you caught above the bathing pool was also the one who assisted at the break-in?"

I found myself shifting uncomfortably in my seat. "Not one hundred per cent," I replied. "Ninety-nine."

"And how about Hanworth and the kid recognizing each other? Is that definite?"

"Well.... not completely. Hanworth was a bit vague. But if the English lad didn't recognize Hanworth, why did he write 'Isaac' on his notepad?"

"Maybe it was a code meaning 'saw someone new at the house'."

"Now who's presuming!"

She smiled. "I'm speculating. It's not quite the same thing. So now I've started, let's speculate some more. Is it possible Hanworth is more innocent in this business than he seems? Could his account of being lost and stumbling over the waterfall be the simple truth?"

This time I could be unequivocal. "Stumbling over the waterfall, yes. But he was very afraid, and it wasn't of me. He believed somebody was after him. That is certain."

"After him enough to want him dead?"

"From his behaviour, I'd say that's what he thought they had in mind."

"And you're sure he gave you no clue as to their identity?"

"No. He wouldn't talk about it. But it stands to reason it was the Americans. It's a fair bet whoever returned my rifle to its cabinet was also the person who committed the murders with my shotgun. And the Americans were the ones who had my firearms last."

"Yes," she said. "But fair bets are like presumptions; they aren't admissible in court."

I looked in her eyes and tried to divine what was going on behind them. She'd asked some intelligent questions (which is more than could be said of Superintendent Adcock); they weren't the sort of questions you'd ask of someone you'd already convicted in your mind.

"You believe me, don't you?" I asserted.

She hesitated, biting her lip. "I don't believe you're a natural liar, Mr Radman. I'll go that far. As to how much of what you've told me is plain truth, well...."

"Can I confide in you, Mrs Czerny?"

"Be careful. You don't know who I am."

It was an odd reply for her to make but I was captivated by her, by her receptiveness, by the way she was taking me seriously. I wasn't going to let an odd reply spoil it. I said: "I've never begged for anything in the whole of my adult life, but I need friends...." I looked at her with all the earnestness I could muster and somehow got the words out: "Please help me."

"It's not a good idea for you to choose me. My profession will get in the way."

That was a blunt rebuff. I couldn't afford to accept it, either in practical or emotional terms. I risked giving her a smile, a rare commodity for me these days.

"Look," she said, "I'll see what I can find out. And quit trying to win me over with your boyish charms. I'll get back to you."

"I appreciate it more than I can express."

"Yes, well, I guess I'd better be going. So long, Mr Radman."

"To you it's George."

She returned the smile. "See you, George," she said with genuine sympathy in her voice.

For a little while after that interview I felt as if I'd rejoined the human race. My spirits revived markedly. The idea of escaping returned to the realm of dreams. Deborah Czerny was going to be my white knight.

*

Prison life is essentially monotonous; each day is much like the previous one and the next one. There were three exceptions to this rule. The first was the visits from my mother and Malcolm, which took place in a room set aside for that purpose. The second, less frequent but more regular, occurred on Sundays, when there was a sort of religious service. A lot of the inmates took part in that — which surprised me considering their behaviour the rest of the time — but I wasn't one of them. In my view, if God existed He was being grossly negligent where looking after me was concerned and didn't deserve my worship; and if He didn't exist the exercise was meaningless. (I gathered inmates who attended were hoping to convince the parole board they had reformed and could be granted earlier release than would otherwise be the case.)

The third break in the routine was another regular one in that, as a prisoner on remand for a serious offence, I had to be transported periodically to the court which had decreed originally that I be locked up. This journey marked the high point of the drab prison cycle. I was presented to the court for all of a minute, observed by all and sundry, remanded in custody automatically, and returned to jail. It was a completely pointless business as far as I was concerned, and a misuse of petrol and everyone's time.

[*Note added by author Harry Senthill: the authorities agreed with Mr Radman on this point and replaced in-person court appearances with a video-link from prison within a couple of years.*]

I made the first of these court appearances before Mrs Czerny introduced herself. I made the second before Peter came to see me, apparently rather pleased with himself, and told me about Colwick Hall. How strange that the passage of time which had always been marked out by the sun and the moon and the seasons should now be marked out by long trips handcuffed in the back of the security firm's van, and by chats with prison visitors!

Colwick Hall I knew to be an imposing mansion about eight miles north via Scotsmans moor — somewhat further by road — from where I lived. It had once been the family seat of the local nobility, but financial hardship forced the last of the line to abandon the place while I was a university student. A rock star had acquired the property, living there surprisingly quietly, before selling it a few years back to a secretive group of people who, so rumour had it, ran the mansion and its grounds as a kind of kibbutz, though they weren't Jewish.

What my cousin was able to add to this limited knowledge of mine was an American dimension. He'd been attending an agricultural show and had heard from one of Colwick Hall's farming neighbours that the estate was held in the name of a company based in the U.S.A.

Peter's informant thought the residents were 'a bunch of Commie dreamers being bankrolled by some Yank idealist'. Regrettably he wasn't able to confirm the American connection extended to personnel. He believed the occupants were mostly, if not entirely, of British and Irish origin.

As leads go, my cousin's information didn't strike me as particularly promising. However, it was something that could be followed up and I asked him to enquire further, warning him to be discreet. If Colwick Hall did prove to be the source of my troubles, at least one member of the commune — was that the right word? — was a murderer.

I briefed Peter about Mrs Czerny and requested that he pass on to her the things he'd told me. Unfortunately I only knew her name and the newspaper she worked for, which wasn't a lot of help. He said he'd do what he could.

It turned out I could have saved him the bother, for Mrs Czerny paid me a second visit the following day.

"Hi George," she began in her curiously erotic way. "Don't get excited. I promised I'd report back. That's all I'm doing."

"That doesn't sound very hopeful."

"I'm sorry. The best I can say is that I've discovered nothing which incriminates you."

"But nothing that vindicates me either?"

She shook her head.

We both started talking simultaneously, then stopped and waited for the other to say something.

"You first," she said.

"I was about to remark I'm glad you're here, even if

you haven't much to tell me, because I've got something to tell you."

"You have?"

"Yes. There's a place called Colwick Hall. I don't suppose you've ever heard of it." I stopped because she was frowning.

"I've heard of it," she said.

"It might be worth checking," I continued. "It's possible a few Americans may be living there. Seems like a commune of some kind. Also it's occurred to me, since the Americans who broke into my house were preaching religion, to wonder if there's a religious element to the Colwick Hall set up. It might be interesting to find that out."

"I see," she said vaguely. "How did you learn about this place?"

"From my cousin." As I spoke I became aware of a developing sense of unease. She wasn't reacting quite right.

"Fine," she said, still vague. "Look, George, I'd better give this to you straight. My.... editor has ordered me not to get involved with you. I'm here researching a story and you.... Well, he thinks I'd be going off on a tangent. I have to stay focussed."

"Are you trying to say goodbye to me?" I asked; and when she failed to respond immediately, the additional words: "Please don't do that," sprang involuntarily to my lips.

"I warned you. You don't know who I am."

"You're a journalist. That's who you are. You could make a difference."

"It's not my job."

"You're like the rest of them! You believe I'm guilty."

"No, George. As it happens, I believe you're innocent. I just don't see there's a solitary thing I'm able to do about it."

"Well, thanks a lot!"

"You're making this very hard for me."

"Mrs Czerny, this is the rest of my life we're talking about here."

We'd both become heated. There was an embarrassed silence. Then she said: "I'd better go."

She stood up, hesitated, looked down at me (I was still seated) and breathed out heavily as though I'd exasperated her. "Okay," she said in a frustrated tone of voice, "I'll keep my ears open. If I come across anything useful to you, you'll be the first to know. That's a promise."

I treated her to another — this time intentionally — manipulative smile. "Take care," I said, "especially if you go anywhere near Colwick Hall."

That remark engendered a most peculiar expression on her face, rekindling my unease.

"I'll be seeing you, George," she said, and left me to puzzle over a distinctly unsettling conversation.

It was clear Mrs Czerny already knew about Colwick Hall. But what exactly did she know about it? More than I knew, that's for sure. Reading women's minds has never been something I'm any good at, but I refused, nevertheless, to think badly of her. She'd been such a good listener; so genuine, so sympathetic. I couldn't *not* trust her. Whatever was going on she was on my side.

My illusions lasted for a mite less than twenty-four hours. Peter called in to see me unexpectedly with the sole purpose of reporting that the New England Sentinel had never heard of anyone called Deborah Czerny and furthermore that they had only one reporter in England and he was a man. Nor had any of the national or local Northumberland papers had any dealings with her. Peter warned me to be wary of her.

It was a bitter disappointment. I couldn't speak for a while after my cousin had left, and woke several times during the night dreaming of her. In each dream she was walking away from me. In one, I was hanging from a scaffold.

5

Solicitor Smith, the prison psychiatrist, and now Deborah Czerny. Three times my optimism had been dashed. Three times I had been thrown back into the nest of vipers which I was trying so hard to get out of. I decided three times was enough.

I had, I realized, been using Mrs Czerny as an excuse for not proceeding with the planning of my escape. That excuse no longer existed. Indeed, it struck me that that woman, by her dishonesty, had given me a sign. It was as if, through her, the whole world had said: "You've had it, mate. You're on your own." No judges, barristers, jurors, solicitors, policemen, pretend-journalists were going to save me. If I couldn't save myself my life was over, actually or in effect. So why let it be ended to their schedule? It was time to do or die.

The prison was a mass of concrete, steel, locked doors, warders, security systems. Even with the assistance of other inmates — and I didn't trust any of them — a break-out would be extremely difficult. But there was another option available to me and it didn't require a genius to spot it. At regular intervals I was taken out of the prison and driven the long distance to the courthouse. That had to be my route to freedom.

Peter called in again the following day. He had seen how badly his news about Mrs Czerny had affected me and was very worried for my wellbeing.

Shortly into the conversation I said: "I'm thinking of

asking them to let me have a breath of fresh air next time I'm in court. They'll say no the first time. And probably the time after that. But once they've had the opportunity to think about it, they'll agree."

Peter nodded. "You think so?"

"I'll be wearing handcuffs. Why shouldn't they?"

"Indeed."

We talked for a while about my mother.

Then Peter said: "I'm going to buy a car. I've had my eye on it for a while. Fast. Automatic transmission. Only problem is it doesn't have any security. If the driver's door is unlocked anyone could get in and drive off. I'll have to see to that."

"I should think you will."

We talked for a while about my house and Land Rover.

Then I said: "How's Richard? Is he out in his trawler much at the moment?"

"It's keeping him busy. I've been meaning to suggest though that it's time he visited Agnes."

"In Norway?" I said loudly.

"He reckons he can make it if the sea's calm. He'll need a crewman though."

I smiled. "They'll be queuing up."

Shortly after that, Peter left. I knew from now on I'd see him regularly before each of my future visits to the courthouse. I'd tell him when I was ready. He'd tell me about the car: one with automatic transmission that someone in handcuffs could drive. He'd tell me how to recognize it and where it would be parked. Richard would be ready to sail if I got to Berwick. But not for

Norway. Aunt Agnes, rest her soul, had lived in Scotland. British territory but a different jurisdiction. It might give me an edge. So, if I could escape from the courthouse, the clan would lay on the logistics. The Radmans aren't 'the law' in these parts like they once were, but the locals know to treat us with respect. We're a resourceful family.

*

The next time I made the journey to court — the third such excursion — I took the opportunity to be much more observant than usual. As the noble occupant of the bench took his standard minute to confirm I was still alive and in custody, and to decide that society must surely collapse if my status was altered by the tiniest detail, I was gathering data and assessing the options. How many people were in the court? Which of them could put up a fight? What windows were open? How were they secured? Could they be broken? How far were they above the ground outside? What was the local road layout? What about traffic and parked cars? What about places to run to and places to hide? Were there any objects within reach that could do duty as a weapon? As each question acquired an answer, my confidence grew. I was sure, if I was determined, capable of effective violence, and willing to gamble everything including my life, there was a reasonable possibility I could break out.

Back in the van and heading prison-wards, I continued to observe and plan. The handcuffs, fastened in front fortunately, would be a problem, if not the greatest problem. They would hinder my escape and mark me out conspicuously as I fled. The key to unlock them was with the two private security guards escorting me from prison to court and back. They were sitting in the front and separated from me by a solid partition. Was the key brought into court or left in the van? Should I spend time trying to obtain it? If not, where could I get bolt cutters and a hacksaw? Even if Peter laid them on, could I manipulate them to cut a chain between my wrists? Would I be able to force someone else to do it for me?

Such a lot of problems. But all I knew was I'd had as much as I could take of these people and their misguided justice. Sometime in the next few weeks, I was going to give those implacable court officials something to wake them up.

I wasn't able to see out of the van but, being familiar with the journey, could judge roughly where we were by how much time had passed. I knew we were getting close to Durham. However, Durham jail is in the middle of Durham town, and we hadn't got that far yet. We were still travelling fairly fast on a main road.

I felt a sudden, surprise deceleration and heard the driver say: "What's this idiot doing?"

The van came to a halt. The next thing I knew, I heard gunfire. A fully automatic weapon by the sound of it.

A voice, very close by, shouted: "Get out! Get out!"

Neither of the security guards said anything.

"This side," commanded the voice. "Move! Hands where I can see them. You! On the ground face down. You! Keys. You've got five seconds to get him out here or your friend dies."

"All right, all right," said one of the security guards. I

76

could tell from his tone he was petrified. Keys jingled.

The van's rear doors opened, letting in a blast of daylight. I got out, curious to see who was going to all this trouble. It certainly wasn't the family. They wouldn't mount an operation like this.

There was a standard 'white van' blocking the carriageway ahead of the prison van. A crash barrier down the middle of the road made manoeuvring round it impossible. The white van had obviously come from a slip road a few metres back the way we came. There were two men. One young, one older, maybe thirty-five. It was the latter who was wielding the artillery. I didn't recognize either of them.

"Get up," he ordered the security guard on the ground. The man hastened to obey, moving to stand beside his fellow guard.

"Run!" commanded the gunman, pointing his weapon at them. My god, did they run!

"Come with me," the gunman said to me.

When I didn't immediately jump to it, he added: "I'm out of here. The police will be along shortly if you'd rather go with them."

That convinced me to hasten after him. He was, after all, saving me a lot of bother, and if his intentions were harmful I'd be dead already.

He paused to shoot out a tyre on the prison van and then we ran to a fence bordering the road. We climbed over that, as did the gunman's young accomplice. On the other side of the fence was a residential road bordered by some houses. There was a car parked there. The getaway car! The young man got behind the wheel. The gunman ordered me to sit in the back with him. We slammed our respective doors more or less simultaneously and the car moved off. The entire rescue — if that's what it was — had taken less than two minutes.

I said nothing, limiting myself to occasional glances at the men taking me to.... wherever we were going. The gunman had a smug look on his face: the sort that goes with having done a good job and knowing it. His eyes were intelligent, his demeanour self-assured, and he was chewing gum.

He reached across with his right hand and said: "George Radman?"

"I might be."

He smiled. "Bryce Nordstrom."

We shook hands, jangling my handcuffs.

"I didn't think that was your real voice you were using back there," I remarked. "Too plummy."

"I never have quite mastered English English," he said jovially, "but it suffices. There'll be a manhunt getting underway shortly and I didn't want them looking for an American."

"Do I get an explanation for what's happened?"

"Sure, but later. Right now I've got to concentrate or your period at liberty is going to be undesirably brief."

We stayed on residential roads, driving inconspicuously. Quite soon we came to a supermarket where we pulled in and parked. Nordstrom got out, came round to my side of the car, and threw a raincoat over my handcuffs as I stood up. I noted he left the gun behind on the floor of the car.

"You see the blue campervan?" he said. "That's ours.

This car we ditch. We walk separately over to the store. You look in the window, act casual, and then make your way slowly to the camper and get in the back. Don't worry about the woman inside. She's with me. I'll go in the store briefly and then join you."

I did as I was told. The young woman inside smiled at me when I got in. Three minutes later Nordstrom joined us, taking the wheel. We left the young man who'd assisted with my 'rescue' behind. I didn't see where he went.

We were immediately on the move once more, heading south. Nordstrom had bought a packet of cigarettes and lit one. I declined the offer to light up myself, explaining my lungs preferred unpolluted air.

"Uh-huh," Nordstrom said, and opened his window a little so the smoke mostly went outside. Speaking over his shoulder to me, he continued: "My boss bitches about smoking too. Clean body, clean mind, that's what he reckons. Me, I say that if God had meant us not to smoke, He'd have made it so it wasn't a pleasure. Or else not invented tobacco in the first place."

"I'm sure there's a counter argument," I said, "but I can't think of it right this minute. There are other things on my mind."

"I guess so. You didn't like my Limey accent; how's your Yankee one?"

"What's that got to do with anything?"

"Give him the documents, Naomi."

The young woman with me in the back of the campervan did as instructed. I found I was looking at a U.S. passport, correctly stamped, a U.S. driver's license, and a wallet with plastic cards, some American bank notes and a picture of a middle-aged woman with two teenage boys. There were also a return ticket from Heathrow to Logan and a pair of glasses.

"Who's Walt Westlebury?" I said, reading the name on the passport.

"You are," Nordstrom replied.

I looked at the photo IDs. There was a degree of resemblance, I suppose, but not convincing. (I assumed the documents had been prepared by someone working from newspaper photos of the 'alleged murderer'.) The hair was the main discrepancy. Mine was dark brown and parted on the right. Westlebury's was fair, shorter and parted on the left.

Naomi, who informed me she was a qualified beautician, got to work: comb, scissors and an application of hair dye. My eyebrows were not forgotten and I was advised to shave at least twice a day so that my facial hair didn't give me away. There was other hair as well, I pointed out, but Nordstrom interjected that if they suspected me sufficiently to make me strip down they'd get me on fingerprints anyway.

Soon, still keeping carefully off main roads, we came to a small wooded area. We halted there. Nordstrom produced bolt cutters and used them to remove my handcuffs. Next he took off his wig and swapped the number plates on the campervan. Then came a complete change of clothes for both of us — all traceable to America, Nordstrom informed me. The bolt cutters, handcuffs, discarded clothes and old number plates went into a plastic sack which he knotted and threw deep into the trees. "The stuff will be found eventually," he said, "but it won't matter by then."

We resumed our southward journey, dropping Naomi off at a bus stop on our route.

I began to think I was going to get away with this, and so did Nordstrom judging by how much more relaxed he seemed to become as the miles passed.

"The story's this," he explained. "You and me, we're father and son-in-law on a week's tour of England. We live in Boston. Left our families behind. Due to fly back tomorrow. Unless things get unexpectedly hot in these parts I won't actually be coming with you but that's what we tell anyone who asks this side of Heathrow."

"I don't know what to say," I remarked honestly enough. I was feeling a trifle overwhelmed.

"Later. Right now, listen up. We're not out of danger yet. The police will be expecting us to be fleeing as fast as possible, so they'll have roadblocks on all the main routes pretty damn quick. That's why we're keeping to back roads. The trouble is Westlebury and Nordstrom have to get to London by tonight, so once we're clear of the immediate area we'll be joining the A19. We may be stopped. If we are, you need to talk like an American. Try copying my accent. And remember to get the story straight. We're here on vacation. *Not* holiday. Study the documents Naomi gave you. You mustn't hesitate if you're asked questions with answers the police can immediately verify. And don't worry about the campervan. It's fully legit, unlike the white van and the car we left at the supermarket. They were stolen. Now, put on the glasses."

The glasses, I found, had real lenses in them, making everything slightly blurred.

"Keep the glasses on whenever we're in public. Don't take them off for any reason. Understand?"

"Yes."

"One final thing. If anyone calls out 'George' or 'Radman', *do not react.* It's an old trick and it's vital you're prepared so you don't fall for it."

"Got it. I have to admit I'm impressed by the planning."

"American!" Nordstrom scolded. "Try again. Listen to me." He repeated word for word what I had just said.

I made my comment again, imitating him quite well, I thought.

"Better," he agreed. "Keep it up."

"Now tell me what's going on," I said, obeying him.

"You mean you want to know my angle?"

"Yes."

"My angle's this. I bust you out of jail, get you out of this country, and in return you give me some information. Sounds like a good deal to me."

"Let me guess. You're another journalist."

"Journalist? No sir."

"So who do you work for?"

"I'm not authorized to tell you that. Let's just say I'm one of the good guys."

Not a helpful answer. It gave me a dilemma. My recent experiences led me not to trust Americans. Should I trust this one? I thought about Deborah Czerny and how she'd duped me into providing her with information on false pretences. With her I'd erred on the side of being open and trusting and had come to regret it. With Bryce Nordstrom I resolved to adopt the opposite tactic and to reveal as little as possible until I had a better idea of what I was involved in and who, if anyone, was genuinely on my side. Of course I didn't say that. What I said was: "What do you want to know?"

"I want you to tell me about Clifford Hanworth."

"Clifford Hanworth?" I said bitterly. "Who's he?"

"What do you mean?"

"The police say it's a false name."

"Well, there you go. That's the first thing you've told me I wasn't aware of. What's his real name?"

"I've no idea. I don't think the police have either."

"That's a shame. Where did you find this guy?"

That was exactly the sort of question I wasn't going to answer. Not truthfully, anyway.

"I didn't," I said. "He knocked on my back window not long after some burglars had paid me a visit."

"Did he say where he'd been?"

"Only that he'd got lost."

"How about what he had with him. Anything unusual?"

"He wasn't equipped for the moor. That was unusual."

"You sure he wasn't carrying anything odd?"

"Like what?"

"I was hoping you could tell me."

"I didn't search him. He was my guest."

Nordstrom was silent for a moment so I took the opportunity to ask a question of my own. "Don't you want me to tell you why I killed him?" I thought I was being clever, putting it like that.

"Now that would be a dumb question, being as you didn't."

"That means you know who did."

"I can't help you with that."

"Not when it might prevent a serious miscarriage of justice?"

"It's been prevented. You're on your way to freedom."

"Yes. On the run in a foreign country."

"That's not an issue I want to get into. Do you know if the cops found anything significant when they checked Hanworth's body over?"

"Only that he'd been almost decapitated."

"No, I mean possessions."

"If there had been anything remotely suspicious on him I'm certain they'd have challenged me about it. They couldn't have found anything."

"One other point, Radman. You said you thought I might be, quote, another journalist. I'd like you to explain that."

"Somebody claiming to be a journalist interviewed me in prison. It's not important."

"Name?"

"I don't recall."

Why was I lying about Deborah Czerny? Considering the way she'd deceived me, I had no reason to protect her. Then again, I had no reason to hand her over to Bryce Nordstrom either. She was a woman and I'm a sucker. Put it down to that.

"Describe him," said Nordstrom, assuming I was talking about a male journalist.

I described Mr Solicitor Smith.

"Nothing to do with us," said Nordstrom. "You're sure he wasn't a real journalist?"

"No. I checked."

"That I do not like. It makes me think we're right to get you out of the country soonest. Sounds like there may be some opposition nosing in on this."

"In on what? Come on, Nordstrom, I've levelled with you. Tell me what I'm mixed up in."

"No can do."

"Then perhaps I won't go to America."

He laughed at that. "The only other option is jail. Now you've gone on the run no one — absolutely no one — is going to believe you're innocent."

Having the truth spelled out so bluntly left me momentarily speechless.

"You're a pawn on a big chessboard," he commiserated. "Pawns get sacrificed. Just be grateful Uncle Sam has decided to shunt you off-line instead of leaving you to rot."

That remark brought an end to our conversation. We travelled on in relaxed silence.

Yes I was a pawn. But who were the chess masters? Nordstrom had referred to 'we' and 'Uncle Sam'. Did that mean he worked for the CIA? His obvious professionalism and the quality of the Walt Westlebury documentation suggested strongly that he did. But there were also arguments against. For example, if he wanted to question me, why not simply talk to me like Deborah Czerny had, in prison? Why go to the risk and expense of getting me out of custody? I could understand the CIA taking an interest in a fanatical compatriot like Deep Voice, but not in spiriting a 'pawn' like me out of England. There was a hidden agenda being pursued here. Somebody was expecting to gain an advantage from my departure. It didn't strike me that that someone was the CIA. And what about the CIA hints Nordstrom had dropped? Had that been deliberate or careless? What did he *want* me to believe? Whatever it was, it was probably the opposite of the truth.

And there was one other — crucial — question that I couldn't ask him. Now that I'd had a conversation with him, I'd formed an opinion about his voice. When it had been proposed that I be 'sacrificed' in my bedroom the night this affair had begun, the voice of the man who'd argued against it, pointing out I was 'unclean', and the voice of Bryce Nordstrom sounded to me like one and the same. If they did indeed belong to the same man, then I was travelling in the company of someone — CIA or otherwise — who had quite possibly committed two brutal murders. Consequently I had to be very careful what I said, what I did, and what I revealed. I had an uncomfortable feeling that if I put a foot wrong I could at any moment become murder victim number three.

6

We encountered no roadblocks on the A19 or on any other of the roads to London. Taking turns at driving, we reached the outskirts of the capital late in the afternoon. To guard against the small possibility that the police might somehow have come to know about the campervan, we left it in a multi-storey car park near Ilford railway station and completely covered our tracks by buying a couple of rail tickets into central London from an automatic vending machine, rather than from an interviewable booking clerk. We then made our way to our hotel variously by train, tube and on foot.

The hotel was expecting us, Nordstrom having reserved a couple of single rooms a few days earlier. We played the brash American tourists. My attempt at mimicking Nordstrom's accent might not have fooled a native but it was good enough for London. Indeed the only serious difficulty I had with my acting was wearing Walt Westlebury's glasses; they strained my eyes and made me prone to misjudging steps, especially steps downward. It was hard to resist taking the damned things off.

After a sumptuous meal — a glorious experience following on from several weeks of prison fare — Nordstrom and I bade each other goodnight and retired to our respective rooms.

Naturally I had an urgent decision to make; namely, whether to stick with my dubious rescuer or to strike out on my own. Equally naturally I deferred reaching a conclusion on the matter until I had watched the evening news. I imagine that's what I was supposed to do, for Nordstrom made no attempt to restrict my movements or spy on me — not that I could tell, anyway. And when I saw the news I could understand why he reckoned he didn't need to.

"The headlines tonight: a major manhunt is launched in north-east England following the escape from custody of alleged murderer George Radman...."

They'd made me the main news story! Start with a camera shot of the prison where I had lately been residing. Cut to a serious-faced reporter standing a few metres in front of the prison van, now ringed with blue and white police tape, and still exactly where Nordstrom and I had left it. Recount my escape, not remotely accurately, for the general enlightenment of the viewing public, and then get the reporter to answer studio questions about what is being done to re-apprehend me. Show a picture of the fugitive — quite a good one — and provide a description of Nordstrom — quite a bad one. Use standard footage of a police roadblock and motorists being questioned. Invite comments from one of the detectives who'd interviewed me with Superintendent Adcock: basically I was violent and desperate and believed to have gone to ground locally; there had been unconfirmed sightings of me in Newcastle; airports and seaports were being watched in case I had somehow managed to bypass the police encirclement of the area; anyone seeing me should dial 999; on no account should I be approached. End the news item by interviewing a woman who claimed to be my friend (though that was a surprise to me since I didn't recognize her). She described me as a loner — not a matter-of-fact loner, of course, but a something-wrong-with-him loner — and voiced all the predictable clichés: bit of an odd-ball, keeps himself to himself, etc. Shot of the reporter, nodding and grim-faced, saying: "And now back to the studio."

It is not conducive to peace of mind to know that a large proportion of your fellow citizens are looking for you. It is, frankly, unnerving. About the only good thing I'd heard in the four-minute report was that the security guards were shaken but unharmed.

Other than that it was entirely bleak. Nordstrom's questions in the campervan had led me to conclude Hanworth had been carrying some object of interest, nature unknown. It was a conclusion that fitted with the search of my house by Deep Voice and company. But any thought I may have had of going home and searching for this object, whatever it was, which Hanworth must have hidden at some time before I dragged him on a blanket to my house, had to go straight on the scrap heap. So did my intention of calling on Colwick Hall and checking out the commune living there. While the police were concentrating their search in Northumberland that was the one place I daren't go, not even as Walt Westlebury.

If the moors were out of bounds, where else could I make for? Remaining in England I'd be exposed to the constant danger of re-arrest with no compensating benefit. Which left somewhere abroad — precisely what was on offer if I fell in with Nordstrom's plans. America was a good place to hide. Give it a few months. Once the heat was off and I'd been forgotten, that would be the time for me to return and try to clear my name. For now I was better off out of it.

The decision was one I slept on, but come the morning the position looked the same as it had the night before. Nordstrom emphasized that fact by knocking loudly on my door as I was getting dressed. My pulse went over one-twenty and I opened up, certain — and dreading — that I was about to be confronted by Superintendent Adcock. The thought of living with that kind of fear every day henceforward was enough to make relocating across the Atlantic an irresistible option.

"Still okay for America?" Nordstrom asked after I'd let him into my room.

I nodded.

"Thought you might be," he said.

He proceeded to brief me about what to expect on landing at Logan airport; how to get from there to Walt Westlebury's apartment in Boston; how to let myself in — he gave me a couple of keys for the purpose; where the nearest shops were; how to make a transatlantic call from a payphone (so I could telephone my mother); where to find a small stash of dollar bills of various denominations hidden inside a particular piece of the apartment's décor; and what to do about other trivial matters that were likely to arise.

He also advised me about passing through security at Heathrow. "There'll be people there watching for you. If they're obvious, ignore them. Don't let them catch your eye or you'll betray yourself by looking away too fast or looking back too long or just not looking right. If the people watching for you are not obvious, you'll have an easier time. Remember you're a U.S. citizen. Your papers can't be faulted by less than a very close inspection. If anyone stops you, act tough: you know your rights, that sort of thing. Threaten them with the American embassy. Play up the part of a tourist going home and you should be okay. And one other point: can you read with those glasses on?"

"Yes. Funnily enough they actually make reading easier."

"Good. Don't take them off on any account. It'd be a dead giveaway."

"I'll remember that."

"Anything else you need to know?"

"What do I do when the pocket money runs out?"

"Don't worry about that. Likely we'll sort something more permanent out for you fairly quickly. Keep to the apartment as much as possible so we'll be able to find you."

"You realize I'll want to come home eventually?"

"Miracles we can sometimes manage. But the impossible.... Don't hold your breath."

Not a remark calculated to elevate my spirits.

After breakfast we went through my luggage — a single large suitcase — in case I was stopped and questioned about its contents, and then made our way to the nearest Underground station. It was there we parted. Nordstrom's final words as the train doors closed were: "If you're forced to miss your flight, it'd be best if you don't describe me accurately. Not that it matters. I don't exist."

He was a professional, all right. Probably CIA. But I still didn't get why they were taking so much trouble over me.

*

I encountered no difficulties at Heathrow. There were several tallish men hanging around, men with alert eyes and bored faces, who might have been plain-clothes policemen or customs officers or MI5 or whoever watches airports for absconding murderers, but they gave me no trouble; they could easily have been wholly innocent. I ignored them, kept the glasses on, talked American English when spoken to, and played the part of Walt Westlebury with gusto. Judging by the results, it must have been a good performance.

Not that there weren't some tense moments, especially while waiting for the plane to take off. And I remained fidgety after that until we were safely over the Atlantic and I could relax and read a newspaper that I'd bought.

Guess who was on the front page? And two inside pages! Apparently the writer still had to call me an 'alleged' murderer, but any other lies were fair game. According to him I was a bully at school (actually, my being a loner made me the target of bullies); I'm a drunkard (I don't drink alcohol at all); I'm suspected of being a racist right-winger (I'm not a racist and I have no interest in politics); I'm illiterate (I have an English O-level and two university degrees). And so on. I remembered what had been said about the newspaper industry when Princess Diana had died. That was less than a year before. Now I knew first-hand what it was like to be the victim of a newspaper hatchet job. What makes it so infuriating is that you can't fight back.

Sickened by the newspaper I tried to doze. And discovered that Heathrow's nervousness had been replaced by a different malaise. I began to feel intensely lonely which, given I'm a loner, was saying something. It came home to me I was going into exile, escaping unjust persecution in my own country at the price of becoming a stranger in a foreign land. Freedom in America had to be better than imprisonment in England. But England was where my roots were, and my family, my land, my memories, my identity. England was my home. I vowed that someday, somehow, I'd be back. England and I weren't done yet.

*

The ten-hour flight was uneventful. So was my arrival at Logan. I followed everyone else, nonchalantly pretending I knew what I was doing and where I was going. An official checked my passport and wasn't remotely taken aback when I tried out my fake accent on him. I seemed as close to being anonymous as you can get at an international airport, and that's pretty close.

After the usual delays sorting out luggage I emerged into the open to be confronted by a Boston June day, surprisingly similar to the day I'd left behind: scattered clouds, blue sky, dry. The only noticeable difference —

and barely noticeable at that — was that the air was a few degrees warmer. The main incongruity for an arriving passenger from Britain was that the sun was much too high in the sky and the clocks were five hours too early.

I hired a taxi and got driven to the Westlebury address. The taxi driver was a chatty sort, and in order to divert him from my ignorance of things Bostonian I told him about the vacation (*not* holiday!) I'd just taken in England. He'd never been across the Atlantic himself but had a range of opinions about different facets of British life gleaned, I suspect, mainly from watching television. He demonstrated his idea of an English accent — hopeless — and disconcerted me by remarking I'd picked up the way of talking a tad myself. He seemed like a nice fellow, so on arrival at my destination I paid him a tip, something I never do in England. I stood on the sidewalk, suitcase in my hand, and watched him drive cheerily away.

The road I was in was long and straight, bordered by parked cars. The house fronts were a continuous brick wall, the division between one house and the next being inferred by the entrance doors and location of the many windows. Each front door was approached up a few steps.

Taking out of my pocket the keys Nordstrom had supplied, I let myself in through the appropriate door and found myself in a dim hallway. The carpet was worn and dingy, the paintwork flaking, and there was a peculiar smell — tobacco mixed with disinfectant — in the air. Somebody had a hi-fi turned up too loud.

I went up a floor and unlocked the door to the

Westlebury apartment. This was more encouraging. The residence consisted of a lounge with other rooms off. It was neat and tidy and nicely decorated. The only negative factor was the blasted hi-fi, which was louder still, coming through the ceiling and probably located in the room immediately above.

Having checked the apartment out, my first priority was to ring home. There was a phone on a small table but it was silent — not broken as far as I could tell, but disconnected. Disappointed, I went out into the street and wandered about until I came across a payphone. But that was only the first hurdle. I hadn't enough change to fund an international call and so had to wander about some more until I found a number of stores. In one of these I was able to buy a pre-paid long-distance phone card (and also a few food items which took my fancy). Then it was back to the payphone. I punched in Malcolm's number and it was he who answered.

"Hello, Malcolm," I said. "It's George. Is Mum at home?"

"George? Where are you? Are you okay?"

"Yes, I'm fine. Reasonably."

"Your mother's not here. She's in hospital, I'm afraid."

"What's happened?"

"Nothing serious. At least I don't think so. They've taken her in for observation. Chest pains, heart irregularity of some sort, high blood pressure. I'm pretty sure it's stress."

"Oh, this is awful," I said, and meant it. There was no doubt where the stress was coming from.

"What can I tell her?" Malcolm asked gently.

"Tell her I'm okay and not to worry. And give her my love."

"Of course."

"What's going on at your end at the moment?" I asked.

"You mean about you?"

"Yes."

"The latest on the midday news is that they've found a getaway car in some supermarket car park or other. There's been the usual appeal for witnesses. But the big problem, family-wise, is that the police seem to be convinced your break-out is some sort of clan affair. They're giving Peter a hard time. He's been 'helping them with their enquiries', as they put it, since yesterday afternoon. Actually I'm not sure he isn't under arrest. All your other cousins have been interviewed too. I gather they've even been questioning the Berwickshire Radmans."

"They're nothing to do with us!"

"So I believe."

"This just gets worse and worse. Poor Peter. Just because he's the head of the family. He's had no involvement whatever. I'm really sorry, Malcolm."

"You did what you thought was for the best. In your place I might well have done the same at your age. Everyone's bearing up. It's your mother I'm worried about."

"That makes both of us. Listen, this phone call is probably being monitored. When it's over, report it to the police immediately, otherwise you run the risk of becoming an accessory. Mum's got enough troubles without you being arrested as well."

"I'll do that."

"I'd better go now. I'll call again in a day or two to find out how she's getting on."

"One thing before you hang up, George. I've had a Deborah Czerny here looking for you. Can I...."

"Tell her nothing," I interrupted. "She's not to be trusted. Make sure the rest of the family knows."

"Okay. I'll pass the message on."

"Thanks. Well...."

"Good luck, George. I hope I have better news for you next time."

"So do I."

I returned to my apartment in a thoroughly mixed-up state emotionally. There was anger at the police for pursuing what looked like a vendetta against my family, worry over my mother, affection for Malcolm for his trust and sympathy, and despair over how I was ever going to prove my innocence and get out of this mess. And there was irritation at the person — using a polite word — with the infernal hi-fi blaring away upstairs, making a local contribution to my mental turmoil. If there'd been someone culpable around to hit, I'd have hit them. But there was only the empty, impersonal apartment and the daylight streaming in through the windows when my brain was telling me it ought to be getting dark, and nothing to do except allow myself to sink into homesickness.

Having crossed five hours' worth of time zones I was ready to sleep by six p.m. There was no obvious benefit to forcing myself to adjust to Boston time in one go, so I settled down on the bed, a finger uncomfortably in each ear and a pillow over my head. I slept despite the hi-fi.

I awoke at ten to find a hush had descended on the building. I lay still for a few minutes to make sure it wasn't merely a gap between one record and the next, and went back to sleep.

At eleven, somebody rang Mr Westlebury's front door bell. It could only be the Boston cops here to arrest me. As I struggled into my clothes I decided I wouldn't resist extradition. What purpose would be served?

I opened the door expecting to see uniforms, but I had it wrong. Two men stood there, both a few inches taller than my five feet six, both mid to late twenties. Smart haircuts, smart clothes, white shirts, carefully knotted sober ties. Apart from a five o'clock shadow on one of them they looked like a couple of graduates applying for a high-paid job.

"Mr Radman?" one of them asked.

Not wishing to give anything away, I responded with: "Who are you?"

He smiled. No hostility. "We're friends of Jed Nordstrom."

'Jed' Nordstrom I noted immediately, not 'Bryce'. That confirmed my identification of Nordstrom as one of the two Americans who had forced their way into my house on the moor. But where did that lead me? Anywhere that made any difference?

"How are you settling in?" the man continued.

"Hard to say yet. I was asleep."

"Okay, I get the message." The man sighed as if

wishing to convey reluctance. "Now don't get up-tight. I realize you want to go back to bed. It's just that our boss would like to ask you a few questions."

"At this time of night?"

"You know how it is. We've got one bitch of a problem over in England and we need to clear it up as soon as possible. Day's already dawning in your home town. No time to lose."

"So who's 'we'?"

"We are the people who sprung you from jail; we made it possible for you to leave England; we are paying for all this;" — he looked around the apartment — "and we will see you make out in America if that's what you want. Is an hour of your time that much to ask?"

"That's all it'll take?"

"Tops."

"And it really can't wait till tomorrow?"

"Sorry."

"Oh all right," I said wearily. "Tell your boss he can come up."

"He isn't here," the man said, sounding slightly shocked. "The boss doesn't do visiting. He expects people to come to him."

"Look," I said, "I'm really not up to travelling. I told Nordstrom everything I know."

"Maybe he didn't ask the right questions. We'd really appreciate your cooperation."

I put the Westlebury overcoat on, turned out the lights, locked the door to the apartment and followed the two men down the stairs.

Out in the street they indicated a big American four-door sedan. The car was empty. Before I got in, it occurred to me to ask to see their identification documents. Just to be on the safe side.

"The boss will show you all the ID you need to see shortly," said the driver.

I didn't like that answer. "Then it'll have to wait till morning," I said and made to re-enter the apartment block.

They obstructed my way. The talkative one casually opened his jacket slightly so I caught sight of a shoulder holster. That I didn't like even more.

Without being threatened, I'd just been threatened. I began to think going with these two men would be unwise. But how not to? Fighting with armed men was out. So was running. Selecting to bide my time I shrugged and allowed them to usher me into the front passenger seat, after which the talkative one with the five o'clock shadow took the wheel and his colleague got in, sitting directly behind me. They both seemed at ease. I fastened my seatbelt. They followed suit and the car moved off.

In the apartment I'd been drowsy, barely capable of thought, and easy prey to the two men's suave politeness. (Is that why they'd chosen late at night as the time to call on me?) Now I found I was beginning to think more coherently. These guys were clearly working for the same employer as Nordstrom. That meant I was safe, since if their employer wanted to harm me, why go to the trouble and expense of flying me to America first? Nordstrom could have done the deed easily enough in England. They really did intend just to talk to me. I could hardly refuse them that. Therefore I should ignore my misgivings and go with them.

But there was another way of looking at the situation. I recalled the friendly sergeant saying: "My boss would like a word with you." And I fell for it, never suspecting his smile, never perceiving until too late that I was being asked to hang around while they fitted me up for one of the worst nightmares imaginable. Now, here in Boston, these friendly men had made a nearly identical request: "Our boss would like to ask you a few questions." On this reckoning I should, conversely, take heed of my misgivings and *not* go with them.

"Is it far to this boss of yours?" I asked.

"Might as well tell you, Radman," the driver answered. "I misled you a little back there. The interview is likely to take an hour but we've a way to drive. Why don't you go back to sleep. I'll wake you on arrival."

"Great," I said sarcastically.

The scales were tipping towards getting out of the car as soon as possible. Nobody in their right mind would go on a long journey in a foreign country with men they didn't know. Hell, I wouldn't even do that in England.

I laid my head back on the headrest and closed my eyes.

Momentarily I was alarmed when the man behind me began speaking, not much above a whisper, but it turned out he wasn't talking to me. Or even about me. "Are you okay with the route?" he said.

"Sure," the driver confirmed.

"Only you took several wrong turns getting here."

"Thanks for the reminder."

"Just as long as we get home before three. I'm kind of tired."

"Aren't we all. So shut up distracting me, or likely I'll end up driving us into Boston harbour."

I noted they talked of 'home', not 'the office'. That decided me. I definitely wasn't going with these people.

I continued pretending to be asleep.

And now I faced a moment of truth. Suppose I tried the peaceful approach and politely asked the two men to let me out of the car. Would they agree? Answer: almost certainly no. If I insisted, would they try and stop me? Answer: almost certainly yes. Conclusion: I'd have to employ a degree of violence. The consequences of choosing that option were terrifyingly unpredictable. Understandably I hesitated.

"The turn we want for Interstate 93 should be just up ahead," remarked the man in the back.

"Look," the driver responded, "who's driving this car, you or me?"

"Didn't want you to miss it, that's all."

Interstate 93? That sounded like some sort of motorway. Once we were on that, any violence I employed would get us all killed in the resulting high-speed car crash. Get out, George. Get out now! I didn't pick the moment. I simply went for it. The first the driver knew he had more than navigation to worry about was when the side of my hand karate-chopped his Adam's apple. The space was too confined for it to do much damage but it bought me a few seconds. I rammed my foot down on top of his on the accelerator pedal and jerked the steering wheel so the car turned to the right.

The man behind me was fast. He got a forearm round my throat, but the headrests were in the way and hindered his effectiveness.

Slewing across the road, the car mounted the sidewalk doing about forty and smashed obliquely into a mostly-glass store front. Airbags inflated for an instant, leaving me winded but uninjured. The man in the back, who'd unfastened his seatbelt to deal with me, cannoned between the headrests and between the airbags and pushed the windshield out with his skull. He finished up with his head on the dashboard and the rest of him draped between the front seats.

For a moment there was an eerie silence. Then an alarm bell began jangling very noisily somewhere overhead.

The driver had evidently had enough. Obviously dazed and probably in pain from the blow to his throat, he got out and staggered away.

On my side, the impact had forced my door open, enabling me to alight quickly and easily. The car had spun round before coming to rest and I found myself standing in the road, the car between me and the damaged store front.

A passing vehicle had pulled up and disgorged an occupant. He approached while I dithered, momentarily nonplussed and indecisive.

"You okay, bud?" he asked, shouting against the alarm bell.

"Yeh," I replied equally loudly. And then, referring to the body between the front seats, I added: "He's not though. Has anyone called an ambulance? Did you see where the driver went? I think he had some kind of seizure.”

“He ran off that way,” said the man, gesturing.

“Darn. First attack he’s had like that in years and it has to hit him behind the wheel. I’d better go after him. Good friend of mine. Don’t want him to injure himself.”

I wasn’t, of course, remotely interested in the driver’s wellbeing. I merely wanted an excuse to clear out before anyone else came along who might want to take me away in a big car. I fancied I could already detect a flashing light in the distance.

I made off after the driver. The street lighting was good but there was no sign of him or anyone else ahead of me. We had crashed quite close to a major traffic junction — the turning for Interstate 93? — enabling me to quickly get out of sight of the main road we had been driving along. Almost at once I came across the man I was purportedly chasing. He was on his knees, leaning against a wall and looking decidedly unwell. He didn’t even give me a glance. I took to my heels.

I ran and ran. Right turns, left turns, anything to throw off potential pursuit. I sought narrow passages and backstreets and found them. Of the people I encountered, the bold ones stared and the timid ones pretended not to notice. No one tried to stop me or gave chase. Running isn’t a crime in Boston any more than it is in Northumberland.

Eventually I succumbed to fatigue and came to a halt. The panic — for that was what I quickly realized it was — passed off. But not the fear. Cities scare me at the best of times, and this was not the best of times. I hadn’t the faintest idea where in Boston I was. I couldn't even obtain a kind of flimsy reassurance from getting a compass bearing off the stars; the street lighting and the tall buildings made that impossible.

My utter quandary was rendered even worse by the thought that not only was I adrift in a foreign city near midnight, but that some organization, possibly the CIA, would very soon be out there searching for me, and with a very substantial grudge to give impetus to their efforts. It was enough to make me feel staying in an English prison wouldn't have been so bad after all.

7

In the streets to which my taking flight had led me there were few passing cars and only the occasional pedestrian. I didn't want to try stopping anyone to ask directions; I had just assaulted one person, seriously injured or killed a second, and caused a car crash. The last thing I wanted right then was to talk to someone who might be able to identify me later, someone who could point me out in a line-up and thereby independently corroborate what the witness at the crash site said about the man fleeing the scene. Determined therefore to keep myself to myself I wandered aimlessly for a while, like a lamb which can't find its mother. Soon though I became more rational. I selected a quiet street to walk down, convinced it was heading in a direction which was taking me away from the crime, took a couple of turnings for no better reason than that they seemed to make sense (in a completely undefinable way) and shortly came upon a broad main road. Looking to my right I saw the weirdest sight imaginable. Perhaps two hundred metres away were several cars with flashing lights. A few people were standing around. A loud alarm bell was ringing. It was as though I was observing a repeat performance of the accident I myself had caused.

The realization swiftly dawned on me it *was* the accident I'd caused. I recognized the road. Somehow in my dash from the scene I had turned right a couple of times more than I'd been aware of, so that instead of heading away from the crash I'd walked back to it. Needless to say, I increased my distance from the flashing lights as quickly as possible.

By now another issue was intruding into my mind. The stress and the cold night air were having an effect on my bladder. (That's another reason why I hate cities. Alone on Scotsmans Moor the discomfort could be relieved in a few seconds.) It tipped the balance in favour of risking talking to someone; specifically, a taxi driver. I watched out for taxis and saw several drive past. They ignored my attempts to hail them, which made me feel a fool. Nevertheless I persisted and was eventually rewarded. A cab stopped, I got in, and the driver asked for my destination. I gave him the name of the street where Walt Westlebury lived. It was the only residential street name I knew of.

When we arrived I had him drive the full length of the road before dropping me off. I paid him a little more than the fare on the meter and expected change, but he didn't produce any. Indeed he seemed disgruntled not to be given a sizable tip, which made me all the more determined not to offer him one. I had to conserve my dwindling financial resources. He didn't need the money as much as I did. He drove off muttering uncomplimentary things.

The street was very quiet: no traffic, no people, only a few windows with lights in them. It being midnight, that was what one would expect. There was nothing suspicious in the immediate environs to alarm me. Yet the feeling of imminent danger was intense.

At first sight, my returning to this location was utter

stupidity. Westlebury's apartment was the most dangerous place for me in Boston. Anyone with hostile intent was bound to show up there to look for me. So why had I come back? Partly it was for the same reason a frightened rabbit makes for its burrow. The apartment was the nearest thing I had to a bolt-hole. More important, there were logistics to consider. Inside were food, a change of clothing, warmth, shelter, toilet facilities, bed, money. All highly desirable and free of charge. I had returned to the Westlebury residence, despite its hazards, because there was nowhere else for me to go, not in Boston, nor, come to that, in the U.S.A. at large.

Ready for anything, including having to dive out of the path of a hail of bullets, I circumspectly approached the front entrance to the apartments, ascended the steps and unlocked the main door. So far, so good. From a back room a TV was faintly audible but otherwise there was complete silence. I went in.

Checking the hallway repeatedly as I advanced, I climbed the stairs to the landing, creeping noiselessly. I inserted the key in the door to the Westlebury apartment. If there was someone lying in wait inside I doubted they'd start shooting — my understanding was that they had questions to ask — but I wasn't taking any avoidable risks. As the door swung open I stood to one side, out of the line of fire.

The interior was in darkness, as it should have been, and not a murmur could be heard.

It occurred to me the light in the hallway had me at a disadvantage. Reasoning a precaution was better taken late than not at all, I went to the light switch and turned it off. Then, feeling the need to make one final check of my rear, I went downstairs and glanced out into the street. It remained deserted. No one had got out of the various cars parked against the kerb.

I returned to the open apartment door. A small amount of illumination persisted coming from the floors above and below, but I decided not to worry about that. Even if the place could be made totally dark, going inside would still be dangerous. And it couldn't be shirked. There was no advantage in delay. I went through the doorway fast and low.

No gun fired. No one struck out at me. There was no sound of movement or breathing. I closed the door behind me and locked it.

The thought began to gain currency in my mind that the organization which was after me might be a little low on manpower at this time of night. Suppose the driver of the car had been too badly hurt to stay in the game. Suppose there was no one who could take his place at short notice. I might yet have a few hours unmolested.

Feeling a little less tense, I drew the thick, heavy curtains, turned on a light, and confirmed the apartment was empty and undisturbed.

I was now able to get some coherence into my thoughts. My main concern of course was to work out what my next move should be. The more I thought, the fewer the options seemed to be. I found myself cursing my folly in leaving England. I should have given Nordstrom the slip and gone to ground somewhere comparatively local. Yorkshire perhaps. At least there I'd have known what was what. But here in Boston I was so uninformed on how things are done that ignorance thwarted me at every turn.

As an example, consider finance. I had what Nordstrom had given me, plus the sum hidden in the apartment — which was quickly transferred to my wallet — minus what I'd spent so far. The question was, what would I do when the money ran out? I'd either have to beg or steal or starve — all unthinkable options. Alternatively I could try to find work. That was a brilliant solution until my ignorance was taken into account. Then it started to look unviable. Presumably a Bostonian would know how to go about obtaining employment. But me? Do they have job centres here? Situations Vacant columns in newspapers? And what sort of experience have you got, Mr Westlebury? Well, I'm an ecologist, a crack shot with a rifle and I probably know more about sheep than anyone else in Boston. Sorry sir, there's not much call for sharp-shooting environmentalist shepherds in these parts. And if I found a job to apply for, what documents would an employer want to see? Would I need a bank account? A social security number? An address? The conclusion was plain. Ignorance would make it very difficult for me to get work. Therefore, since begging, stealing and starving were unacceptable, I had to be out of America before I was out of money. And that was just one of the ways in which my freedom of action was constrained by what I didn't know.

In fact I ended up deciding I had no options at all other than travelling to Washington, marching boldly into my country's embassy there and telling them who I was.

Not for the first time, thinking about the future was making me seriously dejected. To dispel the mounting gloom I tried turning my mind to the immediate present and answering an urgent practical question: should I remain in the apartment or evacuate it?

I was already clear on why I had returned to the Westlebury residence. They were all valid reasons. But.... The apartment was a magnet. Anyone looking for me would start there because it was the only place they *could* start. And I was in no doubt the driver of the car, or colleagues of his, would soon be seeking me earnestly. They'd shortly be knocking on my door, and this time they wouldn't bother to smile and be polite when they did so. It was obvious the dangers of remaining in the apartment greatly outweighed the material and tactical advantages it bestowed. It had to be abandoned. The only consolation was, given the absence of trouble so far, the evacuation could be carried out in an orderly fashion. I permitted myself an hour. That would give me time to have a good breakfast — I was still running on British time — pack some lunch, assemble all the necessities I'd need to take with me, tidy up generally, and pause to go over everything in my mind and make sure I was leaving nothing important behind.

I began by shaving — very necessary since my beard was dark and my hair was dyed fair. Then I prepared a substantial breakfast.

I soon found I had badly underestimated how long it would take to carry out all the chores I had listed for myself. Shaving, cooking and eating took up the hour I'd allocated for everything.

It was while I was hastily packing some lunch that I heard a noise, an almost imperceptible vibration, that seemed to come from the vicinity of the entrance to the apartment. I snapped off the lights and went to listen.

Minutes passed without any further sounds being made. Had I been imagining things? Perhaps there were mice in the building. Quietly I engaged the security chain, pressed myself flat against the wall and opened the door a fraction. All I could see outside was darkness. All I could hear was silence. If there was anyone out there they did nothing, a response so contrary to my expectations it convinced me everything was okay. I had been spooked by my own ears playing tricks on me. I returned to my packing.

Nonetheless I now found myself hastening with something akin to panic. I was in the apartment on borrowed time. I had to get out and it had to be now.

I stuffed the packed lunch in a carrier bag, pocketed a few personal items, checked I had Walt Westlebury's identity documents, and went to the window overlooking the street. I could see nothing suspicious. The time was just after half past one. Time to leave.

I went to the door, the security chain still in place, and opened it a little. The light was on in the hallway. I unhooked the chain and checked outside cautiously. In both directions the hallway was deserted.

That hall light should not have been on. Nobody had been moving around out there who'd need to see where they were going. I didn't like it. But on the other hand, logic told me not to worry. Somebody hostile would not have left the light burning since they'd have realized it would put me on my guard. Therefore it had been switched on innocently, even if I'd not heard by whom.

Ultimately it was an academic issue. I had to leave the apartment. This was the way out, light or no light. I stepped into the hallway, closing the door.

I'd gone all of four silent paces when I heard behind me something I didn't want to hear. It was the sound made when a gun is cocked.

There was no room for manoeuvre to left or right. The only possibility of escape was to throw myself down the stairs. But I didn't do that. Whoever was holding the gun had wanted me to know he was there. The sound was a warning. And that meant he didn't simply want to shoot me dead; executions are best done without providing advance notice. I stopped in my tracks and awaited his next move.

A voice whispered: "Hands on your head."

I obeyed very slowly, informing him when my arms were clear of my body that I was going to drop the carrier bag with my packed lunch in it. I didn't want to make him jump. The bag thumped to the floor softly and my hands completed their passage to my head.

"Turn around," said the voice, still whispering.

I complied. It was the car driver, the man with the five o'clock shadow, only now it was more like designer stubble. He was holding his pistol at the end of an outstretched arm. I was an unmissable target this close to.

"We're going back into the apartment," he muttered. "Open the door."

Again very slowly, I lowered my right hand, reached into my pocket and took out the key. His eyes never left me for a moment. He uncocked the gun by touch, which I took for a good sign as it meant he didn't want to pull the trigger accidentally.

I inserted the key in the lock and as I did so he suddenly moved forward and hit the back of my neck with the gun barrel. I was stunned for just long enough for him to turn me so my back was against the door. He punched me in the stomach. I was prevented from doubling up by his body keeping me upright. That enabled him to punch me a second time, lower down, getting my testicles. I was out of the fight.

He completed the job I'd started of unlocking the door, and dragged me inside by an arm. Having reclosed the door, he kicked me in the ribs a couple of times before I had a chance to get up.

Then he raised me partly off the floor with a forearm round my neck from behind. "As Abraham is my witness, I hate you, Radman," he whispered, the whispering plainly the result of my hitting his throat in the car. "You hurt me. Now I'm going to hurt you."

Partly throttling me with one arm, he took to punching my back with the fist at the end of his other arm.

After a minute or two of this unpleasantness he calmed down and stepped back. Then he ordered me to stand up, and when I tried to comply he kicked me in the stomach and put me down again.

"Stand up," he snarled. Repeat performance: when I'd got onto my hands and knees, he kicked me back down yet again.

This was clearly an enjoyable way to pass the time: tell me to get up, and when I struggle to obey kick me. I gave up. That brought forth a couple more kicks in the ribs and then he gave up too. Game over.

He sat down in Walt Westlebury's armchair, gun pointing in my direction. And we waited. Waited for what? For me to recover so he could have some more fun? For reinforcements?

I moaned and played the part of someone injured rather worse than I was. When that produced no response, I just lay there and ached, thinking hard. The trouble is, when someone's pointing a gun at you, there's not a lot you can do. Except be ready to grab any chance that arises, and not to hesitate if and when it does.

Time passed. A lot of time. Whatever he was waiting for — probably someone with a replacement car — I reasoned the morning would bring the answer and I couldn't leave it that long.

Eventually I felt recovered enough to try and bring matters to a head while it was just him and me. "I need to go to the bathroom," I dishonestly informed him.

"Tough," he said.

I made to get to my feet, very slowly as if in great pain. His response was going to be one of two things: to threaten me with the gun in his lap or to play the kicking game again. Either way I was ready. What might have worked for him when I was beaten to the ground wouldn't work now. Mustn't work now. In my mind I was back revisiting my plan to escape from the courthouse in England. Aside from the gun, which made the situation a lot more deadly, the odds were a damned sight better here: he was my only opposition.

He went for the kicking option. As he lashed out I

launched myself towards him, taking the force of his kick against my shoulder and causing him to topple backwards towards the armchair. I followed through.

The gun, which he hadn't put down, fired. I felt like I'd been slashed across the stomach by a very hot knife. But almost immediately I had the hand holding the gun in both of mine. And that gave me my first surprise and piece of luck. He wasn't as strong as I was. I could tell that from the moment we began grappling.

We both quickly ended up on the floor.

My essential next move was to get the firearm out of his hand. I tried to pull his thumb back off the grip; he countered by using his free hand to stop me.

His thumb wouldn't budge. Neither would my hands, which were too strong for him to dislodge. We wrestled around on the floor over this blasted gun for a minute or so and then I had my second piece of luck. Unintentionally I found I'd got his little finger loose from the grip, and then intentionally I pulled it back and broke it. He screamed like someone with laryngitis: very few decibels.

His grip on the gun weakened. I pulled it out of his hand and pushed it away from us towards the wall. I know I'm 'George Radman, the murderer', but funnily enough I didn't want to kill this man. I needed to know who he was, and he wasn't going to tell me that if he was dead.

The fight descended into a playground brawl. Or it would have done but for an unfortunate development. The gunshot wound I'd sustained, which had initially become completely numb, suddenly sent a stab of pain right through me. It distracted me for a second and he got away from my grasp.

We both began to get to our feet. He was faster than me. But I was between him and the gun. So he chose as a weapon a chair from the dining table and swung it at me. Because of his broken finger he could only wield the chair one-handed. It enabled me to dodge, falling back towards the wall. And the gun.

He made to swing the chair a second time. If I'd hesitated, if I'd paused for even a fraction of a second to think, the chair would have fractured my skull before I'd reached even the most basic conclusion. So I didn't hesitate. I couldn't. I grasped the gun. Shooting from the hip — impossible to be accurate unless you're an actor in a Hollywood western — I compensated by pulling the trigger three times. Two of the bullets — I don't know which two — hit him, one just above his heart, the other, judging by the result, in his stomach. He tumbled over, the chair striking me on the upper arm and inflicting nothing worse than bruises.

I kept him covered for the few seconds it took my brain to fully register what had happened. By then it was the end for this particular enemy. There's nothing worse for blood-letting than a bullet in the stomach. It was pouring from him. He retched and blood came out of his mouth. His eyes, though fixed on me, had already become glazed.

Damn! I still wanted to know who he was, more so now than ever. To that end, and thinking also of my limited funds, I decided to help myself to his wallet. Holding his arm out of the way, I opened his jacket. The contents of the inside pockets were not yet bloodied. I grabbed the things that came to hand. Then I left him, still breathing but beyond my help.

Shots had been fired. Residents of neighbouring apartments would have been woken up. Somebody had probably called the police. Unless I wanted to spend the rest of my life in an American jail — an even worse prospect than being locked up in an English one — I had to move, and move fast. Fortunately the bullet wound in my side was only bleeding a little and I was so hyped up it was unable for the time being to put me out of action. I hunted out a spare shirt, and also the first-aid box from the bathroom, put on my Westlebury overcoat in order to hide the bloodstain, and hastened to the door.

The gun I decided to leave behind. That was for three reasons. Firstly, it was a murder weapon. The received wisdom is that you dispose of such things lest they incriminate you. Secondly, possessing a firearm would only give me a false sense of security. If I had to use it, doing so would only dig me yet deeper into the mess I was already in too deep to escape from. Better to avoid getting into such a predicament in the first place than to rely on a gun to get me out of it. And thirdly, for the first time in my life I had killed a human being. It didn't feel good. I didn't want to do it again. Ultimately though, dumping the weapon was a snap decision. I wiped it clean of fingerprints and tossed it onto the floor. A present for the police department.

I swiftly exited the apartment. A kid on the floor above — he of the loud hi-fi I supposed — called down, asking if everything was all right. I didn't look at him, didn't answer, kept my face turned away. I gathered up the carrier bag from where I'd dropped it, added the spare shirt and first-aid box to the sandwiches already inside, and proceeded steadily downstairs and out into the street.

I was surprised to find it was daylight. A quick check of my watch revealed it was approaching five. There were no people around: not in cars or on foot.

I walked falteringly until I was out of sight of the apartment and then tried jogging. A few seconds of that was all I could manage. The discomfort in my side turned rapidly into a searing pain and compelled me to place each foot on the ground gently and with the minimum of movement to the rest of my body from my pelvis upward. I could sustain a painful one mile an hour at most.

It might have helped if I'd known where I was going, but I didn't. I had no destination whatsoever in mind. My only aim was to get away from the scene of the crime. The prospect of the Boston police turning up and arresting me for murder, given my experience of such things in England, was literally terrifying. For that reason everything, and I mean everything, took second place to the imperative to flee. The only concession I made to rationality was to glance once in a while at the blood on my shirt and waistband. It seemed to be spreading but there was no heavy leakage taking place. I could live with it.

Because I was forced to walk so slowly, I avoided crossing roads wherever possible. The traffic at this time of day was light but I still felt vulnerable when not on a sidewalk.

Eventually I came across the entrance to an MBTA

station. There was a choice of 'inbound' and 'outbound'. The former seemed the better bet, in that from downtown Boston I could head in any direction, including to England via Logan airport. There were also likely to be more crowds to hide in and places where I might rest: public spaces and museums, for instance.

I alighted at Park Street, whereupon I promptly worked out, after studying a plan of the MBTA system, that I should travel onwards to the airport. I decided to forgo the city centre and make for this new destination because I reckoned there'd be crowds there too and I'd be that much closer, in practical terms, to England. (It can't be denied my plans were changing by the minute — a symptom that goes with being in a situation which is completely out of one's control. Tactically speaking it's a very bad sign.)

This second MBTA journey was rapidly completed and I was able to do what I'd been urgent to do since leaving the apartment; that is, examine the bullet wound. Safely hidden in a lavatory cubicle, and with the first-aid box open and ready for use, I looked at what my clothes had been concealing.

The bullet had grazed me. (I'd say 'merely grazed me' but bullet wounds are never 'merely' anything.) It appeared to have ploughed a furrow about four inches long in my skin to the right of my navel. A mass of congealed blood made it impossible to estimate the depth of the track, though from the kind of pain I was experiencing it seemed the underlying muscle tissue had been nicked. I hoped that was all it was; I didn't want to start herniating. The bleeding had stopped except in one small spot. I cleaned the area up, put an antiseptic dressing on it, and changed into the spare shirt.

Satisfied I had done my best I left the lavatory, found a place where I could buy a coffee, and sat down to drink it. I took my time, sipping slowly while I thought about what on earth I was going to do now.

Get on the next available flight to England, I told myself. I'd been in America less than twenty-four hours and I'd killed someone already. Not to mention the second occupant of the car I'd crashed, whose condition was unknown but he was probably dead too. That was no way to go on.

What was particularly worrying was that I had to add the Massachusetts police to the list of those persons pursuing me. I didn't think they'd be able to tie me in to the car crash — at least not yet — but the late designer-stubble body was a different matter. It was, I suppose, just possible that the Westlebury neighbourhood was the sort where people prefer not to get involved, and maintain an attitude of being blind, deaf and dumb. If so, there might be hours or even days before I had to worry about officers of the law. If not so, on the other hand, and someone — the hi-fi-enthusiast for example — had reported the gunfire, then I was already a wanted man, albeit in my Walt Westlebury guise.

And of course it wasn't only the cops I had to bear in mind. The dead man had friends. They knew what I looked like, they knew my false name, and they were surely extremely keen to find me. Definitely I should leave the U.S.A. while I could.

The one thing that gave me pause initially was a silly,

trivial matter: I'd left Mr Westlebury's glasses behind in the apartment. Probably it wouldn't be of any consequence but it troubled me nonetheless. The last thing I needed was to be subjected to an inquest if my photo IDs didn't match with their owner. It was just one more problem to solve. Somewhere I'd have to find someone selling a matching pair of glasses and buy them.

Hesitating over the glasses led me, for the sake of argument, to consider delaying my departure more long-term. The bottom line in that case was money. I had to keep enough cash with me for a one-way ticket to London. Sooner or later I was going home. If I lost that option, it seemed to me I lost everything. So how much spending power did I have at my disposal? I got out my wallet and also that of the man I had shot. Combined, the two yielded a comfortable amount, good for at least a few weeks as long as I was frugal. Money wouldn't be a problem in the short term.

The dead man, I learnt from his driver's license, was named Asshur Hampete. He had been carrying some sort of medical card which told me the same thing. The remaining items I had taken from him were a couple of envelopes with mail in them, and a photo in a hard jacket showing the deceased with his arm around a girl looking at him with adoring eyes. This last gave me a pang of conscience. A few hours ago I had blown a big part of her life away and she didn't look like she deserved it.

I took out the photo and examined the back. In faint pencil was written: 'Asshur and Elisheba in the sight of Abraham,' and a date eight months previous. I hardened my heart. It was that or start crying.

Of the two envelopes, one contained a letter and a pamphlet praising the virtues of a particular brand of credit card. (There were no cards in Asshur Hampete's wallet.) The other contained a couple of handwritten pages signed by 'Mom'. Another life I'd blighted.

The address on both envelopes was the same:

> Mr A Hampete
> Sarai Lodge
> Melody
> New Hampshire

followed by a zip code.

This information set my thoughts running in a new direction. One of the lesser reasons for leaving America straightaway was that there was nothing for me to do there. But now I had an address to check on. Should I do that? Would it get me anywhere? What would I find other than an apartment block and an unhappy young woman?

Put like that it would be a wasted journey; but then again I might learn something useful. After all, currently I knew almost nothing about Mr Hampete. In particular I didn't know who he worked for. Was it the CIA? His behaviour in the apartment suggested not. Both his cruelty and the ease with which I'd overcome him fitted with his belonging to a more amateurish outfit. Hampete's girlfriend Elisheba could reasonably be expected to know the nature of her boyfriend's employment. If I called on her, I might be able to trick her into answering my questions, especially if she didn't know her boyfriend was dead; since I'd removed Hampete's identity documents after I'd killed him, I reckoned the police might take days to identify him and get round to informing Elisheba. On the other hand his employers could well inform her sooner. Was it worth a try?

It might be reasoned Hampete's allegiances would prove pretty irrelevant to my ultimate goal of establishing my innocence of a double murder in England. It might indeed turn out that way. But the fact is, if Hampete wasn't CIA then presumably neither was Jed — or was it Bryce? — Nordstrom, since the two of them were closely connected if not actual colleagues. And Nordstrom I saw as potentially crucial to clearing my name. Not to mention that identifying Hampete's employers could well make a huge difference to whether I lived long enough to achieve any goals whatever, ultimate or otherwise, in England or anywhere else.

Hampete was an enigma worth cracking in another respect too. I thought about the writing on the photo: 'Asshur and Elisheba in the sight of Abraham.' What had Hampete said to me in the apartment? "I hate you, Radman, as Abraham is my witness." Something like that. And if my memory served me correctly, the young man watching my house from above the bathing pool had mentioned Abraham too. Abraham? Could this be a reference to the Biblical character, being invoked in the same way as Catholics might call on Mary Mother of God? Or was Abraham a church minister, say? Either way, the name had a religious feel to it, as did the way it had been used. And that brought me full circle to Deep Voice and his talk of God and sacrifices that long month ago in my house on Scotsmans Moor.

124

In fact, given the pretty safe assumption that the young lad who'd taken part in the burglary was also the young lad I'd caught the following morning, there was a neat square of connections here. Hampete knew Nordstrom, Nordstrom knew Deep Voice, Deep Voice (and Nordstrom) knew the young lad, and the young lad and Hampete shared an interest in 'Abraham'. I reasoned that if I could pin down the identity of one of the four people, that knowledge might lead me to the other three. Asshur Hampete was the only one I had a certain name and address for, so he was the one I should pursue.

I just about convinced myself to stay a day or two longer in the U.S. But then the doubts launched a counter-attack. Think of the risks! Surely it would be both safer and more profitable to pursue what could be called the Northumberland mysteries: the nature of the commune at Colwick Hall; the offence Clifford Hanworth had caused to someone, that made them want to take his life; the object he'd supposedly had with him that Deep Voice and Nordstrom had been looking for when they broke into my house; the identity of the 'opposition' Nordstrom had referred to when he interviewed me following my rescue from the prison van; and the mystery of who Deborah Czerny was and what she had to do with everything else.

The arguments were finely balanced. I had to choose between putting Northumberland on hold in order to investigate Hampete in New Hampshire, and returning forthwith to England. I tossed a coin. It came up for England. And then I knew what I was going to do.

8

Melody proved to be a clean, opened out sort of place, no more than half a mile from one end to the other. Main Street, where the bus deposited me, was wide and not spoilt by an endless procession of cars passing through. I liked that. The stores appeared business-like and prosperous, selling a broad range of goods. There were also a few civic buildings and a cinema. I don't normally have much time for towns but I make the odd exception and Melody felt like it could be one of them.

As in Boston earlier in the day, the weather was on my side. It was dry — the main thing — mostly cloudy and surprisingly cool. That was fortunate as I had to keep my overcoat on to conceal the bloodstain on the waistband of my trousers. My spirits revived.

I began my visit to the town by hunting out somewhere I could dump a blood-stained shirt and a first-aid box. That accomplished, I wandered into a store selling camping gear; I wanted to check out an idea which had occurred to me on the bus while eating my sandwiches.

The thing was, my anonymity needed to be preserved. I had not the faintest idea how much cooperation there was between the law enforcement agencies of Massachusetts and New Hampshire, but it seemed sensible to assume it was effective and that consequently with Walt Westlebury a wanted man in the former state it would be risky to claim to be him in the latter. That ruled out my staying in hotels and guesthouses, for the owners would want to know my name, and conceivably expect to see some proof. (Quite possibly proof would *not* be required but I was so infernally ignorant of American ways I couldn't say. Ignorance was hamstringing me worse than a ball-and-chain.)

Hence my interest in camping. Melody was completely surrounded by dense forest, which meant it was also surrounded by a lot of places where one could lie up at night undetected. All I needed was some basic equipment.

The store exceeded my expectations. Everything an out-of-doors type might require, from the primitive to the ridiculously luxurious, was there. And with a storekeeper to match. I got chatting to him while selecting my purchases, taking the opportunity to practice my American accent. The way he talked suggested he was lonely, but he came across as a nice guy, so I didn't object to him. Indeed, he proved full of useful information. Bears? Only a few. Won't kill you unless you do something so dumb you really get up their nose. Moose? Half a ton of stupidity on legs. Won't kill you unless you do something so dumb etc. Ticks? Get some nasty diseases from ticks. Poison ivy? Don't touch it, even with your clothes. Skunks? Be very nice to them unless you enjoy having people avoid you. And so on. I paid for a waterproof sleeping bag and a backpack to carry it in, plus a tin-opener and a small knife which I intended to use for eating. I'm glad the advice was free or I'd have run up a much larger bill.

My purchases complete, I managed eventually to get

out of the store without being abrupt and made my way to the restaurant just off Main Street which the storekeeper had recommended. I hadn't arrived in Melody until mid afternoon, evening was now imminent, and with it the urge to have a cooked meal. The food proved to be good, but the service let the place down. It was cheerful and efficient enough, but after I paid my bill with the exact money the staff seemed to go kind of frosty on me and I left feeling very uncomfortable and wondering what I had done wrong.

My last port of call for the day was a new shopping mall on the edge of town. This was a place the storekeeper had pointedly not recommended. It had already caused Main Street's grocery business to close down, and some of the other stores — not his own, fortunately — had been hit. As it happened, it was groceries I wanted, so there I had to go.

The walk proved trying because the town was laid out primarily for cars. Although there weren't that many, they were frequent enough to make crossing roads tricky, given my top cruising speed of one mile an hour. Somehow I reached my goal without apparently tempting providence too much (not that providence seemed to need much tempting with me these days).

I bought some tins of food for next morning's breakfast and thereafter took to the forest. The weather stayed dry, the temperature mild, and the sky cleared before dark to reveal, as I peered up through the trees, a beautiful night sky made majestic by a full moon. Finding somewhere suitably obscure to pass the hours of darkness was easy enough and I had a good night's sleep.

I certainly needed it. Bears, moose, ticks, poison ivy and skunks all kindly left me alone.

Overnight the bullet wound and the underlying muscle stiffened up greatly but there was no sign of infection, which is what I was mostly worried about. Other than that, my abdomen was a mass of bruises from Hampete's kicking and my testicles were tender. I can't say I was sorry I'd killed him.

Come the morning — a spirit-restoring sunny one — I breakfasted, visited the mall for the toilets there, and then went in search of the public library, which I soon discovered at the end of Main Street. My intention was to use it to locate Sarai Lodge.

I had no luck until I asked the librarian if she happened to know where the place was.

She said: "You aren't fixing to join them, I hope."

Considering I was asking directions to an apartment block, this was a nonsensical reply.

"I'm just curious," I said.

"Aren't we all," she remarked in a way that signalled the conversation was over.

"Can you tell me where this lodge is?" I persisted.

"Oh, if you must know, two, three miles out of town. Nothing much to see, though. If you're not one of them they won't let you in. They'll stop you at the gate."

Clearly, Sarai Lodge was not an apartment block. So what was it? Hunting for an answer I said: "Are we talking about some sort of country house?"

"You might call it that. But see here, if you're not one for joining them, and you're not a local man, why'd you want to know for?"

"I met someone from Sarai Lodge down in Boston. We got talking."

"Recruiting in Boston now, are they?"

"I wouldn't say that exactly."

"Well, they sure go in for recruiting round here. Mostly go after kids, not locals, high school drop-outs, rich kids with no brains, that kind of person, the sort given to walking the mountain trails looking for something. I mean spiritual things."

I tried what struck me as a long shot. "These people who live at Sarai Lodge," I said, "does the name Abraham have any significance to them, would you happen to know?"

She gave me a look which suggested she was considering allocating me to the with-no-brains category and said: "I can't think why else they'd call themselves Abramites."

Stupid question. I felt sufficiently embarrassed by my ignorance I made a self-deprecating remark, thanked her for her help and left the library.

I was perplexed. Making sense of what the librarian had told me wasn't easy. Abramites? What the hell was that supposed to mean? Was Sarai Lodge another commune like Colwick Hall? I was beginning to think it must be. In which case talking to Hampete's Elisheba wasn't going to happen. Not if they — whoever 'they' were — weren't going to let me in.

I felt in need of further enlightenment and fortunately I knew just where to get it. My talkative storekeeper greeted me like an old friend. He happily sold me a local map and, as expected, eloquently regaled me with a history of Sarai Lodge when I mentioned the place. The key facts were that it had formerly been the Franklin Pierce Hotel, a plush hundred-and-twenty bed luxury complex, till it ran out of money maybe twenty years back and had been left to become derelict. The Abramites acquired it around five years ago, renamed it and brought it back to life. From what he described, it was as I'd come to suspect: a New Hampshire equivalent of Colwick Hall; that is, a mansion possessing large grounds enclosed by a wall.

Then the storekeeper gave me the juicy details. The guy in charge had been a tele-evangelist — and had made a great deal of dough thereby — before inexplicably selling out to Satan, changing his name to Abraham something-or-other, and founding the cult. More recently he'd got into trouble with the IRS for cheating on his taxes and had decamped abroad. As for his followers, they took part in orgies; their recruitment policy broke up families; they were survivalists waiting for a nuclear war to happen so they could take over the world; worst of all, and incomprehensibly, they repudiated Jesus Christ as their Saviour. I half expected him to tell me they ate babies. He plainly didn't like them. I was cautioned, for my own good, to keep away.

I assured him I'd take his advice and asked him to pinpoint on the map where the place was so I could avoid it. He innocently showed me. It was slightly over two miles out of Melody on a back road off the highway. The back road ran past the lodge rather than to it, and connected to another through-route which led to a town called Bewel and then elsewhere off the map.

I emerged from the store sooner than anticipated thanks to another customer coming in. My initial intention was to walk the two miles to Sarai Lodge straightaway but I quickly gave up on the idea. The wound was hurting too much.

I pondered the problem for a while and then hit on a neat solution. If these so-called Abramites wouldn't let me into Sarai Lodge anyway, why go there? Why not ring them up instead? I might learn just as much. So I looked up their number and gave them a call.

"Hello," said a male voice.

"Hello," I said in reply. "I'm up here touring the area and I heard from a couple of hitchhikers a few days back you have some interesting ideas on religion."

"Like what?" he said unenlighteningly.

"Oh, just that you've got a different slant on things," I answered, waffling while I thought up a proper response to his unexpected question. "That Abraham has greater relevance to modern life than we give him credit for."

"They said that?"

"Yes. Have I got it wrong?"

"Might have."

I waited for him to say something else but he didn't. "Is there someone I can talk to?" I ventured after a pause.

"Like who?"

"Well, I don't know. If I knew, I'd ask for them by name." And not waste time with a moron like you, I added silently.

"Just a minute." There was a pause while the phone ate up my credit and then he said: "Try the mall. Girl giving out pamphlets."

"Thanks," I said and hung up.

The mall was a painful and inconvenient distance to walk and I wondered if it was worth the bother. If the girl with the pamphlets was anything like the joker on the phone I'd have a wasted journey. As ever I had a choice to make: the mall, or back to Boston and thence to England.

The decision hinged on what, with luck, the girl would tell me. I was coming to conclude that Hampete and his colleague were (had been!) paid-up members of the Abramite.... What? Sect? Cult? Church? If that was the case, I could reasonably conclude I was tangling with some religious band of brothers rather than the CIA. The girl might also cast more light on the Abramites in general, something with the potential to provide a link to Deep Voice and Nordstrom and their theological prattling during their search of my house.

Okay, I was being highly optimistic hoping to get answers to these questions, but I'd come all this way and it had to be worth a try. Just let the girl not be at the mall, or go moronic on me, though, and I'd darned well stop feeling sorry for Hampete's girlfriend Elisheba.

She wasn't there. Or possibly I was looking in the wrong place, though the mall's open spaces were not that extensive.

The wound was giving me hell so I sat briefly. That brought relief, but when I stood up to get moving again it hurt worse than ever. I cursed Elisheba something rotten.

And then I had a piece of luck. I found an Abramite pamphlet. It was on the ground, trampled and dirty, but not wet or torn. I picked it up and took it into a burger bar where I proceeded to read it while eating the speciality of the place, plastered with ketchup and onion rings.

'DO YOU EVER WONDER WHERE THE WORLD WENT WRONG?' was the headline, superimposed on a picture of a naked baby, very much alive but lying in an open coffin. That was the front page. On the back was a list of various publications and the address of Sarai Lodge, followed by its telephone number and some meaningless hieroglyphics which began 'http:'. The two inside pages were a mass of words, mainly extolling Abraham as the GREAT FATHER who fell from grace and set the world on its post-Flood course to ruin. The burden of the writing was that we should go back to Abraham and live as he did while not making HIS MISTAKE. Then the world would be SAVED and all would be happiness and fulfilment, both material and spiritual. Abraham's mistake, it was revealed, was to be tricked out of sacrificing his son Isaac by the GREAT SERPENT, which had fooled him by appearing unto him disguised as the Angel of the Lord.

Sacrificing his son Isaac. Another clue that I couldn't fit into place. The boy who had been watching my house had written Isaac on his notepad. And Deep Voice had proposed sacrificing me. What I was discovering meant something more than I was discerning. But what?

Abraham's mistake aside, the text was littered, as one might expect, with chapter and verse references, mostly ascribed to the books of Genesis and Exodus. The whole thing left me cold, though I suppose if you were young and looking for answers to impossible questions you might find something in it.

134

I was musing on whether this pamphlet was of any use, when the waitress who'd served me came round with a damp cloth, wiping tables.

"You into that stuff?" she asked, glancing over my shoulder.

"This?" I said, waving the pamphlet. "Not really. It caught my eye on the ground outside. Strange sort of thing."

The waitress lowered her voice and remarked: "See her sitting over by the window? She's one of them. Hands those tracts to people sometimes. Not to old folk like you, though."

"Right," I said, privately mildly disconcerted to be called old.

"Me," the waitress continued, "I quite go for the mature type myself," and she gave me a smile and a wink that warmed my heart. Sweet kid.

When I'd finished eating I paid my bill and then sauntered over to the woman by the window. Early twenties, short stylish brown hair, brown eyes, flawless complexion, trim figure, prettily dressed. There was nothing obviously odd about this particular Abramite. Quite the reverse.

"Excuse me," I said, standing before her.

She looked at me but said nothing, not with her voice and not with the neutral expression on her face.

"I've been reading this pamphlet," I explained. "The waitress tells me it's one of yours."

"So?"

"I think it's quite interesting."

"Why?"

I had that sinking feeling. She was indeed like her colleague on the phone. "It's refreshingly different," I observed vaguely.

"So's the Reform Party but it doesn't mean I want to vote for them."

"Well no, that's true. On the other hand, if I asked a politician to tell me what his party stands for he'd be keen to fill me in."

"You haven't asked."

Before I could oblige there was a can-I-have-your-attention cough by my side and I turned to find the waitress looking at me.

"Did you leave anything at the table?" she asked politely but with distinct firmness.

I was wearing my overcoat, and my backpack was in my hand, but I glanced over to where I'd been sitting anyway. "No," I said.

"Was there a problem with the service?" she persisted.

"Definitely not," I assured her.

"Well, did you forget then?"

"Forget what?" I said, feeling very uncomfortable because I had no idea what she was talking about.

Her face reddened.

"She means her tip," said the Abramite.

It was my turn to blush. In England some people tip, some don't. I don't. Recalling the surliness I'd encountered in the past from taxi drivers and staff in restaurants when I'd paid them with the exact money, it began to occur to me that in America not tipping might be a social offence.

"I'm sorry," I said to the waitress and smiled. "I was

too busy thinking of Abraham. How much would you like?"

Instead of mentioning a figure, she reminded me what the tab had come to. Evidently I was supposed to know the percentage.

Desperately I said: "I want to make amends. What would you *like*?"

Diffidently she quoted an amount which was around twenty cents on the dollar. I gave her thirty. She danced away, rewarding my generosity with a beautiful display of wiggling hips.

I looked back to the Abramite. Her expression was a little less neutral, a little more encouraging. "I'm Tamar," she said.

That put me on the spot, in that it was no part of my plan to abandon my anonymity. I settled hastily on the first name that came into my head and gave her that. (It was the name of the Minister for Agriculture in London, whom I'd recently come across in connection with a controversy over organophosphate sheep dips.)

"Shall I tell you what I'm thinking?" Tamar asked, and continued without a pause: "I don't reckon you're a forgetful man. I think it's more a case of ignorance. And that voice of yours. I can't place it. You're not an American. I have to guess Canada."

I realized with some chagrin that my fake accent still wasn't making the grade. "You're right," I agreed, humouring her. "I'm over here on vacation."

"Over?" she echoed thoughtfully. "People don't usually come over from Canada. They come down. 'Over' is for England. Or Australia."

"Well, I came 'over' from Newfoundland."

"That where you live?"

This wasn't the kind of interview I'd had in mind. The information was flowing the wrong way. "It's not important," I stated. "I'm not going to recount my life story right now. If you don't want to tell me about the Abramites just say so and I'll go away."

"What do you want to know?"

"Mainly I'm wondering why I've never heard of you. Have you been around for long?"

"Seven years or so."

"Are there many of you?"

"Four hundred and thirty-six, last time I checked. Plus infants. We're a select group. Only a few are chosen."

"And you all live at Sarai Lodge?"

"Not all, no. We have branches in Brazil and South Africa. And England."

As she said the last named country she looked at me as if expecting a reaction. I think maybe I should have shut up at that point, but I was hot on the scent and didn't.

"That's interesting," I said. "I've been to England. You don't know where your branch is over there, I suppose?"

"Place called Colwick Hall. I can't recall the exact address."

"Never heard of it," I replied.

"Be surprising if you had, being as you're from Newfoundland."

"I guess so."

"Look," she said, taking the conversational initiative

once more, "I'm only a canvasser. You need to talk to one of our recruiters. He'd be able to give you facts and figures, the addresses of our branches, explain what we believe, even tell you whether you've any chance of being chosen. Why don't I make an appointment for you. Say ten a.m. tomorrow. You could meet here."

I found myself getting the feeling that comes with being polite (instead of dismissive) to an uninvited salesman. She was manoeuvring me into committing myself to something I didn't want to get committed to. "I don't wish to be any trouble," I said. "I'll pass on making an appointment."

"Uh-huh."

"If I want to take things further, who should I contact?"

"Not me."

"Can you give me a name?"

"I don't think so."

I had obviously said the wrong thing. Monosyllable responses were back in fashion. "Oh forget it," I said and turned away.

"Where are you going?" she asked. "Don't get mad."

Our eyes met.

"I like you," she said. "You've got an inner strength that really turns me on. Maybe we could get together."

"We're together at the moment," I pointed out.

"No," she replied, suggestively moistening her lips with her tongue. "I mean privately. I want to lie with you. You'd enjoy that, wouldn't you?"

I was so astounded it made me speechless.

"Where are you staying, big boy?" she asked.

"You're beautiful," I said, forcing my reluctant voice box back into operation, "and I'd love to share my bed with you...."

"But?"

"But it really wouldn't be a good idea."

"HIV positive, huh?"

I shook my head. I was trying not to hurt her feelings.

The neutral expression returned to her face. "Think about it," she said, no longer warmly. "Give me a call. The number's on the back of the pamphlet."

She looked away and stayed looking away. Interview terminated. I walked out into the open air feeling distinctly hot under the collar, and not just because the sunshine was making the day quite warm, there being no wind to speak of.

I made my way slowly downtown, not for any particular reason, while the embarrassment passed off. I'm no innocent myself where sex is concerned but never in my life had so explicit a proposition been made to me so casually. It appeared the rumours of orgies might have more truth in them than I had credited.

I arrived in due course at the long-distance bus pick-up point. Naturally that set me thinking about what justification there was for my tarrying in Melody. The uncommunicative bunch at Sarai Lodge were highly unlikely to shed any light on my remaining questions. And the journey to Melody had already more than paid for itself thanks to one major advance: I had established that Colwick Hall, a mere eight miles north of my house on the moors, was occupied by Abramites. There was no way that could be a coincidence.

So let me think this business through. How did the facts shape up?

Start with the English lad's notepad reference to 'Isaac'. According to the Abramites, the Biblical Abraham should have sacrificed Isaac; my conclusion now was that Clifford Hanworth had been marked for death and 'Isaac' was a code meaning 'to be sacrificed'; i.e. murdered, in anyone else's language.

Next Nordstrom. This 'professional' was the only person who knew I had left England. Therefore anyone else who knew — as Hampete had — *must* have been told by Nordstrom, which meant Nordstrom and Hampete were working together. One of them was giving orders to the other, or they were being directed by a shared superior. From his conduct and what he had said, I was certain Hampete was an Abramite. So Nordstrom must be an Abramite too. Or possibly he was someone who had infiltrated the Abramites in a (CIA?) spying capacity.

Then there was Deep Voice. Although he and Nordstrom had been partners in Northumberland, I ruled out Deep Voice as an employee of a spying agency because of his 'sacrificial' tendencies. Did that make him an Abramite? If Nordstrom was an Abramite the answer was yes. If Nordstrom was an infiltrator, he was maintaining a pretence of being an Abramite so the answer was still yes.

What about the other players? I reckoned Clifford Hanworth was either a renegade Abramite, or an innocent victim (much as I myself had become), or a member of Nordstrom's 'opposition', whoever they were. As for pretend-journalist Deborah Czerny, she was either an

Abramite trying a subtle way to get information from me, or one of the 'opposition', possibly an ally of Hanworth, possibly not.

It seemed I had for the first time a semi-coherent picture of what it was that I had got involved with. Some pieces of the puzzle were fitting together at last. And the conclusion was plain: the Abramites at Colwick Hall were the source of all my troubles. Target acquired.

I felt pleased. A key part of the mystery had been solved, now that I knew the probable location of the two Northumberland Americans. My next move was obvious. I should return to England, visit Colwick Hall, establish Deep Voice and Nordstrom were there (*if* they still were!), and identify them for the police. One of Superintendent Adcock's main charges against me was that I had invented the Americans. If I produced them, he'd have to take my testimony seriously. It might not prove me innocent but it would sure as anything cast doubt on my guilt.

To head home as soon as possible was thus an easy decision to take. Unfortunately I had three practical problems to overcome first. Number one arose from my assumption that Nordstrom possibly worked for the CIA (or similar). My behaviour in America would have the agency hopping mad. Instead of being a pawn on their chessboard, I had gone rogue. They were sure to be staking out Logan airport watching for me. Ditto, number two, would the Boston police, anxious to detain me in connection with the dead body in my — that is, Walt Westlebury's — apartment. Finally, number three, was the problem of documentation. I had no idea about visa requirements for U.S. citizens travelling to Britain. Ignorance was once again threatening to confound me.

As there was no bus to Boston for several hours, I called into the library to see if I could answer my visa question, and to discover what options there were as regards alternative international airports to Logan.

Then, with those issues resolved, and with an hour still to spare, I walked to the restaurant off Main Street which I'd used the previous day. When they caught sight of me in there, the smiles vanished like snowflakes on a pond. I went straight over and apologized for not offering them recompense for the fine service they'd provided on my previous visit and promised, if they'd forgive the oversight, to leave double this time around. It's gratifying what saying sorry can do for world peace. The smiles were restored and they treated me like a VIP.

The restaurant was air-conditioned, which was a good thing since I had to keep the overcoat on to hide the bloodstain, and the day was becoming too hot to wear much more than a shirt in the open air. That boded to be a problem if the temperature continued to rise into the afternoon.

I ate a good meal and then, as the place wasn't busy, sat for a while drinking a coffee slowly and pondering on whether to risk Logan, which I was familiar with, or go for an airport further afield.

I had just reached the dispiriting conclusion that I simply didn't know what I was doing, when a man approached my table. Tall, unremarkable appearance, prematurely balding, twenty-something.

"Mind if I join you?" he said.

In England, with several free tables to choose from, it would have been almost an affront to ask such a thing. Perhaps, I thought, this was another American custom I infringed at my peril. "Sure," I replied, playing safe.

He'd bought himself some complicated bread-roll affair. Before taking a large bite he said: "You a tourist here?"

"That's right. Been walking out in the forest. Nothing serious. Strolling really."

"Where are you staying?"

"I'm not. I'll be out of here on the next bus."

I didn't like his questions. Was he a plainclothes cop?

"Nobody with you?" he asked between mouthfuls of roll.

"No."

"Must get mighty lonesome out in the forest on your own."

"I like it."

"Some folks do, I guess." He smiled, wiped his hand on a paper napkin and offered it to me across the table. "Jared Carlison," he said.

I gave him my Minister for Agriculture pseudonym and we shook on it.

"I recognize the name," he remarked. "Have you befriended a young lady here?"

"No."

"Somebody looking for you. Don't know her name." He paused, frowned, chewed more of his roll and described someone who could only have been Tamar.

"I had a few words with her, that's all," I commented, concealing my consternation.

"She must be real keen on you. Brought some of her friends along. Asking questions. Not much luck of course. They're from the crowd at Sarai Lodge, so townspeople tend to be guarded."

He continued chewing vigorously, seemingly completely unconcerned by what he had told me. I, on the other hand, sipped at the dregs of my lukewarm coffee while consternation was replaced by alarm. Wasn't this typical of how my life had been going recently! I sort everything out in my mind and straightaway something happens that doesn't fit the picture and I know I must have got something wrong somewhere. Nothing I'd said to Tamar could justify a search being mounted for me. So where had my reasoning been at fault?

Try this for size, Radman, you idiot. I already knew Nordstrom told Hampete I was in Boston. Hampete was an Abramite, and I was already sure it was the Abramites who'd wanted to question me in the middle of the night the day I arrived in the U.S. So Hampete wasn't the only Abramite who knew I was in Boston; they all knew. Including Tamar. She must have been given a description of what I looked like and had had her suspicions aroused by the business with the tip. I'd then been unwise enough to admit to being foreign and having a knowledge of England. No wonder she'd wanted me to make an appointment. No wonder she'd tried to tempt me into telling her where I was staying. She thought I might be George Radman.

Hang on, though. All her evidence was purely circumstantial. She couldn't be sure about me. The only thing her friends would want to do initially was check me out. Maybe I could bluff them.

But no. Oh my god! Not only did I have Walt Westlebury's documents on me; I had Asshur Hampete's as well. If they searched me, there wasn't a bluff in the world that could explain away those things in my pockets. I had to get out of Melody fast.

"Look," I said calmly to Jared, "I can't think of any reason why Tamar would want to find me. These Abramites must be odd sort of people. I really don't wish to meet them. You couldn't give me a lift out of town, I suppose?"

"Well, ordinarily.... But you seem like a nice guy. So okay. Just remember when you get home to say a word or two about New Hampshire hospitality."

"I will," I assured him, feeling very relieved. It must have shown in my face.

"No sweat," he said. "Stay cool. I'll go fetch my car. When I pull up outside the door I'll sound the horn a couple times. You come right out and get in and we'll take off."

He stuffed the last of his roll in his mouth. "Give me two minutes," he said.

He paid his bill and went out. I noted he left the tip on the table so I did the same and paid my bill too. There was just sufficient time to dash into the restroom. Dry paper tends to float in the pan rather than flush away, so I forced Hampete's mail round the bend manually before pulling the handle. His wallet proved impossible to dispose of effectively. The cisterns had lids which were screwed down so I couldn't hide it in one of them. There were hot-air blowers instead of paper towels to dry your hands on so the garbage bag was practically empty. Out of time I dropped it in there regardless. That accomplished I didn't feel quite so much like I was about to be caught with my pants down. It was only a pity I couldn't unload the Westlebury documents as well; I needed them in order to cross the Atlantic.

A car pulled up outside. A horn sounded. I hastened out of the restroom and into the street. As I did so, another man who had seemingly come into the restaurant to talk to one of the staff, ended his conversation and followed me out. Close behind me. Too close.

Alarm bells ringing deafeningly in my brain, I bent down, looked at Jared through his open passenger door, and said: "I've changed my mind. I'll wait for the bus."

I shouldn't have been that polite. The man behind me pushed against me. I partly fell into the car. Before I could reverse direction, he bent over me and held his hunting knife in front of my face, too low down for potential witnesses to see but clear enough to me.

"Get in the car or bleed to death," he said.

"Okay," I said.

He'd have to back off slightly to give me room to stand far enough up to get my legs inside. It might give me an opportunity to disable him. But I wasn't given the chance. As I raised my head from the car seat, I became aware Jared had a small aerosol canister in his hand. I got a faceful of whatever was inside it.

I was blinded. I couldn't breathe. It was worse than being winded. Involuntarily my hands went to my eyes.

The man with the knife practically scooped me up, got

my legs inside the car, slammed the door and got in behind me. My wrists were pulled away from my face. Before I could resist or strike out, a thin wire loop was dropped over my head from behind and tautened round my neck. But not that taut. My wrists were released and the car moved off.

"Listen, Radman," said a voice from the back seat. "If you don't struggle I won't harm you. If you do...." I felt the wire tighten for a moment.

Struggle? My eyes were hurting like hell, tears were streaming down my cheeks, my nose was burning and I was fighting to get my breath back. That was occupation enough for the time being.

A minute or so later the car stopped to pick up a fourth occupant. "Yeh, that's him," the new arrival said. I recognized her voice. It was Tamar.

We were on the move again within seconds. I didn't need to ask where we were going because I already knew the answer. Friendly, helpful Jared Carlison had been an Abramite all along. And now I was in their clutches. I had the sick feeling I was never going to see England again.

9

By the time we got to Sarai Lodge my eyes and lungs were functioning again, albeit I was still in some discomfort, particularly my eyes. Unfortunately, sight I required more than anything else. To be able to see was essential in order to assess what was between me and freedom.

The first thing I managed to notice through the tears in my eyes was the wall, well over two metres high. We drove alongside it for a time until coming to a gate. This was also two metres or so high, climbable in an emergency, but with a strip of razor wire stretched across the top which would cause problems.

As we approached the gate it was opened automatically, permitting us to turn off the road and enter the grounds.

We came to a halt almost at once adjacent to a gatehouse. This was a small but substantial structure and had a window spanning the full length of the side facing the driveway. Inside I could see various lights and telephones and switches.

I watched the man within press a button, and the gate closed behind us. He came out, and over to our car. Military-style uniform. Revolver in a holster attached to his belt. Carried himself like a conscientious don't-mess-with-me type. Probably more show than substance.

He examined my three companions' passes through the car's windows. Inference: if he didn't recognize these brethren he was more likely a hired security guard than an Abramite.

"And who's this?" he asked, indicating me.

"Someone we caught snooping," Jared answered. "We're going to have a word with him."

"Has he been frisked?"

"Check him if you like."

The guard opened my door and patted me perfunctorily in various places where I might conceal a weapon. He pretended not to notice the wire loop being held around my neck or the tears on my cheeks. For that reason I didn't appeal to him for help. He knew I was in trouble and he didn't give a damn. Search concluded he shut my door and said: "I'll let them know you're coming."

The car pulled away.

The grounds were extensive. In contrast to the dense forest beyond the boundary wall, I beheld mostly neatly mowed lawns. Sarai Lodge itself, oriented obliquely so that the driveway curved as we drew nearer, was huge. The front of it was all windows and whitewashed walls, topped by a tiled roof. It had four floors in all, the bottom one fronted by a veranda except in the central part where there was a lobby extending outwards to the driveway.

We stopped in front of this lobby, and after about a minute the tinted-glass entrance door slid aside and three men emerged, the oldest one around thirty years of age, very well dressed and clearly in charge. He came straight round to my door and opened it, smiling broadly. He was about to speak when he saw the wire. The smile turned into a glare and he ordered the man sitting behind me, using a tone of voice associated with addressing an incompetent subordinate, to let me go. The wire was whisked away.

The smile switched back on. "Mr Radman," he said, extending a hand. "So pleased to meet you. I'm Jacob."

I got out of the car and we shook hands. It was unreal.

"What makes you think I'm Mr Radman?" I asked, wondering if I could work the bluff. It was worth attempting.

He grinned and said: "Well, you aren't the English Minister of Agriculture." He was obviously very pleased with himself. "Yes, I looked the name up," he continued. "And in any case, if that was who you are, you'd have a passport to prove it. But I'll bet the only documents in your possession belong to a Mr Walt Westlebury. Are you going to admit it or do I have to search you?"

"All right and no, respectively," I replied.

"Good," he commented. "Honesty is so much the best policy, don't you think?" And then to Tamar he said: "Well done, my dear. I shall ensure you are blissfully rewarded tonight, perhaps even personally."

I tried to give her a hard look, but with my eyes watering and tears still dribbling down my cheeks, I doubt it was effective. She ignored me anyway.

"Don't be too sore at her," Jacob said, clapping an arm round my shoulder. "You must admit she's very observant. No one expected you to turn up in Melody on your own initiative. We could hardly believe it when she reported she'd met you."

He began gently steering me towards the building. I didn't resist. There were too many men supporting him, not to mention the armed guard at the gate if I did manage to make a run for it.

"I hope you will pardon the way you were brought the final few miles," Jacob went on. "It wouldn't have been necessary only I'm afraid you've acquired a reputation for being a rather violent man."

"Reputations can be exaggerated," I replied.

We came to the entrance to the building and involuntarily I hesitated.

"Come in, come in," said my host.

Again I judged resistance would be futile.

As we stepped into the lobby and out of the sunlight I remarked: "It's an impressive place you've got here."

"Excluding our children, two hundred and fifty God-respecting souls. Another eighty in England. Fifty or so each in Brazil and South Africa. I guess you know Colwick Hall?"

"Vaguely."

We passed a couple of swing doors fastened open, and turned left into a long corridor.

"As to your reputation being exaggerated, I fear it is not so. Look what you did to our two brothers we sent to Boston to bring you here. One shot dead; and shot with his own gun, no less. The other, God mercifully stretched forth his hand and saved, but only after you put him in hospital with a fractured skull and internal injuries. Neither of these men was noted for being a pushover."

"As far as I'm concerned, Asshur Hampete was noted for being a cruel odious thug."

"Cruelty has its place. We are made in God's image and I can assure you our cruelty is but a spark compared to the raging fire of Almighty God's cruelty when He is roused to make manifest his wrath."

Oh, wonderful! The only good thing to come out of this grim turn to the conversation was that Asshur Hampete's accomplice hadn't been killed in the car crash. It meant there was one less thing for my conscience to be troubled by. And one less reason for the Abramites to inflict their spark of cruelty on me.

After forty-eight paces paralleling the veranda, we turned right into another corridor. Another twenty-six paces and we came to a particular door on the left, which Jacob opened. I could see steps leading down to a basement. Again I hesitated.

"It would be more dignified if you walk down, Mr Radman," he advised, turning on a light by means of a switch in the corridor, and going ahead of me.

I had a bad feeling about that basement but now was not the time for heroics. There were four men standing behind me, easily capable if they acted together of demonstrating the *un*dignified way of descending the steps.

The basement was sizable, ten metres by ten metres. There were some empty wine racks over against the far wall where I assumed they'd been pushed to make more room elsewhere. There were no windows and no doors other than the one I'd come in by. On the floor was a mattress with a folded blanket on it. That was the sum total of the furniture save for a chamber pot and a roll of toilet paper. The air was chilly.

"Good," said Jacob as I reached the foot of the steps. "It's a touch primitive, I'm afraid, but we had very little time to sort something out. We usually do better for our guests. I trust you can find it in you to forgive us."

I was bemused by the whole business: the incongruous politeness, the implied threats, the stomach-churning fear I was struggling to keep hidden and under control.

"If I'm a guest I want to leave," I said.

"Of course you do. And so you shall. But first our leader, Abraham Reborn, would like to ask you some questions. Regrettably he cannot be here in person. We'll need to set up a video link. Once you've told him what he wants to know and we've checked out your truthfulness you'll be free to go."

"Can you give me a timetable?"

"Everything should be set up by tomorrow afternoon. Say twenty-four hours from now."

"I can hardly wait."

He looked at the other men and asked: "Have you searched him for weapons?"

"The guard at the gate," said Jared, shrugging.

"Hasn't our brother Asshur taught you anything!" Jacob scolded. "Why didn't you tell me sooner?"

None of the men replied, all apparently overcome with instant sheepishness.

"If you wouldn't mind putting your hands on your head, Mr Radman," Jacob requested.

We went through the motions.

"And what's in there?" he asked, indicating the backpack I'd been carrying with me.

"Sleeping bag and a map," I answered.

He checked it and quickly found the small knife and

154

the tin opener. He picked the backpack up, complete with contents, and threw it to Jared. "We'll return it when you leave," he said to me. "As you're our guest I'm sure I don't need to ask you to respect our property in the meantime. Try to resist the temptation to do any damage. It would be totally pointless."

He gestured to the four men, and I stood there and watched them ascend the steps. The door was shut. I heard a key being turned. And then the light went out. In darkness I felt my way over to the bed and sat on it.

I was conscious of having been psychologically manipulated. They were encouraging me to believe there was no need to put up a fight; just answer a few questions and liberty will be restored. And it was working. While it was possible violence could be avoided, I'd be a fool to do anything precipitate. I was playing along with Gentleman Jacob and overlooking the fact I'd been abducted and imprisoned. According to the textbooks I'd be bonding with my captors next. Watch it, George, or you'll lose touch with reality.

I gave my eyes, now rapidly recovering from whatever they'd been sprayed with by Jared, a while to adjust but it made almost no difference. The outline of the door at the top of the steps became visible, and that was all; the basement proper remained impenetrably dark. It was a shame, non-smoker that I was, that I had no matches or lighter with me. It compelled me to do everything by touch.

I began of course by checking the door really was locked, and yes it was. The wood of the door was sound and the lock was imbedded rather than screwed to the rim. There'd be no sneaking off while everyone was asleep unless I acquired a key.

That reduced my options to only two: to take Jacob at his word, stay passive and wait to be released in due time; or to use violence. The latter course of action meant waiting until someone entered the basement and attacking them. With that in mind my focus of attention shifted to hunting out a weapon. I tried breaking the chamber pot but it wouldn't shatter. My efforts merely dented it. The wine racks proved equally unhelpful. They were an antique of some sort, seriously heavy and made of very hard wood, but when I brought one onto its side, with a crash which was either ignored or not heard above, the thing remained undamaged so far as I could tell. Certainly my attempts to pull it apart were unavailing. That left the light bulb. Eventually, though, I rejected it as a means of offence. For one thing, the light would be turned on before anyone entered the basement. If the light didn't work because I'd removed the bulb they'd be instantly on their guard. For another thing, the glass is of too thin a type to be effective for stabbing and gouging, and there's very little handle to hold onto. I decided it wouldn't work. It would only make them angry. That reduced the 'violent' escape option to unarmed combat — something the wound in my side precluded at least for the time being. The prognosis didn't look at all good.

They brought me three meals, at seven p.m., seven a.m. and shortly after midday (judging by my watch). Wounded, lacking weapons and unconvinced yet of the need to use force, I refrained from aggression. Not that they gave me the opportunity for any. The routine was the same each time. The light came on, the door was unlocked and two men entered; always the same two. One carried the meal on a wooden tray. The other functioned as a bodyguard. He clasped a short cosh in his hand; hooked onto his belt was an aerosol canister like the one Jared had used on me. The meal was placed on the floor. The two withdrew, taking the tray and the chamber pot with them, and locking the door behind them. Half an hour later they returned to collect the leftovers and replace the chamber pot, cleaned and sanitized. Finally, darkness was restored. The food was on paper plates and there was no cutlery; I had to eat with my fingers. Water to drink with the meal was supplied in a soft plastic cup. In escape terms the whole arrangement was pretty foolproof.

The fourth time the light came on it was three p.m. Four men descended the steps. One of them said: "Abraham is ready to see you now. For everyone's protection we need to put these on." He held up a pair of handcuffs.

I could fight or I could submit. I reckoned I could disable maybe one or even two of them, but the others would have me. So I submitted.

They led me, hands cuffed behind my back, up the steps and to a room on the second floor, probably a converted bedroom. There was a table in there with a video camera on it. On each side of the camera were a desk lamp and a loudspeaker. All five pieces of equipment were pointed at a chair some way back from the table. Jacob was already present. The four men followed me in.

"Bit like an exam," said Jacob, smiling. "I'm sure you'll make the grade. Please sit down."

I sat. My pulse rate was up and my throat was dry.

The desk lamps were turned on. The main room light was turned off. Nobody spoke.

"Well, what have we here?" a disembodied voice said, coming from the loudspeakers. Deep, resonant tones, American accent. Quite unmistakable.

"Answer Abraham," said Jacob affably.

"Good evening, Mr Reborn," I said. "I take it it is evening where you are?"

"Same old problem with your ears," said Abraham 'Deep Voice' Reborn. "I asked you a question and I didn't rightly hear an answer."

"You know who I am. We've met before."

"Indeed we have. George Radman, is it not?"

"Correct."

"Now tell me, George. Last time we spoke you lied to me. I have had much tribulation on account of that. Why did you lie to me?"

"I didn't lie to you. As I recall, you asked where my visitor was and I said I'd had no visitors. That was the truth."

"Do you want to make me angry, George?"

"No, of course I don't. Clifford Hanworth knocked on my door after you'd left, not before you arrived. If you don't believe that, there's nothing I can do about it."

"When exactly did he call on you?"

"Around five thirty."

"George, you must think my brain is scrambled. I can understand him seeking sanctuary with you when we're

158

close on his tail, but why would he do that hours later?"

"Because he was very cold and he'd injured his ankle. He could barely walk."

"Okay. Let's say I buy that. It means you and he had a couple hours to talk. I want to know what he told you."

"We didn't talk. He wouldn't even admit anyone was pursuing him. All he said was that he got lost on the moor in the dark."

"Oh, he was lost all right, brothers. Truly lost. Worse lost even than Sodom and Gomorrah: a soul seeking damnation; a manservant of the Great Serpent that has its coils around this dear Earth of ours. And he was gathered to his people that they should punish him for his mighty transgressions.

"But, say now, we have another lost soul brought among us who bears false witness in front of God's chosen people. He too consorts with the Great Serpent. What shall be done to him?"

Nobody made any move to answer, least of all me.

"Listen close, George," Abraham continued. "Clifford Hanworth is gone where he can do us no harm. Now, I didn't want to kill him, leastways not in that shack of yours. No sir, not me. It wasn't my idea he should hold a knife to that boy's throat. 'Don't come any closer,' he says to me. I figured, since the boy was one of the chosen ones, God would save him, so I went closer. I was kind of surprised, I'll admit, when God didn't put forth his hand. Have you ever seen a throat sliced open, George?"

"No."

"And you don't want to, believe me. Quick as a flash I realized God had sent me a sign, telling me his wrath was upon Hanworth and I should gather him to his people right on the instant. You see that, George?"

"I wouldn't know. I wasn't there."

"Take your time, George. I want you to think about it. Hanworth was an evil man and deserved to die. Why, surely you can appreciate I was acting righteously. I take care to do nothing impure in the sight of God. The day is fast coming when Abraham's children shall inherit the Earth and I will lead them all."

He stopped as though he'd lost the thread of his discourse, and then said: "The Great Serpent has sunk its fangs into you, George. You must suck out the poison and spit it away or your soul will be ruined. You must stop your deceiving and your lying. Will you do that?"

"Okay," I said, humouring him. I was being interrogated by a lunatic and had no idea how to handle it.

"Good. I know Hanworth must have told you a lot of stuff, but I won't tax your resolve to be honest too far. Not me. Yes indeed, I'll only ask you one question. Will you answer one question honestly, George?"

"Okay," I repeated.

"Where's the videotape?"

Silence. Total silence.

"What videotape?" I said at last.

The noise from the loudspeakers suddenly shot up by about ten decibels. "That is a vexatious answer," Abraham yelled. "The tape Clifford Hanworth stole from me. Where is it hidden?"

"Why should I know?"

"Because he had it on him. Why do you think we were chasing him! And because it wasn't on him when I

160

gathered him to his people. He gave it to you and you hid it."

"He didn't give me anything. I didn't hide anything."

"Liar, liar, liar," Abraham shouted, sounding near to tears.

"Just tell him where it is," Jacob interjected quietly.

"He must have left the damned thing out on the moor before I ever caught sight of him. It could be anywhere," I said.

"Radman," Abraham shouted, "you are a worse transgressor than Onan the son of Judah. And the Lord slew him for his transgression. God is sorely vexed with you. Sorely!" And then his voice calmed. "I know you haven't watched what's on that tape, you having no electricity at your shack, so there's no reason why I shouldn't spare you. I will spare you, George. But God has commanded me to find that videotape even if it's the last thing I ever do. I can't disobey God and I will have that tape. Where is it?"

"It's got to be out on the moor," I repeated. "I don't know where."

There was a crash as Abraham struck something — his desk presumably — on which his microphone must have been resting. "Pluck out his eyes," he ordered.

The five Abramites in the room stirred uneasily.

"What?" said Jacob.

"Pluck out his eyes. The light of the Great Serpent shines from them."

"What with?" said Jacob, sounding very disturbed.

"He is keeping me in darkness," Abraham shouted. "Let him also know darkness."

"Go and fetch a knife," said Jacob to the man nearest the door. "Make it small and sharp and clean. Sterile. You understand?"

The man left the room. Two of the others, one on each side of the chair, pinioned my shoulders.

I was about to beg for mercy but the words never came. My stomach went into spasm and I vomited up some of my most recent meal. There were times in my life when I'd been scared, but I'd never experienced terror like this.

Everything seemed to be suspended. While they waited for the arrival of the knife, I struggled to get the gastric acid out of my mouth by spitting and swallowing in turn. My mind wouldn't function any more. I couldn't think.

Eventually I said gruffly: "What do you want me to do? Invent one hiding place after another until you get tired of going to look?"

"You know where the videotape is," Abraham responded. "God has told me you know."

"If He's told you that, why doesn't He go the whole way and tell you where to find it?"

"This goes beyond vexatiousness," Abraham asserted, his voice rising again. "Now he mocks God. He reviles Him. We will sacrifice him for these monstrous sins. We shall gather him to his people. But first pluck out his eyes."

Right on cue the door opened briefly to re-admit someone. I glimpsed a stainless steel knife. It was passed to Jacob.

"Who shall do it?" asked Jacob miserably.

"It is a test," said Abraham. "God tests us all from time to time. This is your test, Jacob."

"Hold him still," Jacob commanded.

One of the men not pinioning my shoulders pulled my head back. The knife was brought that close to my face it went completely out of focus. Jacob was squeezing the hilt so tightly his knuckles were white.

"Please don't do this, Jacob," I muttered. "I haven't been cleaned. It isn't worth two cents on the dollar." A final anguished throw-away line courtesy of Jed Nordstrom. Hopeless despair.

Jacob remained motionless. Then he said: "After this, he is to be sacrificed? Is that right?"

"It is God's will," Abraham replied.

"Does a sacrifice without eyes count as clean? Chapter one of the book of Malachi teaches us we would have defiled it."

The loudspeakers went silent as though the microphone at the other end had been switched off. A minute went by. Nobody moved. The knife, inches from my eyes, dropped lower.

"You pass the test," said Abraham suddenly as the speakers came back to life. "Beat him till he agrees to answer my question. But take care not to damage him. He must not be defiled."

I was hauled out of the chair. And then the problem. Beating someone *and* not damaging him are contradictory instructions. They settled on punching me in the abdomen.

They were unaware of my bullet wound. When Jacob had patted me down, he'd missed the bandage or not realized its significance. And now this Abramite bastard hit me in the worst possible place. I screamed in pain and collapsed onto my knees.

That produced what I assume was a puzzled pause.

"Where's the tape?" I heard Abraham demand. "Hit him again."

Two of them raised me back onto my feet and supported my weight so that the punching could resume. Again and again.

The room seemed to be getting dark. My sight failed. I was losing consciousness and I didn't care. Oblivion welcomed me like a port in a storm.

10

They must have decided not to proceed any further with the interrogation. Perhaps they realized I was telling the truth when I claimed not to know the whereabouts of the videotape. The alternative possibility, that I would rather be blinded or tortured to death than hand it over, was blatantly ludicrous. There are a few things I would give up my life for, but some lousy movie isn't one of them.

I revived as they were carrying me down into the basement. My clothes, most of which I had soiled by one means or another, were taken away and I was washed with wet cloths. Then they placed me on the mattress, threw the blanket over me and departed. And there I lay, curled up like a foetus, and cried my heart out. My spirit was completely broken.

Breakfast next morning followed the usual routine. I couldn't eat it.

A little later someone I'd not seen before removed the dressing on my bullet wound — a wound they'd found when they took my clothes off — examined what he saw as if he had medical knowledge, and put a fresh antiseptic pad on it. He spoke to me but I was still too dazed with shock to take in what he said.

Between meal deliveries I passed the time drifting in and out of sleep and weeping quietly. It wasn't till the evening, and the third meal supplied that day, that hunger finally overcame nausea. I ate as much as my stomach could take, which wasn't a lot, returning thereafter straightaway to the mattress. Huddled up under the blanket I found what little comfort there was in this dreadful place.

The second day following my interrogation passed like the first, misery from start to finish, punctuated by three meals which I consumed without enthusiasm. My clothes, freshly laundered, were returned with the breakfast but I couldn't be bothered to put them on. The bed was where I belonged.

At the start of the third day something snapped back into place in my mind and I wanted to massacre Abramites. I got dressed. My appetite returned in full so that I devoured breakfast voraciously. And the two men who brought it I watched more closely than I had before.

They were both slightly taller than me and a lot younger. And heavier: what you might call fat-bellied types. That meant they could pack a lot of momentum into a punch. It also meant they could take more punishment. On the debit side they'd be slower on their feet. I was confident I could put one of them out of action, though it would be difficult and unless I got lucky (some chance!) would take time. To settle two of them, on the other hand, wasn't a realistic option, especially as the one with the cosh and the aerosol canister always kept his colleague between him and me. The only man who was ever within reach was the one I least needed to worry about. Abramites may have weird beliefs but these two at any rate weren't stupid. Starting a punch-up in the basement wouldn't enable me to escape.

Not that I relapsed into defeatism. Quite the opposite. I clung to the recollection of what 'they' say about the

Radmans: *a Radman makes a good friend — and a bloody awful enemy.* The saying originated long ago when we Radmans had to defend our estate and our livestock against all-comers and especially against marauding Scotsmen from across the border. I thought about my ancestors — and not all that far back in the past either – and how they would have reacted had they found themselves in my place. It made me determined not to be the first to let the clan down.

Until the moment of my interrogation I'd only known the location of my enemy and not his identity. Somebody out there had decided to victimize me. Somebody out there was treating me with disrespect. Somebody out there needed to be taught a lesson. But who? Well, I had a name now as well as an address: Abraham Reborn, Colwick Hall, Northumberland. And I had a goal in life more compelling even than proving my innocence of two murders. There was a score to settle.

Considering I was locked up and completely at the mercy of my captors, thinking of retaliation might seem seriously premature. So it was. But it motivated me. And motivation was what I desperately needed. Pending an opportunity to escape I embarked on an exercise program: press-ups, sit-ups, running on the spot, anything that didn't need light or space or equipment and would keep my muscles and joints ready for action. I also practiced moving around in the basement in the dark till I knew the room intimately. The bullet wound in my side continued to pain me and impose irksome restrictions on what I could do but it was definitely healing. Every day it bothered me less — even to the extent I was able to put the wine rack I'd pulled over when I was first incarcerated, and which I'd been completely unable to lift at the time, back into its upright position.

I also tried extracting information from the two fat-bellies, with mixed results. When asked why I was still being kept a prisoner and when I could expect to be released, all they said was: "You'll find out." So could I speak to Jacob about it? That apparently was an impertinence, my even uttering his name; I would speak to Jacob when Jacob wanted to speak to me, and not before. But when I tried asking for a bath, the question proved more productive. My aim of course was to have a chance to see other parts of Sarai Lodge. What I was told in response to my request was: "Don't worry about it. You will be made clean soon enough." These two Abramites had no reason, I suppose, to believe there'd be any connection in my mind between being cleaned and being murdered (or 'sacrificed' as Abraham called it) or they might not have said what they did. I shrugged off the remark in the best tradition of tactical deception, but after they had gone and I was back in the regular between-meals darkness I did some serious worrying.

To be executed you had to be cleaned. Did it follow if you were cleaned you were going to be executed? Perhaps not, but Abraham had explicitly stated during my interrogation that I was to be sacrificed, so in my case the answer was almost certainly yes. So why, given I was marked down for sacrifice, delay the event? Why not simply clean me and do it right away? I couldn't begin to guess and that made me worry even more.

I continued to bide my time, watching for a weak spot

in their defences. The trouble was, the routine was always the same. Three times a day: light on, bring in meal, leave, return to remove left-overs, leave, light off. There was never any variation which made them vulnerable. The two fat-bellies always stuck to the tried formula and I couldn't eliminate both of them as long as they did so.

Still, it was a problem that had to be solved, and quickly before they decided to clean me. I began working on a manoeuvre based on throwing my drink at the light bulb, which hung down from the ceiling and was completely unprotected. If I could hit the target and shatter the glass the resultant darkness and surprise might give me enough of an edge. But what then? Suppose I was able to leave the basement and lock the two fat-bellies in. That would be the easy part. I had to get out of the building past two hundred and forty-eight other Abramites; out of the grounds past an armed security guard; and away from the inevitable resultant pursuit. Any one of the tasks would have been difficult to accomplish. Taken together they turned my vague plan into not much more than a fantasy. Nevertheless I was determined to make the attempt. Even if I failed I'd have at least gone down putting up a fight.

And then, just as I was psyching myself up to mount the operation, something totally unexpected happened. It was at night. I woke because someone was pushing me.

"Not a word," said a female voice whispering so quietly I could barely make out the words. She had a flashlight which she shone briefly in her face. I didn't know her.

"Check your watch," she said. "It's one fifteen." In

the light of the flashlight I checked, and she and my watch agreed.

"Twenty-eight hours from now, tomorrow at dawn there's some kind of special ceremony planned. Summer solstice or something. I think it involves you. I've got two keys here. This one is for the basement door, and this one is for the front door to the lodge. Tomorrow night at one fifteen, I'll arrange a diversion. Probably start a fire in the cafeteria. Give the confusion a few minutes to build up then leave the building. Outside the gate you'll find a parked car. Get in."

"What's going on?" I whispered.

"No questions now. I'm risking my life every second I'm down here. Got to go."

And she fled up the steps and shut the door behind her.

Utterly bemused, I went up the steps myself and tried the appropriate key in the lock. It turned. Locking the door I went back down to the bed and considered the situation. It immediately occurred to me I could leave right now. Why wait? Answer: because a diversion and a getaway car solved two of the most intractable problems I faced. *If* she could be trusted to deliver. But then if she couldn't, tomorrow night was as good a night as tonight. I decided to wait and see.

The next day passed off normally. Same old three meals.

And then they broke the routine.

After the evening meal I went to bed. As had been my practice since resolving to escape I didn't undress, not even taking off my shoes. Sleeping clothed had the advantage that I was ready for action if a situation arose which I could exploit.

I was sleeping fitfully because of my need to be awake at one fifteen, when the light came on. Four people came down the steps: my usual two fat-bellies, a largish young woman and Tamar.

I glanced at my watch: twelve thirty. This was not the plan.

"Move you over onto this towel," the woman said. "You got to be cleaned."

No, this was definitely not the plan.

I lifted my head and looked at the large towel she was placing on the floor. Beside it Tamar laid a bowl of steaming water. The woman had a flannel in one hand and soap in the other.

"Get stuffed," I said, putting my head back down. I knew this was it. I either got out now or settled for a bullet in the brain. My body began gearing itself up. My mind was icy calm.

"Make it easy on yourself, fellah," the fat-belly who usually carried the cosh advised. There was no cosh this time — he probably didn't want to risk defiling the sacrifice — just the aerosol canister in his hand.

"Okay, okay," I said. "I could do with a bath anyway."

I got off the bed and stood by the towel.

"Call if you need help," said aerosol man.

"Sure will," said the woman. "Fancy sleeping in your clothes. Let's see what you got underneath."

She pulled my upper clothes free of my trousers, told me to raise my arms and thereby stripped me to the waist.

All the time I was watching aerosol man in the periphery of my vision. He looked relaxed, bored even. Good.

Addressing Tamar she said: "You be mixing up the foam. There's one scrubby beard to remove here. And he'll look better without the chest hair too."

Next she turned her attention to unbuckling the belt on my trousers. Maybe I'm sensitive in that area, for it made me decide to go for it, then and there.

"Hey," I said.

She looked at me at just the moment my fist hit her square in the face. I put everything I'd got into that punch. She gave a high-pitched gasp and fell backwards. One down.

Tamar, on her knees mixing shaving foam, looked up, stupefied. The two fat-bellies were not within immediate reach. I snatched up the chamber pot, not empty unfortunately, and brought it in an arc over my head. I'd found by experiment some days ago that I could just reach the light with it if I jumped up. The bulb smashed. The basement was suddenly completely dark, the Abramites having closed the door at the top of the steps behind them. As of now I had the advantage. For me the basement was normally dark; for the fat-bellies it wasn't.

As I'd predicted, they were slow. Aerosol man tried to spray me but he aimed too high. I ducked under it and brought my fist up between his legs. A scream ensued which I extinguished with the same fist directed horizontally into his groin. He still didn't go down so I hammered his head with the chamber pot.

The other fat-belly I'd lost track of, but Tamar,

intending to escape I think, blundered into me. I grabbed her and ran her head first into the nearest wall. She sagged in my hands and I let her drop. Two down.

I could hear someone trying to go up the steps. Not easy when you're panicking and effectively blind. I found the second of the fat-bellies on the fourth step. I grasped his ankles and pulled with all the strength I could muster. That stopped him. They were stone steps he fell onto.

"Please," he said. Silly man. Knowing from his voice where his face was, I grabbed his hair and bashed his head against the nearest step several times. Not unconscious, I think, but moribund. Three down.

Meanwhile, aerosol man, somewhat recovered, had just crashed into the wine racks, obviously completely disoriented. I located him easily enough, shoving him hard so he fell over. Then I pulled the wine rack — the very heavy, hardwood wine rack — over on top of him. Four down.

I disengaged the aerosol canister from his unresisting hand and promptly trod on something that shouldn't have been there. It was a safety razor. I picked it up and put it in my pocket. Every little helps where weapons are concerned.

Success now hinged on speed. I found Tamar, who was the only hostage available to me who was portable. She wasn't out cold, though that was luck rather than judgement on my part. I hauled her to her feet. She put up some token resistance and then submitted. It was apparent to both of us that if it came to a trial of strength she wasn't in contention.

I held the aerosol canister against her cheek. "Do you

know what this is?" I asked. "If you do anything I don't like I'm going to spray this right in your face at close range. Do you realize what the consequences of that will be?"

She knew. "Please don't," she whispered.

"We're going up the steps and then we're walking calmly to the gate. When we get there you're going to persuade the guard to let me out of here."

"He won't listen to me."

"He'd better or I'll have to kill you."

"Oh god," she said miserably.

I marched her towards the steps, accidentally treading on the other woman as I did so. She moaned.

Then I fell over the comparatively harmless fat-belly by the steps. The idiot was recovered enough to grab one of Tamar's legs, mistaking her for me. I sprayed the aerosol where I judged the fat-belly's face was. Going by the results I was well enough on target.

Tamar and I reached the top of the steps. The basement door wasn't locked so we entered the hallway. It was deserted.

When the four Abramites had entered the basement they'd left the key in the lock. I ordered Tamar — the only one whose hands were unencumbered — to lock her three partners-in-cleaning in. She obeyed.

We turned right and set off. "One sound out of you," I said to her. "Anything at all."

A few more than twenty-six paces but near enough. Then left. I counted out the forty-eight paces to the entrance lobby, again having to add a few extra. We went through the swing doors that had been fixed open when

I'd arrived but were now shut. The lobby was in darkness.

I went to the main door, which was the kind that slid aside rather than opened on hinges. I had to put the aerosol canister down in order to get the key out of my pocket. I tightened my grip on Tamar as a precaution but she made no protest at all.

The key fitted in the lock and turned. I picked up the aerosol canister and took one last glance behind me. No movement, no sound, no people. Freedom entailed a quiet, steady walk to the gatehouse. Perfect.

Triumphantly I pulled the sliding door aside.

And activated the most god-awful, deafening intruder alarm I'd ever heard. Not only that. The alarm was tied into floodlighting in the grounds which came on and lit up the lodge as effectively as bright sunlight.

In this new situation I realized Tamar would just slow me down. Without warning I sprayed the aerosol in her face and released her. She sagged to her knees, making a choking, wailing sound.

I set off at a run for the gatehouse guarding the exit from the grounds. My pace was a measured one. I didn't want to give the impression to the security guard that I was fleeing desperately. Think of it from his point of view. If he's at his post — I had no idea whether the gatehouse was manned overnight or not — and not asleep, he'll at least be drowsy. The commotion gets him fully awake but his judgement is unlikely to be at its best, not at midnight. If I behaved as a fugitive, or behaved aggressively, he might open fire. Whereas if I was only moderately in a hurry he'd assume I was an Abramite and want to ask me what was going on. I needed to convince him by how I approached that I was a source of information rather than danger.

One potential problem: there was a phone connection between lodge and gatehouse. I had to hope nobody in authority was in a position to know why the alarm had sounded. If that was the case, all anyone could tell the guard would be platitudes. If it wasn't the case, I'd find out soon enough.

The guard was there, all right — a different one to the man who'd seen me taken into the lodge — looking towards the floodlit building and dithering.

I ran towards him, waving a hand in the air. (Only one hand; the other was holding the aerosol canister out of his sight.) Wearing nothing but trousers and shoes I certainly must have appeared like an Abramite dragged hastily out of bed.

Somehow I forced myself to slow to a walking pace, determined to avoid doing anything that might put him on edge. You're one of the chosen, George. Act the part.

"It's okay," I shouted as I got closer. "This is an operational readiness test." I thought the jargon would sound authoritative. "I have to make certain the gate has been secured. Have you activated the perimeter defence procedure?"

"Have I what?"

Good. I had his attention and he wasn't thinking about his gun. "It's in the manual. You know. The red one."

"Manual?"

I didn't need to say anything else because he was within range. He had allowed me to come right up to him.

I gave him a dose of the aerosol. He grunted and his hands went to his face.

I acquired his gun from its holster without resistance. Several people were running from the lodge towards me. I could have directed a bullet over their heads but the more terror I inflicted the better my chances of escape. I aimed at the nearest of the runners and fired. He fell to the ground because he'd been hit. Everyone else fell to the ground because they didn't want to be next.

Satisfied, I hastened into the gatehouse. It only took two seconds to spot the right button. I pressed it and the gate began opening.

The phone was ringing. Guessing who was on the other end, I picked it up and shouted: "Call off the pack, Jacob, or people will die." I didn't wait for a response.

The guard had found the gatehouse door, mainly by chance, but he wasn't really blocking it. I elbowed him aside and ran through the gate.

I was quickly at the road. Melody was to the right, Bewel to the left. In all my planning I'd never expected to get this far and hadn't chosen in advance. With no time to think it through I turned left.

As I resumed running, I suddenly found myself in the beam of headlights. A car was coming towards me, heading for Melody. This was no time for subtlety. I stood in the middle of the road and aimed the gun at the windshield.

The driver got the message. Or nearly so. He braked and swung the steering wheel to his left, so the car ended up broadside on to me, the passenger door invitingly on my side of the car.

To my surprise, instead of trying to speed off, he waited.

Not wanting to have to shoot at an innocent party, I gave him no time to reconsider. I got to the car door. It should, on any reasonable calculation, have been locked, but it wasn't. The thought flashed through my mind that after a month of atrocious luck it was about time a few things happened to redress the balance.

I got in swiftly, pushed the gun against the driver's ribcage and said harshly: "Get me away from here."

The driver didn't protest; didn't delay at all. The car completed a screeching U-turn and surged forward towards Bewel.

I settled back in my seat and tried to make out in the darkness who this imperturbable man was who'd managed to be in the right place at the right time. I realized I had the gender wrong. The driver was a woman.

"Hi, George," she said, while keeping her eyes on the road ahead. "You're running early. Good thing I allowed plenty of time or I'd have missed the excitement."

I'd heard three American voices in Northumberland. Two — Abraham Reborn's and Jed/Bryce Nordstrom's — had been scarred into my memory in the course of a traumatic event. The third I remembered for milder reasons. And I was hearing it now, deep for a woman, and speaking my name more sexily than ever. Of all the baffling things that had happened to me recently, this one would surely take the top prize. I had just been rescued by that most untrustworthy of pretend-journalists, Deborah Czerny.

Fighting Back

June 21 - June 28, 1998

11

There was no time to ponder this extraordinary turn of events; Jacob had declined to call off the pack.

"We are pursued," Mrs Czerny announced. "Would passengers please fasten their seatbelts. There may be some turbulence."

I looked back. A pair of headlights was following us. I belted up as instructed.

"Maybe it's someone driving innocently along the road," I remarked optimistically. "We can't be sure."

"They're at least matching my speed," she replied, "and that's despite I'm going much too fast for safety. Besides, I was out here last night in case you decided to leave twenty-four hours early and I didn't see a single car. They're chasing us. No doubt about it. Let me know if they close the gap. I've got to stay focussed ahead. You get moose on these roads."

I glanced at the speedometer. We were doing over sixty. Striking half a ton of stupidity on legs at that speed would probably leave little for the Abramites to do beyond praising God for gathering me to my people on their behalf.

In case it had to be employed, I checked the gun. It was a six-chambered revolver. Five bullets remained. Enormous things they were. Americans aren't content to blow holes in people; they've got to blow big holes in people. This gun fired cannon shells. I was disturbed to realize I'd probably just murdered some poor overenthusiastic Abramite in the grounds of Sarai Lodge. Wounds inflicted by this firearm were more likely to prove lethal than not.

The car slowed rapidly as Mrs Czerny remarked: "Left to Bewel. Right to the highway."

I tossed a mental coin and said: "Left."

She turned right with a squeal of tyres and a surge of acceleration.

The road we'd been travelling on, which I was seeing without stinging eyes for the first time, albeit in the light of headlights, had been little more than a dirt track. The new road, taking us away from Bewel, was only slightly better. It seemed to be almost a tunnel between two walls of overhanging trees. There was no way off it. Behind us the pursuing headlights came into view intermittently, as often as the rises and falls and minor bends in the road permitted. It was impossible to say with any certainty whether the distance between us and the Abramites was decreasing.

We came to a section of the road which ran downhill and then turned sharply to the right.

"Can you handle that gun?" Mrs Czerny asked suddenly.

"Same as a rifle," I said. "Point at the target; hold the barrel absolutely still; pull the trigger."

As we took the right turn, the sound of the road changed. We were on a bridge.

"I'm not going to be able to lose them," she said. "Shoot out the tyres. I'll wait for you down the road. Don't hang around to let them shoot back. And try not to kill anyone."

The car screeched to a halt. I got out quickly. She accelerated away.

For a heat-of-the-moment plan it wasn't bad. The Abramites would have to slow to pass over the bridge because it was narrow and because on the far side — the side I was now on — the road bent sharply leftwards. There was a stream flowing beneath the bridge, and the road ran alongside it briefly before climbing up and disappearing into the forest.

That much I gleaned from the headlights of Mrs Czerny's car as it drew away. But now I was in the dark — there was no moon — with no more than half a minute and perhaps as little as ten seconds to settle a lot of tactical issues: where to take up position; when to fire; how to get away afterwards; and everything to be accomplished with a maximum of five bullets. At least the weather was dry and the air was still. That helped a little.

Time was almost up. I could hear the Abramites' car approaching. I ran to the bridge and leaned against one of the end pillars which was holding the whole structure in place. I knew before it happened I wasn't going to be able to shoot out the tyres, not staring into headlights on main beam. Nor could I shoot out the headlights. One maybe but not both. The car came into view. I stepped out into its path, the gun pointing at where I judged the driver's head to be. I gave him two seconds to duck, and then fired. I hoped his reactions were fast enough. But if not — well, that's the way it goes.

The car ran onto the bridge and veered slightly off course, scraping against the wooden planking that served to keep vehicles from going off the bridge and into the stream. Nobody seemed to correct the error. Indeed the driver, ducking or dead, allowed it to get worse.

The car was now about to run me down. I fell rather than jumped sideways out of the way. It swept past, demolishing the support I'd initially leaned against. The tyres squealed as the brakes were applied but nobody turned the car to the left. Consequently it came off the road and careered headlong, doing not much less than thirty, into a substantial tree. The tree shrugged off the pinprick. The car didn't. The engine died. Motorized pursuit was at an end for the night.

I slid and stumbled down the bank and into the stream, where the flowing water made sufficient noise to cover my movements. From there I passed beneath the bridge. It was my intention to go downstream a way and then climb up to the road and locate Mrs Czerny.

I'd gone about five metres when somebody appeared at the top of the bank. I could see him because the idiot was waving a flashlight about. Never, never, never hunt an armed adversary in the dark with a flashlight. I took aim and waited, motionless.

Someone called out: "Can you see him?"

I watched the flashlight. If its beam came anywhere near where I was standing I'd have to kill the holder before he could bring it to bear on me.

He was concentrating on the bridge and the space underneath it. I willed him desperately to carry on doing that, not because I was afraid of discovery but because I'd hurt too many people this night and I was sick of it.

For perhaps as long as half a minute his life hung in

the balance. Then, quite casually it seemed, he flicked the beam downstream and I shot him.

That was the signal for me to move further away at speed. There was return fire. Not being able to do anything about it, I took no notice. In any case, they'd given up using lights to try and find me. They'd grasped that lesson. They were shooting blind, at random.

I climbed the bank up to the road. By then the shooting had stopped. Somebody could have run along to make an interception so I kept low and played things very cautiously. Consequently it took me a few minutes to get sufficiently clear I could risk jogging.

Quite aside from enemies, jogging proved inherently hazardous. It was so dark I couldn't see my own feet. And the road was only a slightly different colour of black from the forest on either side. Several times I came unnervingly close to smacking into a tree. Ditto Mrs Czerny's car which was pulled over hard on the right with the lights off.

I tapped on the driver's window. There was no response. I was about to open the door when it occurred to me doing that would turn on the interior light. Not a good idea at this stage. Instead I whispered: "Mrs Czerny?"

"Okay, George," she said from close by. "Sorry for the melodrama. I had to be sure it was you."

We wasted no time getting into the car and moving off.

"Mission accomplished?" she asked.

"Yes."

"How'd it go?"

"Could have been better. If you've got money to invest, put it into the funeral business."

"That bad?"

"I think I've killed four people tonight. And there was one in Boston too. That's the height of my achievement in your country: littering it with dead bodies."

There must have been something in my voice that conveyed how I felt about it, for she said quietly: "It's over now, George. We'll get you home."

That choked me up so that I couldn't speak and my eyes watered and I was glad it was dark.

Perhaps she sensed that also, because she said nothing further until I broke the silence myself to ask where we were heading.

"Bewel," she replied. "I'm staying in a motel there."

"I thought that was back the way we came."

"It is. I'm going the long way round. I didn't want to drive right over in case we were unable to shake those people off."

I shivered.

"You cold?" she asked.

"Slightly. My trousers are soaking wet."

She turned up the heating and said: "I'll go buy you some clothes in the morning."

We joined the highway for a few miles and then left it again. It was nearly two a.m. when we pulled into the motel in Bewel.

We managed to sneak in without being seen, which was well and good given my strange attire and the handgun I was carrying.

Mrs Czerny's room was actually two rooms: a well-furnished bed-sitting-room containing a double bed as its central feature, and an attached bathroom. She took charge of the latter, saying: "I'll run you a bath." She didn't offer me a choice.

"I could do with one," I agreed. "I've not had a decent soak since leaving England. And," I added ruefully, "when I escaped from Sarai Lodge there was this chamber pot with urine in it, and it went everywhere."

"Needs must," she said with a smile in her voice.

So I had a bath and washed my hair and cut my nails and shaved with the razor I'd acquired from the Abramites, and removed the dressing from the wound in my side. The site was healing nicely and didn't need to be covered any more. I emerged from the bathroom a new man, wrapped in a bath towel.

Mrs Czerny was waiting outside and obviously approved of the transformation. "My!" she said. "I can see you're feeling better."

Apart from family, she was the only person who'd shown me any genuine sympathy since the nightmare began. On an impulse of affection I kissed her on the lips. She didn't pull away but she kept her mouth shut. I felt like a coarse oaf.

"I don't think I should have done that," I said, looking down.

"We hardly know each other," she remarked, though not with anger.

"That's what I mean."

She touched my elbow lightly and said: "I'll be out in a minute. Make yourself comfortable."

She took rather longer than a minute. At first I lay on

the bed staring at the ceiling, and then my attention was drawn to the Bible on the bedside table. I began leafing through the pages looking for Abraham. Someone called Abram came to light in Genesis chapter eleven. There also was Sarai, Abram's wife. That made sense, I suppose, to name the Abramite headquarters after Abram's wife. Further on there was a lot of stuff about Sodom and Gomorrah, after which I came to the bit about Isaac being sacrificed. By this time Abram had inserted a 'ha' into the middle of his name, though I missed where that happened so Abram and Abraham might have been different people.

I was reading through the Isaac business carefully when Mrs Czerny reappeared wearing pyjamas.

"I didn't know you were religious," she said.

I shook my head. "Studying up on the enemy."

She pulled back the bedclothes. Not having any clean or dry clothing to wear, I was naked. And embarrassed. As she'd said, we hardly knew each other.

It wasn't that that bothered her, though. "What happened there?" she asked, seeing my bullet wound for the first time.

"It was when I was in Boston. Somebody shot me."

"Was that when they kidnapped you?"

"Not then. I got away from him. He was the first of the bodies I've been littering America with."

"I'm glad we're on the same side. And talking of sides, can I trust you to keep to your half of the bed?"

"If I misbehave, hit me with your wedding ring," I joked.

"My husband's dead, George."

"I'm sorry. I don't know what's the matter with my mouth tonight. I seem to be really determined to screw this up."

"You're tired and you've had a bad experience. Let's get some sleep. We can talk in the morning."

She turned out the light and wished me goodnight.

"Goodnight, Mrs Czerny," I said, and put the Bible back where it belonged by touch.

"George?"

"Yes?"

"Can we get one thing straight this minute?"

"If I just pulled the bedclothes off you I didn't mean to. I'll try not to do it again."

She chuckled. It was a pleasant sound. "It's not that. I'd like it if you'd call me Deborah."

"Goodnight, Deborah," I said, and fell asleep feeling unaccountably cheered up.

*

We were up late, which suited me fine. It was a long time since I'd slept in a decent bed and I was in no hurry to leave it.

Deborah went shopping and came back with a T-shirt and jeans which I could wear temporarily until I was able to buy clothing of my own choice. While she was out I watched television. Nothing demanding. Just a way of avoiding thinking. Thinking had got me into a lot of trouble over the last few weeks and I wanted to take a rest from it. Reality could wait.

We went to a fast food place for a late breakfast and

talked about nothing special: the weather (would you believe!), and American sitcoms, and smoking in restaurants. This last topic we vied with each other to condemn the most vehemently. It was almost fun.

After breakfast I bought a long-sleeved sweatshirt and a light zip-up jacket with some of Deborah's money and we returned briefly to the motel for our things We had agreed it would be unwise for us to tarry in Bewel. It was unlikely the Abramites would show up there looking for me but it was not impossible. We checked out and hit the road, avoiding Melody by heading west.

At a town along the way we stopped for a while so I could telephone home. Again Deborah had to provide the funding. It was a forceful reminder that if she cast me adrift I'd be destitute. Apart from the clothes I stood up in, the sum total of my possessions was a safety razor, an aerosol canister (persons, for the disabling of) and a handgun with three bullets in it.

I rang Malcolm's number and he answered almost at once. The news this time was better. My mother was home again, apparently none the worse for her stay in hospital, though she was taking pills enough to make her rattle. He put her on the line and we talked for a while. Of course I told her I was fine and apologized for not phoning more often, explaining that I'd been lying low — I didn't dare tell her what had actually been happening — and that I would be home soon. After that I came out with the usual absurd exhortation about not worrying, and repeated the advice I'd previously given to Malcolm to report my phone call to the police. I assured her it would do me no harm and the police no good. "That way they won't be able to lock you up for aiding and abetting, or whatever they call it," I explained. Bless her heart, she used a very rude word to register her opinion of telling the constabulary so much as the time of day. (Sharing my father's surname since 1940 had clearly made her a Radman by more than just marriage.) She added that if I thought her language was bad I should have heard Peter. She related how he'd been accused of engineering my escape from custody, and how Superintendent Adcock and his colleagues had browbeaten him for seventy-two hours before releasing him. Insufficient evidence, they claimed. Peter had not been polite when expressing his views on the way he'd been treated. I knew only too well what he meant.

Back on the road, Deborah drove onto Interstate 91, heading south. In due course we arrived at a place called Lebanon, arrival being timed nicely for lunch.

Later, we pulled into a parking lot overlooking the Connecticut River. The view was beautiful, made even more appealing by the bright sunshine, and we gazed at it for a few minutes, neither of us speaking.

Then Deborah said: "For pity's sake talk to me, George. The silence is bugging me."

"All right," I agreed. "What would you like to talk about?"

"Are you for real?" she asked.

I looked at her and couldn't make sense of the expression on her face. I frowned and shrugged.

"I have spent the whole morning driving and you've sat in the passenger seat all that time and hardly said a word. Maybe you're the strong silent type, but this is ridiculous. Don't you want to know where we're going? Don't you want to know how come I was waiting for you outside Sarai Lodge?"

I had a feeling that the reality I didn't want to face was about to put the boot in. "I'm afraid of what you'll tell me," I began, truthfully. "I'm afraid I won't believe you. I'm afraid you'll....

"Let me start again. I'm not putting this very well. Imagine you've been in a lot of pain and you find a place somewhere where there's no pain. You know you're going to have to leave that place soon, but you sure as anything wouldn't be in a hurry. Does that make sense?"

"In a way."

"And it's not just me, is it? It's you as well. You could have told me things. You didn't have to wait for me to ask."

"No, I guess not."

"So why the silence on your side?"

"I don't know. I guess I find being with you a little scary."

I was genuinely shocked. "I'm aware I killed people last night, but I'd never harm...."

"No, no," she interrupted, "I know you wouldn't. That's not it. It's that, well, take what happened at the motel. I turn out the lights and you go right off to sleep. Or this morning. I set out to buy you some clothes and you don't query it. And now I could be driving you to anywhere. You trust me. I'd have to be inhuman not to be touched. But it scares me as well. You don't know who I am."

"It's *what* you are I don't know, not who."

"Different word, same point. I've got a job to do. I might let you down."

"And you might not," I said, and gave her what was intended to be a reassuring smile.

"You and your boyish charms!" she exclaimed almost as if she was angry. "You pulled that stunt both times I visited you in jail. Now you're doing it again!"

I wasn't sure there wasn't some kind of misunderstanding going on here. It wasn't a stunt; it was honesty. I said: "There are billions of people on Earth, Deborah, and I asked for you to be my friend. I'm still asking."

"I know you are," she said sadly. "I just wish you wouldn't keep picking on me, that's all. I guess we'd better get going."

"I thought you wanted me to shatter the silence with a grand inquisition."

"Not really. What I wanted was to establish our respective positions on the issue. If we're not going to talk about something, let's be clear why we're not talking about it."

"Fair enough. No discussion yet. I'm not mentally ready for it. And as for you? You're afraid you'll disappoint me. That troubles you because you know, deep inside, that I'm right about you: you're a good person."

She was silent for a moment, and then said: "Why aren't you married, George?"

"What an odd question."

She leaned across and kissed me on the cheek. "You're too nice to be on your own. Let's go."

The relief in her voice was unmistakable. The silence

really had been getting to her and I'd been too self-absorbed to appreciate how much.

*

Four hours later we were at our destination, a six-storey office block in downtown Bridgeport, Connecticut, where Deborah pulled into a private parking lot. Thereafter she led the way to the top floor of the building.

The elevator opened onto a brightly lit reception area. The impression was one of business-like wealth. A lady staffing the desk issued me with a clip-on plastic card bearing the legend: 'D CZERNY VISITOR'. Since both my identities, Radman and Westlebury, were fugitives from justice, I was relieved not to be asked to sign anything.

That was the extent of the formalities. Deborah explained she had to brief her boss before he spoke to me, and apologized that I would be kept waiting. She handled the matter with great courtesy — indeed she became so much more serious and formal once we arrived at her office she was almost a different person — depositing me in a small room and leaving me with a video to watch.

Thus it was I spent fifty minutes learning about the wonders of Deborah's employers, Rodgers & Schirrel, Private Investigators. Basically the presentation was a glorified advert but it was slickly done and an improvement on browsing back copies of Readers' Digest, which is what you're normally expected to do in English waiting rooms.

Another nice touch: when the boss was ready he came for me in person, not via a secretary. "Mr Radman," he said as we shook hands: "Caxton Schirrel." Six feet tall, well built, good looking, in his fifties, no white hairs (which probably meant he was vain enough to use hair dye), wearing an expensive suit, and with a cultured sound to his voice. The only thing that spoilt him was his handshake. I prefer a firm grip to a weak one but I don't expect it to hurt.

He led me down a short corridor to a roomy office. I noted the very large desk, the picture window with a view across what looked like quite a pleasant town, the posh carpet, the leather-upholstered sofa, the mock-antique coffee table. There was serious money here and no mistake.

I was directed to a chair in front of the desk. Deborah, sitting in a similar chair to one side, gave me a reassuring smile like my mother used to give me as a child before ushering me into the dentist's surgery. I decided I didn't like the office-Deborah as much as the outdoor one. She seemed to have lost something of her humanity.

Schirrel went behind his desk, picked up the phone and said: "I'm not on the premises." That was to impress me of course. It was nice to know he thought me worth impressing.

"Do you wish Deborah to leave?" he asked.

"No."

"Fine. You've seen our video presentation. What did you think?"

I decided to play safe. "You're obviously a successful P.I. firm. You must be good at what you do."

He grinned. I'd clearly got top marks on the first question. On to the second: "Do you want to check in any way that we are what we say we are?"

"Do you mean you aren't?"

"Quite the opposite. If you have any doubts, I want to hear them."

"If this isn't genuine, somebody's spending a lot of money. It wouldn't be worth it merely to fool me."

"Good point. Okay now, what I intend to do here is to exchange information. You need answers; so do I."

He gave me a do-you-agree look and I gave him a by-all-means gesture.

"I'll go first," he said. "We have a client — I'm not going to tell you who he is — who has an interest in the Abramites — I'm not going to tell you why. In the course of our work for this gentleman we needed to get someone into Colwick Hall. To avoid suspicion the infiltrator had to be local. Unfortunately we have no one English on our payroll, which meant we had to subcontract the task to the person you knew as Clifford Hanworth. He's.... He was an English P.I. we've used occasionally in the past. Deborah, here, was sent over to provide a communication link between Hanworth and us in Bridgeport. As far as we know, Hanworth was accepted by the Abramites. He was certainly able to provide us with useful information. Then something went wrong. He's murdered at your farmstead.

"Now, the account of events you gave Deborah when she visited you in jail I'm familiar with. Before I continue, do you want to change or add anything?"

"Change, no. Add, yes. Firstly I can put names to the

196

two Americans who broke into my house: Abraham Reborn and Jed — or maybe Bryce — Nordstrom."

"Reborn's the guy in charge. Nordstrom I've not heard of."

"Secondly, I can tell you what happened to Hanworth that morning. As you know, while I was fetching the police he stayed behind guarding an Abramite lad I'd caught watching my house. Apparently Reborn turned up. My guess is Hanworth knew he was about to buy his plot in the graveyard and decided to take an Abramite with him."

"How did you find these things out?"

"I was interrogated at Sarai Lodge and...."

The recollection suddenly made me feel unwell and I had to stop talking.

"Are you okay, George?" Deborah asked with alarm.

"Yes," I said as the nausea retreated. "God! That's never happened to me before. It was almost like I was back there. Look at me!" I wiped the sweat off my forehead with a trembling hand.

"During the interrogation they told you what had taken place at your farmstead?" Schirrel asked calmly.

"Yes."

"Do you know of anything which could furnish objective evidence in support of your account?"

"Not really."

He regarded me thoughtfully. That, and his kind refusal to acknowledge my momentary distress, completed the restoration of my equilibrium. I forced a smile and commented: "If you have any doubts, I want to hear them."

"Touché!" he said. "There are always doubts, Mr Radman, but very few in your case. Let me explain. Do you recall I was referred to as Dr Schirrel in our presentation video?"

"Yes."

"As the video revealed, I've a doctorate in criminal psychology awarded by a famous university not a thousand miles from this office. This gives me a lot of insight. I note, for instance, that we're not dealing here with your word against someone else's. It's your account versus nothing more than a collection of ignorant police suppositions.

"Now, let's say the police are right to accuse you. How does the psychology pan out? Possibility: the murders were premeditated. In that case you'd have been able to construct a better story than the one you gave Deborah. Not premeditated then. That leaves murder-in-haste. When someone does that they're shocked, frightened, remorseful, confused; a whole lot of things. They can't think straight. If, after the event, you'd had a day or two to come up with a cover story, maybe I'd suspect you. But to come up with a tale like yours in a few hours? I don't buy it. Too elaborate. Too self-consistent. And come to that, too implausible. Conclusion: you're almost certainly no murderer."

"I wish the Northumberland police were as logical as you are."

"Hmm. Don't be too hard on them. You were my prime suspect also at first. That's why I had Deborah visit you in jail and why she claimed to be a journalist. I didn't want you to know Rodgers & Schirrel were after you."

"After me?"

"I take Hanworth's murder personally. My employees, including indirect ones like him, often have to associate with low-life and scum. They may risk their lives for this firm. They need to know — and more important, adversaries need to know — that if the worst happens R & S will bring sufficient resources to bear to ensure justice is done. So I was, and still am, after the murderer.

"But you can relax. Deborah's report, following her interview with you, convinced me you were innocent and probably knew nothing of use to us. Frankly, that meant you were of no interest, so I ordered her to drop you."

"Before you go on, Cax," Deborah interrupted, "Cax agreed that if my investigation enabled me, as a kind of by-product, to furnish proof of your non-involvement to the authorities, then I would do that."

"Right," Schirrel concurred, "though that's mostly academic now. Your breaking out of custody has made establishing your innocence a tough proposition. Actually I'd be interested to know how you pulled that off. The word is it was a family affair. I gather you've a lot of kinfolk in your part of England."

"Mother, uncle, two surviving aunts, seven cousins, a few nephews and nieces, but it had nothing to do with any of them. Nordstrom did it. He hinted he worked for the CIA."

I went on to recount my 'rescue' (probably by the Abramites, possibly by the CIA) and how I'd been provided with the Walt Westlebury identity.

"Westlebury?" said Schirrel. "I've heard of him recently."

"You probably have. The Boston police are looking for me under that alias. I...."

"Stop right there!" said Schirrel harshly. "You must not tell me about any felony you may have committed in the United States. Do you understand?"

"Yes," I said, taken aback.

"Sorry, Mr Radman, but I won't allow you to put this firm into a compromising position." He picked up the phone and asked his secretary to do some research on 'Westlebury'.

"As to the CIA, it's always possible Nordstrom is an infiltrator like Hanworth, but if he is I don't think he was doing the CIA's work when he busted you from the prison van. There'd be no gain to them in doing it. So let's say he was obeying Reborn's orders that day. The question then is, why would the Abramites want you out of England? I guess we'd all like to know the answer to that question. You probably have your own ideas but let me give you mine first, speaking as a criminal psychologist. Between us we should be able to construct a complete picture.

"My initial thought — I'm thinking out loud here, piecing this together as I go along — is to ask what happens when an accused man goes on the run. The answer is that it convinces most folks he's guilty. I know it's not rational but it's true. That then was their first reason for springing you: to guarantee the fall-guy takes the fall.

"Another effect of your absconding is that it isolates you totally, thus removing the small possibility you might be able to persuade the police, or anyone else, to investigate Colwick Hall. That's why they flew you to America. It ensured as far as possible your isolation wouldn't be reversed by re-arrest.

"Right, we've got two significant benefits here, but I don't think they're enough. There's got to be a third motive. That has to be something to do with the time you spent with Clifford Hanworth before he died. They need to know what passed between you. They can't ask you these things in jail the way Deborah did because they daren't do anything which might, even improbably, associate Colwick Hall with you or the murders. Therefore they organize your escape. That way they can question you in private, out of anyone's sight.

"This is working out better than I expected. It also gives us an explanation for why Nordstrom hinted he was working for the CIA. You'd never have told him anything if he'd said he was an Abramite from Colwick Hall. The CIA cover story was aimed at making you more forthcoming."

Schirrel paused and then said: "Okay. Let's test this theory I've been building up. So far you haven't mentioned what you and Nordstrom talked about after he sprang you. By my reasoning his interest should have centred on Hanworth. Did it?"

"Yes," I agreed, feeling distinctly deflated. The way Schirrel put it, it was all so obvious.

"And how much did you tell him?"

"Not much. I didn't trust him."

"That fits too. Maybe they intended to set you up in Boston and walk away. Being merciful once in a while probably makes them feel good. But if you didn't provide

Nordstrom with the information they wanted him to get from you.... Change of plan. They'd want to talk to you some more. So they kidnap you and take you to Sarai Lodge.

"Okay. How do my ideas on what's been going on square with yours?"

"Compared to yours," I replied, "my ideas are still at the starting gate. You're clearly the expert here."

"Yes, but I don't have the key. That's in your possession. Tell me about the questions they asked you at the lodge. That's the key. What do they want from you that's so darned important to them? It's got to be something you know; something Hanworth told you."

That was indeed the key. "It's all a sick joke," I said. "Hanworth told me nothing. I didn't know anything so darned important. I didn't even know anything unimportant. I couldn't help them. The Abramites had been wasting their time."

I'll give Schirrel credit. He was one clever man. "Didn't?" he quoted and fixed me with a thoughtful look.

I grinned. "Hanworth stole a videotape. They thought he'd passed it to me and I'd hidden it."

It was nice to see Schirrel temporarily speechless.

I went on: "But it's my belief he hid it himself out on the moor before he ever came anywhere near me. I'm sure it exists but I've no idea where it is."

"Could it be at your farmstead?"

"No. At least if it was there it won't be there now. The police would have found it."

"Yes, of course. Did you form any opinion as to what was on it?"

"Something the Abramites don't want anyone else to see. Could be anything."

Nothing more was said for a while. Deborah and I waited patiently while Schirrel stared at nothing in particular, lost in thought.

Eventually he said to me: "You must have worked out for yourself I have a girl in Sarai Lodge. It was easy to get her in. Jacob has an unhealthy interest in young women. She it was who told me you were there. Apparently they had some sort of ceremony planned for you at sunrise this morning. I decided it would be worth getting you out of the place. And why? Call it a hunch. You had to be important somehow or the Abramites wouldn't have gone to so much trouble over you. I thought you might prove to be the handle we need to finish the job we're doing for our client. But I was wrong. You don't really matter at all. It's the videotape that's decisive. Hanworth knew that. That's why he stole it and ran."

After I dutifully nodded my concurrence, Schirrel lapsed into deep thought again. And this time I joined him. As far as I could see, my own jigsaw puzzle was complete. At last I knew who Hanworth was, who had been chasing him and why, and who had murdered him, name and address. And I knew who had helped me to escape from Sarai Lodge and why. That meant the mysteries were all resolved. There was nothing left for me to do in the United States.

But England was a different matter. In my own country I had a score to settle and my innocence to prove. Ideally both goals could be achieved simultaneously by getting Abraham Reborn locked up for the murder he had committed. Unfortunately nothing in my life was that simple any more. For one thing, I was literally penniless; I needed help returning to Northumberland. For another, I could no longer find it in me to believe Superintendent Adcock would say sorry and admit he'd made a mistake. He'd insist on seeing my prosecution through to the end. As a result I'd have to stay undercover, so that if the information I supplied was ignored I could deal with Abraham privately and escape thereafter back to the U.S. That was something else I'd need help with. The question was, could I persuade Schirrel to provide the assistance? The arguments ran round and round in my mind.

"I have a notion, Mr Radman," Schirrel said, breaking the silence once more, "you've been only half honest about that videotape. I think you have a good idea where it is."

I began to protest my innocence.

"Hear me out," he said. "Here's the deal. I will supply you with a new identity, complete documentation, and fly you to England. Deborah will go with you. All you have to do in return is retrieve the videotape from its hiding place and pass it unwatched to her. Do that and you won't owe me a cent. And I'll go further. If things don't work out for you over there — I mean you can't resume being George Radman without going to jail — I'll give you the option of joining Rodgers & Schirrel here in Bridgeport. I'm pretty confident you have talents we could harness."

I was astounded. He was offering me everything I wanted, and then some. "I couldn't have negotiated a better deal if I'd tried," I responded. "I don't know where the tape is, but if it's out on the moor.... Well, excluding my cousin Peter, no one knows the moor better than I do. If that tape is findable, I'll find it. I'll do my best."

He held out his hand saying: "I demand no less of every R & S employee. Welcome aboard."

We shook on it (painfully again).

I dared to think my choice of Deborah Czerny to be my friend might yet prove the most inspired decision I'd ever made.

12

I spent the night in a downtown hotel which Rodgers & Schirrel had an arrangement with. The service was good, the food ample, the bedroom warm and secure, and the bed comfortable. It was a shame I could only regard it as an oasis in the desert. Still, these things are to be enjoyed while they last.

Next day, while Deborah was disposing of my recently acquired revolver — even in gun-toting America, walking around with a large, stolen firearm bulging your pocket is begging for trouble — I was taken on a tour of the R & S offices. They treated me for all the world like a prospective employee. I was introduced to various people whose names I promptly forgot, and to the firm's rapid-covering-fire lawyer and joint supremo, Ms Rodgers. Not, as my prejudices had me expecting, a tall, hard-faced, power-dressing, pseudo-masculine tyrant, but the opposite of all these things. In fact she was almost as likable as Deborah.

It was Ms Rodgers who gave me the biggest surprise of the day. The firm's research concerning Walt Westlebury had revealed he was being sought by the police, not as a murder suspect, but because they needed a statement from him. I was amazed to learn that in America, if you encounter an armed intruder on your premises, you can quite legally shoot him dead. The police investigation had concluded Asshur Hampete had been just such an intruder, that there had been a struggle, and that Mr Westlebury had exercised his lawful right of self-defence. There were some awkward questions he needed to answer, sure, but no one was anticipating arresting him. When I explained that in England inflicting even the slightest injury on an intruder will result in your facing a criminal charge, Ms Rodgers expressed the view that the law and the police in my country must be completely insane. "Whose side are they on, for Chrissake?" she asked pertinently. It's a good question.

The afternoon was spent sorting out my new identity. It had been decided I should revert to my natural hair colour but, as an alternative form of disguise, to cut it very short, crew-cut style, which I hated. I was politely criticized for shaving off my ten-day beard; every little dissimilarity with George Radman would have helped. But never mind. What's done is done.

With my appearance settled, they prepared my passport and other identification documents. It was explained to me that, with digital technology, generating what they referred to as 'operational docuware' (it was forbidden to use the words 'fake' and 'forgery') was actually comparatively inexpensive (the word 'cheap' was frowned on too). It was also comparatively fast. I was told to be ready to leave for England tomorrow.

The evening I passed with Deborah at a restaurant — another establishment R & S had an arrangement with — and she told me her life story. Despite her surname she was a thoroughbred Anglo-Saxon Protestant, born and raised in Hartford, roughly fifty miles north of Bridgeport. She married her one and only husband in her early twenties and had had two children, a son who was a high-earning architect, and a daughter of whom she commented: "The less said the better." Her husband had built up a successful trucking business but the stress on him had taken its toll, mainly in the shape of fifty cigarettes a day. He'd succumbed to lung cancer eight years ago. His death had left the company rudderless. It had started to lose money. So Deborah sold it, getting a good price and assuring her financial future as a modestly wealthy woman. Why then was she working for R & S? "I needed to be occupied," she explained. Cax, a friend of her husband's from way back, had been there for her in many ways during what she called her 'dark time', and that included offering her a job. I could see she thought a lot of Caxton Schirrel. As for her daughter, the young woman had gone out of control during her father's last illness and was currently 'dropped out' somewhere in California. "She'll come round eventually if she survives," Deborah remarked gloomily. "Until then she's on her own." She shrugged. "Her choice."

How about me and my past life? I began by talking about my family. My grandfather — another George — and many generations before him had been landed gentry. ('Gentry' I explained were a kind of social class between the nobility and the peasants.) Grandad had had two sons. The eldest, my uncle Percy, had, following long-standing tradition, inherited the bulk of the Radman real estate. My father, Arthur, had been set up in the house which was now mine, with enough acres to make a living from. As for me, I was an only-child and the moors were in my blood. I was competent to assist with ewes giving birth before I could read or write, and I made my first solo hike to Lowhope Crag when I was only ten. It was a harsh life, especially in winter, but a great one. I have a degree in biology and a master's degree in ecology, and I earned my living as an ecologist working in environment conservation until twenty years ago. That was when my father died and I became the owner of his house and land. My father, like Deborah's husband, had died of lung cancer. Sad though these losses were, it made a bond between us. We'd both been there. We both knew what it was like. We both loathed tobacco and all its works. We gave each other genuine sympathy.

Not that I want to create the impression we ended up crying in each other's coffee. Life stories are unhappy in places, and dull when précised into a paragraph, but if you take your time and tell them right (we both did) you can make your opposite number laugh along the way. Deborah was beautiful when she laughed. It was a good evening.

I returned to my hotel that night in a very strange frame of mind. Naturally there had been girls during my time at the universities: casual affairs, one-nighters, even a prostitute, but never anyone truly special. After that, and particularly once I was back on the moors, there'd been no one. You don't meet unaccompanied women on the moors; you meet sheep, and I didn't fancy any of them. It made me, putting it bluntly, something of a virgin in emotional terms and I was taken aback by how large Deborah was looming in my thoughts. I wanted just to be with her and hold her in my arms and laugh with her and cry on her shoulder and oh.... lots of things. A strange frame of mind, as I say.

To redirect my attention onto a less disconcerting topic I sat on the bed and picked up the obligatory hotel-room Bible. This time I started from the beginning, Genesis, chapter one. It was all very familiar in a childhood sort of way until I reached the 'begats' in chapter five. The name 'Jared' appeared in verse fifteen. Intrigued, I began looking at the names that were listed from time to time. 'Asshur' I came across in chapter ten. 'Jacob' was first mentioned in chapter twenty-five.

What other names did I know? I recalled one of my jailers at Sarai Lodge had called the other 'Zeb', and of course there were 'Jed' Nordstrom and 'Elisheba'. I soon found a possible 'Zeb' in the form of 'Zebulun' in chapter thirty-five.

And then my eyes were suddenly drawn across the page from Zebulun to something I'd seen but hadn't registered. Chapter thirty-five, verse eight: 'Deborah, Rebekah's nurse....'

I stared at those words for a long time.

At length I tore myself away from them and resumed scanning for 'Jed'. I had a vague notion there was a Biblical name 'Jedediah'. I didn't find it, nor 'Elisheba', but there was 'Tamar' in chapter thirty-eight. It was beginning to look conclusive. The Abramites took their first names from the Old Testament.

Flipping back the pages, I stared some more at that reference to Deborah, Rebekah's nurse. Was it possible Deborah Czerny was an Abramite? Was it possible the Abramites themselves were behind my facilitated escape from Sarai Lodge? Had they planned all along, even if I stayed passive, to allow me to make a run for it? Even to encourage me to escape by frightening me with the 'cleaning' business? What had Deborah advised when she dropped me by the bridge that night? She'd said: "Try not to kill anyone." Had she been endeavouring to protect her co-religionists? And later she'd said: "I've got a job to do. I might let you down." What did she really mean by that? Could Rodgers & Schirrel be working for the Abramites? Could Abraham be one of their clients? Schirrel wanted me to find the videotape and hand it over unseen. That was, in effect, exactly what the Abramites had demanded of me. Was the whole deal I'd been offered one big fraud? George Radman won't surrender the tape under interrogation, so let's try a subtler way. Let's trick him into handing it over willingly. Good plan, Abraham. This Radman's a real sucker.

'Deborah, Rebekah's nurse....' It all fitted. Far too well. Yes, the Abramites had sustained casualties during my escape, but they could easily have been taken by surprise by the degree of violence I employed, or possibly they thought the price was worth paying. Abraham Reborn hadn't struck me as a man who placed much value on other people's lives anyway. Not when he wanted something badly enough.

Just as I thought I'd got it clear what was going on and who I could trust, all the conclusions I had reached were falling apart. I put the Bible down and fretted myself to sleep.

*

The return trip across the Atlantic, on Tuesday June 23rd,

was a mere fourteen days in calendar terms after the outward flight. Subjectively, the gap between the two journeys was much longer. I had gained a lot of knowledge; I had developed an ability — if not a compulsion — to believe the worst of everybody (and that included Deborah now the euphoria of my escape from Sarai Lodge had worn off); and I had acquired a 'wife'. With some cunning on the part of Rodgers & Schirrel — or the Abramites? — in my third incarnation I was one Geoff Czerny. I was pleased about that. Perhaps next time I kissed Deborah she wouldn't keep her mouth shut.

In view of my Biblical discoveries of the night before, it would have been understandable had I become ill at ease with her. However, that wasn't how I decided to play it. My approach instead was to try all the more to gain her affection, so as to make it as hard as possible psychologically for her to betray me. It was an easy tactic to adopt since I liked her a great deal. I was as close as I'd ever been to falling in love.

We breezed into Heathrow arm-in-arm. I had very few worries about being recognized. After all, if the airport was still under surveillance the last place anyone would be looking for me was amongst the *arrivals*. Even so, I stuck carefully to my assumed American accent, which Deborah said was improving steadily.

Schirrel had decreed that I should keep clear of the moor until at least twenty-one days had elapsed since my escape from custody. With that in mind, R & S had booked us into a posh hotel in Wembley for three nights where we could relax while adjusting to the British time zone. We shared a room with two single beds. I behaved myself impeccably, as any sincere and dignified suitor would.

On Wednesday June 24th, the first day after our arrival, we 'did' the capital: Buckingham Palace, Westminster, the Tower of London, the British Museum. That was Deborah's choice.

On Thursday June 25th, the second day, we went on a train to Birchington, a town on the southern side of the Thames estuary. That was my choice. As I've remarked before, cities scare me and I wanted to go somewhere more open. It happened to be fairly warm with sunny periods and we wandered from the train station down to the concrete sea-wall; and from there to a small U-shaped bay backed by chalk cliffs where we spent most of the time sheltering from the light westerly wind, lazily watching the tide come in and then recede. That wasn't exactly my idea of heaven — the bay wasn't deserted — but it was peaceful and relaxing and Deborah took some of her clothes off, which last was a pleasant compensation. In fact it put me in mind of registering that for a woman of fifty or thereabouts — I had to guess, as one doesn't ask a woman her age — she had a fine figure.

That evening, a fantasy or two still fresh in my mind, and feeling so comfortable with her I'd be able to take a rejection in good humour, I broached the issue of whether, as we were officially supposed to be married, we might not get a bit more into the swing of being husband and wife. We were in our respective beds at the time with the lights on and wearing pyjamas (in my case thoughtfully supplied by R & S). Deborah was looking particularly sexy the way a woman does when her face isn't plastered with make-up and her hair is hanging loose and untidy.

"We've convinced the world, George. Our act couldn't be any better," she said, pretending to misunderstand what I meant.

"That's not what I was getting at. I was wondering if er.... and I don't want you to think I'm sex mad or anything like that, but.... well.... when married people feel good about each other they.... demonstrate their affection."

"And you feel good about me?"

"More than I could ever describe. I'm glad I met you, and not because you saved my life, which you did. I'm glad you're with me now. I'll be glad to wake up and find you here tomorrow."

"You haven't used the L-word," she remarked, not using it herself.

"It's just a word, and if I said it now, after you've challenged me about it, it wouldn't convince you. But I'll tell you this. If a robber entered this room right now and threatened you with a gun, I'd stand between you and him without hesitation. In fact I'd probably kill him. And I wouldn't do that for anyone but you. And my mother."

"Mother!" she said and laughed. "Me and your Ma! Well, I guess you must love your Ma. So that means.... Out of interest, how old is your mother?"

"Eighty-three."

"How old do you think I am?"

The question every man dreads! "I don't know. Younger than me, anyway. I'm fifty-five."

"Think carefully, George. Have you ever lied to me?"

I went back over everything I'd said to her since first meeting her, and I knew I hadn't. "No, never," I said.

"I'm fifty-nine, and no injections and artificial stuff."

"I'm surprised. You look younger."

There was a brief silence.

She said: "Would it hurt you if I said no, not tonight?"

"Not really. I would be disappointed though."

"Would you still be glad I'm here?"

"Absolutely. Being with you just feels right, whatever we do."

"Then please give me time, George. I don't feel that strongly about you yet."

Yet! I liked the sound of that word. We wished each other goodnight and turned out our bedside lights. I fell asleep thinking that Deborah's 'not tonight' was the most endearing rejection I'd ever had.

*

The next morning, Friday June 26th, we got down to work. Our first task was to review back numbers of the national newspapers in a public library. We needed to find out, before returning to Northumberland, how the search for George Radman was getting on. It transpired, gratifyingly enough, that mention of me in the press ceased after the first seven days of my — to date — eighteen days on the run. The news media, if not the police, had already forgotten me. The final, throw-away report in one of the tabloids was to the effect that a tourist party newly arrived back from Spain had seen me drinking at a bar on the Costa del Sol. They were quite certain about it. "It was definitely Radman," one fool was quoted as saying. "I'd stake my life on it. Exactly like his picture on the telly. Bold as brass he was."

Thus reassured about the state of my public profile, we boarded a train to Newcastle, arriving mid afternoon. We booked a room in a modest city centre hotel and hired a medium-sized car. Last purchase of the day was a couple of 1:25000 ordnance survey maps covering the area between my house and Colwick Hall. After that, and a meal in the hotel's dining room, we retired to begin drawing up our plans.

Our big problem — aside from finding the videotape of course — was assessing the degree of threat I was under from sharp-eyed citizens with good memories. So far nobody had jumped on me or thrown up their hands in horror screaming: "Oh god. The murderer!" And that would probably remain the case while I was in Newcastle, a conurbation of a million anonymous strangers. But I needed to search the moor around my house, almost forty miles away by road plus a further three on foot, in a location where individuals stand out. Anyone bearing a resemblance to 'the murderer' would attract the attention of police (assuming they were keeping a watch on the area), of Abramites (ditto), and of hill-walkers passing by casually. Seeing that some innocent fellow on the Costa del Sol had been mistaken for me, *I* could certainly be mistaken for me, so the danger was a very real one. The only counter to it we could come up with was for Deborah to always accompany me. We'd be able to work the 'Geoff Czerny' bluff far more effectively together than I ever could alone.

As to finding the videotape, that's where the maps came in. I spent the evening pouring over them, working out the routes Clifford Hanworth could have taken from Colwick Hall to my home. There were very few options: if he started out this way, such-and-such a feature would lead him over Lowhope Crag and he'd miss my place by miles; if he started out that way, he couldn't cross Talstone Burn except at that location there and again he'd miss my house unless he doubled back, and even then he'd have to force his way through a stand of pine trees. Et cetera, et cetera. In the end I reduced it to three main routes with a number of minor detours off each.

All this work was mainly for Deborah's benefit. I had no intention of trudging over the moor checking under rocks and feeling down rabbit holes. Not unless I was desperate, anyway. I simply didn't want her to realize that, and indeed she fell for my deception nicely. I hated being dishonest with her but I had to discover whose side she was really on: the Abramites', Caxton Schirrel's, or mine. If I played it straight with her I wouldn't find out until too late.

On the flight from Logan, and every evening thereafter before we went to bed, I had been reading through the Bible. It was curiously interesting in a 'this is not what they told me as a child' sort of way. The result was I was starting to feel quite an authority on the earlier parts of the Old Testament. On this particular evening, work over for the day, I read Deborah some strange passages from Genesis in the bedroom's Gideon's Bible:

how Abraham's nephew Lot had been rendered drunkenly insensible and then incestuously raped by his two daughters; and how Abraham had this charming habit when he encountered a local king, of telling the king that Mrs Abraham, i.e. Sarai (or Sarah) was actually a sister and that her womanly favours could be bought for a suitable fee. I pointed out to Deborah that if the Abramites modelled their sexual behaviour on examples like Abraham and Lot's daughters, the rumours circulating in Melody of orgies might not be so wide of the mark.

Her reaction, which is what I was after, was reassuring. Raping her father or being sold by her husband to other men were absolutely revolting notions. With a little prompting she revealed she had shared her bed with only two men: her husband and Caxton Schirrel; and 'Cax' had been a mistake born of her bereavement. It explained why she was hesitant about me. She needed convincing I wasn't going to be another mistake.

On Saturday June 27th, we found the day had begun overcast, with rain predicted for the afternoon. It was tempting to stay indoors, but we were both too impatient for that. We agreed Deborah would take the hire car and reconnoitre the moor while I would continue studying the maps.

Before she set off I persuaded her to give me some money so I could call my mother from a payphone. (That was the one thing I disliked about the current arrangement. On Schirrel's orders, Deborah was keeping very tight control of the purse strings. I was still totally penniless.) Suitably funded, once she was out of the way

I made a call, though not to my mother. It was Peter I rang.

As I hadn't the faintest idea whether his phone was being tapped, I had to assume the worst, so when Peter answered I said in my American voice: "Hi Peter. This is Walt Westlebury. I stayed at your farmhouse last fall. I remember Tupper was on his annual spree." (Tupper, the prize ram.)

"I don't recall," said Peter, sounding puzzled.

"Sure you do. We had a lively discussion about organophosphate sheep dips. I helped you repair a fence. Your father, Percy, was there. Just the three of us."

"Oh yes," said Peter.

"Right now I'm in Newcastle. Flew in from the States a few days ago. I thought we could meet. I don't need reminding of the place; it's where we had a meal with your aunt Mabel on October 23rd. Can you get there this morning?" (October 23rd was my mother Mabel's birthday.)

"Yes," said Peter. "It'd be good to see you again."

"Great. Bring some cash in case you'd like to buy a round of drinks."

"I'll do that. What time?"

"Make it eleven. And let's keep it to the two of us. I'd get real mad if there were any gate-crashers. Know what I mean? See you, Peter."

I hung up.

With an hour to kill I returned to the hotel and worked on the maps for a while. That was a matter of marking crosses along each of Hanworth's three possible routes where the terrain or the vegetation would permit the hiding of a videocassette box. I performed the task conscientiously.

Around ten thirty I set off to meet my cousin. I knew which multi-storey car park he'd be using and that's where I went. My assumption was that regardless of my precautions over the phone the police would be tailing him. Realistically it was unlikely to prove the case but so much was riding on my staying at liberty that I felt compelled to take no unnecessary chances. The car park was the securest rendezvous I could think of.

As usual, there were no parking places unfilled on the lowest floor. I waited by the ramp to the next level. When Peter drove up it I swiftly noted there were no other vehicles in sight following him, and stepped boldly out of the shadows. He saw me, stopped, and unlocked the door behind him. I was aboard and we were on the move in, at a guess, five seconds maximum.

"Where to?" Peter asked.

"Do a circuit and then drive out. After that it doesn't matter. This'll only take a minute."

He tossed me his wallet. "Help yourself."

I thanked him and did.

"What's the situation?" he asked.

"I've found the target: Abraham Reborn, Colwick Hall. He's the one who broke into my house. He's the one who murdered Clifford Hanworth. He's the one who framed me."

"What are you going to do about him?"

"He either goes to prison or he dies."

"Sounds reasonable. Need any help?"

"Not at the moment. I'll let you know."

For as long as I was with Peter he was in a potentially compromising situation. Once we were out of the multi-storey car park, I spent a few minutes looking behind us until I was sure we weren't being followed and then parted company from him as quickly as possible. He barely had time to tell me a truly awful piece of news before dropping me off on a street corner. I said in separating: "Give Mum my love. Tell her I'm almost home."

"Will do. And remember, George. This Abraham fellow has caused the family a lot of trouble. I'm not about to let it go."

After he'd driven off I used some of his money to buy a small torch plus a spare battery for it (just in case the first went flat) and a couple of other items which I expected to come in useful.

It was on my way back to the hotel that I had a bad fright. A uniformed police constable stopped me and asked who I was. I answered in American English and showed him my passport. There was no doubt in my mind why he was questioning me. He was as sharp as a razor. He asked why I was in Newcastle and I explained my wife was over here tracing her roots. Inwardly my thumping heart belied my outward calm. He wanted to know where I was staying and got an honest answer. I was unsure whether it was a mistake telling him that. The thing is, I was playing Geoff Czerny, and that gentleman had no reason to lie about the name of his hotel.

Finally I was allowed to go on my way. I'd taken no more than three relieved steps when the constable called out: "George!"

I turned automatically. I smiled at him and said: "It's Geoff."

"Have a nice day, sir."

"Sure will."

I was very glad to return to the comparative safety of my hotel room.

Deborah got back in the early evening. Something was troubling her but she didn't remark on what it was, so I showed her the maps I'd been working on and their comprehensive display of X's. Impressed and subdued would sum up her response.

So how had she fared in rainy Northumberland? (The forecast rain had arrived at half past eleven and only stopped as she returned to our hotel.) She reported that there was no police presence on the moors and there was no one else keeping my house or its environs under observation. She'd spotted a few hill-walkers but I assured her that at the end of June they were entirely to be expected; it would have been more sinister if there'd been none. And never mind the weather!

I was putting on a display of cheeriness because she had some bad news for me and I wanted to make it easier for her, but my levity seemed to be having the opposite effect. I changed tack, sat her down, and said seriously: "You recall you gave me some money to phone my mum?"

"I'd forgotten. Did she tell you...." Her voice trailed off. Poor Deborah. She couldn't bring herself to say it.

"No. My cousin. I rang him instead. He's the head of the family."

"I'm glad it doesn't have to be me," she said and took

a folded sheet of A4 paper out of the pocket of her jeans. "I called into Alnwick library on the way back," she explained. "I don't know how we failed to spot this when we went through the newspaper back numbers in London. I guess it didn't make the headlines. Except up here."

She handed me the paper and I unfolded it. It was a photocopy of the front page of the local Northumberland daily, dated June 23rd, the day Deborah and I had flown in from Logan. The headline read:

Mystery Blaze At
Radman Farmhouse

The report was to the effect that vandals had set fire to my house overnight on June 21st/22nd. The first anyone knew of it was the following morning when walkers had alerted the emergency services. By then the place had been reduced to a smouldering ruin.

"I'm so sorry, George," Deborah said.

"I've spent the day doing my best not to think about this. Can we talk about something else? What was your impression of the moors?"

For a moment she was taken aback. Then she saw I meant it. "Let's go down to the dining room," she said, immediately sounding less tense, "and I'll tell you my opinion of your locality."

That was a fair proposal and I accepted it.

"I know why you live there," she informed me later as we got to grips with roast and two veg. "I'll bet when the sun's out it's beautiful."

"I think so."

"That's quite a spread you've got."

"Most of it belongs to my cousin."

"I recall you told me it's an inheritance."

"Right. It actually goes back to King Henry V. My ancestor Sir Percival Radman fought for the king in the wars with France, made money out of it — some English soldiers did — and used his new wealth to buy our estate here. Ever since, it's been passed down from father to son. My forebears used to be landlords, 'land' and 'lord' both meant literally. My grandfather, I remember, spent his time hunting and shooting. He had tenants do the farming."

"You mean other people did the work and paid him for the privilege?"

"For the privilege of doing it on his land, yes."

"Do you have tenants yourself?"

"Me? No. The property my father was allocated out of the Radman estate was too small to support more than one family, so he had to work the land himself. I think it was Grandad's way of trying to cut my father's brand of filial defiance down to size, but it didn't work. My father loved what he did and he loved the life. So did I."

"And you will again," she said, misunderstanding the significance of 'did'.

"I don't think so. I had an Aunt Agnes who passed away in 1988. She'd married a Scotsman — in the old days that would have been treason if you were a Radman — and after the war they built up an electrical retail business in Glasgow. When he was seventy they sold the business, which was widely franchised by then, and retired. Seven years later he dropped dead of a heart attack. Agnes never got over it. She died of grief."

"That's real sad."

"Yes it was. Anyway, the point is she and her husband had no children. They left their money to their nephews and nieces, two on his side, eight on hers. That was when we found out how much the electrical business had been worth. I invested my share and it generates a lot more income than I can make in a good year from the pasture. So I sold the sheep to Peter and he pays me a pound annually for the grazing rights to my land. That makes me an ex-shepherd."

"You're in the same position as me financially then. You don't have to work?"

"Yes, that's about right."

"So what do you do with your time. I mean before...."

"Quite a lot of things. During the lambing season, and whenever else he needs it, I help Peter out. Otherwise I practice stewardship: maintaining walls and fences, rescuing people who get into difficulties, clearing up litter — you wouldn't believe how much litter some people drop — and thinning the deer herd."

"Hence the rifle at your farmstead?"

"Yes. Wolves used to do the job, but now, well, if I was a deer reaching the end of my life, I'd rather be shot in the head by a marksman than starve or freeze to death during the winter."

"What about sportsmen? Do you let them shoot the deer?"

"*Never*! Killing beautiful creatures for fun disgusts me. It's sick."

"Does Peter feel that way too?"

"Pretty much. How did he once express it to me? Scotsmans Moor exists for our benefit. But it goes the other way too. The Radmans exist for the benefit of Scotsmans Moor. I think that's what he said."

"He sounds like a great guy."

"He is. And I'm sure he'll like you."

"Why's that?"

"Because I do."

I said that and went right ahead and deceived her.

*

After Deborah was asleep I passed an hour staring at the darkness thinking, now I was too tired to put up a mental fight, of my ruined home. It wasn't the destruction of the building I minded; that could be restored. It was the little things: mementos of my father; family heirlooms of no saleable value but priceless and irreplaceable nonetheless; the simple furnishings I'd never glanced at twice but which I'd miss now they were gone. I wish I could say it was just one more misfortune and that my recent past had inured me to such events. Unfortunately I couldn't say that.

For a while I brooded darkly. There was no way vandals would have burnt my house down. But somebody had; and I could guess who. As to why, that was obvious. Abraham had wanted his videotape back. He wanted it, not because he had a compelling affection for audio-visual data storage devices, but because he didn't want anyone else to view its contents. He had said as much when interrogating me. Since Clifford Hanworth

226

had been in possession of the tape and had eventually been cornered in my house, it was easily conceivable he'd hidden it on my property. It was also just about conceivable to someone unfamiliar with the building's construction that it had been so well concealed the police had failed to find it. Abraham, thinking these things, would have conducted his own search after the police had departed, but as was inevitable his quest proved a failure. No matter. The only person who might uncover the tape was me and I was marked for execution at Sarai Lodge. So there was nothing to worry about. Until I escaped. Thereafter Abraham's next logical move was simple. If my escape was genuine and the videotape was in my house he could pre-empt my retrieving it and showing it to other people by destroying the building. And if my escape was a devious Abramite contrivance, destroying my house was still a sensible precaution. He was behind the blaze. Of that I had no doubt at all.

In the court of my mind I tried Abraham for this latest crime against me and found him guilty. I took into account his other deeds which had put my mother in hospital and left me mentally scarred. And I passed sentence. Until now my intention had been to unmask him and see him brought to justice for the murder of Clifford Hanworth. That would have been sufficient. But no more. Mr Reborn's behaviour called for something special. I sentenced him to death. Prosecution, jury, judge, and executioner.

That decision should have made my future very straightforward: break into Colwick Hall, find my target, and kill him. Unfortunately there was one big complication to overcome before I could play the assassin: I didn't know what Abraham looked like. The only time we'd ever come face-to-face had been in my bedroom in the dark. Somehow I had to draw him into the open and get him, in effect, to say to me: "I'm Abraham Reborn and this is my appearance." Pulling off that coup would be some trick.

But I could worry about that later. Dragging my thoughts back to the immediate present with difficulty, I got up and put my clothes on, making not a sound beyond rustling. My plan — and at first hearing it appears absurdly optimistic — was to sneak out at midnight, drive to the moor, locate the videotape, and put it somewhere secure. After that I intended to start calling a few shots; and they'd be different shots from the ones everybody was expecting. No one else was playing straight, so why should I?

Car keys, torch, batteries, other items I might need, all present and correct. Time 11.45. I crept to the door.

"Where are you going?" Deborah called out. Heaven knows what had woken her up.

I gave her the first excuse that came into my head. "I've got to see the house. I've just got to."

"Wait," she said, getting out of bed. "I'll come with you."

"No," I responded, more aggressively than I'd intended. "It's something I want to be alone for. Don't worry. I'll be back before it's light."

I was so fearful of her coming after me I ran down to the hotel car park and drove off in considerable haste.

There wasn't in fact much time if I was to return

before daybreak. I reckoned fifty minutes would take me to where I intended to leave the car. Then I had to cross the moor in the dark — not a problem in itself but time consuming. Then I had to find the videotape. Then I had to retrace my steps. And all by half past three when the sky would be starting to lighten. As the miles passed I began to think I'd set myself a tall order.

Having parked the car, I kept well clear of the usual track. Instead I approached my house from the direction of Lowhope Crag. As I neared the bathing pool the house came into sight, a dark shape in a dark landscape. No damage was evident at that distance and in that light and I might have disbelieved the reports of a fire if I'd been given to wishful thinking. Other than that there was nothing to remark on — no man-made lights anywhere and no signs of activity or movement.

I didn't approach the house. What would have been the point? Instead I entered the bathing pool from upstream.

It was a quiet night. A gentle westerly wind was blowing. There was seventy to eighty per cent cloud cover, producing a shadowless but incomplete darkness; the crescent moon had already set but the northern sky retains a degree of lightness even at midnight at this time of the year. My eyes and ears were at maximum sensitivity, alert to the slightest unexpected movement. All was stillness.

My destination was the tangle of thorns where Clifford Hanworth had got himself stuck. I'd suspected all along, even before I knew what it was, that the object he'd hidden had to be there. Now I was sure. You see, I'd thought it out. Imagine you're him. You steal a videotape and are pursued for its return. A cassette doesn't weigh much. It's not going to slow you down. And I suspected it would have fitted inside one of the main pockets on his jacket. So you don't leave it hidden out on the moor. You keep it with you until you believe you're about to get caught. Only then would it make sense to hide it. It would give you something to bargain with: "Let me go, Abraham, and I'll tell you where the tape is."

The problem then becomes to identify the point at which Hanworth thought he was going to lose the game he was playing. It was most likely to be when he fell over the waterfall in the dark, slithering and tumbling down through various bits of vegetation and coming to rest, demoralized and with a suspected broken ankle, in a thorny bush from which, to his horror, he was unable to extricate himself. That's when he'd hide the tape; somewhere within reach of where he'd been trapped.

I found the bush easily enough and clambered into the space I had cleared in order to pull Hanworth out. Cursing the thorns which repeatedly snagged me, I felt all round as far as I could stretch. Nothing.

There was no choice but to do something potentially catastrophic. Recalling what had happened to the last man I'd seen employing a torch in the dark, I turned mine on. If there were Abramites in the vicinity — because Deborah had tipped them off by phone or because they were keeping a watch for me anyway — and they'd not detected me before, they certainly would now. I was a regular human lighthouse.

Nobody challenged me. Nobody opened fire. Nobody

did anything. For nervous minute after nervous minute I investigated everywhere Hanworth might have been able to reach, and then somewhat further: crevices, ledges, gaps between branches. There was no cassette. It simply wasn't there.

Bitterly disappointed I got back onto firm ground. The realization came home to me just how easy I'd dreamed the search would prove — so easy I'd not considered a fall-back position. All the trouble, all the danger, and I was going to have to leave empty-handed.

The awful possibility came to mind that Hanworth might not so much have hidden the cassette as disposed of it. It would have been the easiest thing in the world for him to have tossed it into the pool. I could jump in and poke about a bit on the bottom, I supposed, if I really wanted to find a ruined tape. At the very least you'd need specialist equipment to stand even a small chance of getting a signal off it. Stuff that! In any case, it was only a possibility he'd done something so drastic, and hopefully not at all likely.

On my way out of the pool area I found (as far as I could tell at night) the place where I'd temporarily laid Hanworth before fetching the blankets. Again risking the torch, I scrutinized the ground thereabouts. There was nowhere nearby that could conceal anything.

Feeling dejected and angry — it looked like I might have to trudge over the moor checking under rocks and feeling down rabbit holes after all — I made my way back to the top of the waterfall.

Before returning to the car it seemed like a good idea to satisfy my curiosity regarding how Hanworth had managed to fall into the bush. Even in the dark it would have required a serious amount of incompetence.

This was really dangerous curiosity-killed-the-cat work. The beam of a torch up here would be visible for miles. I used it anyway. Being fed up takes me that way.

My attempt to follow his line of descent, while avoiding falling myself, led me to a narrow rock ledge which I could only stand on by gripping a gnarled, firmly rooted hawthorn trunk level with my head. Shining the torch with my free hand I noticed over to my right a disturbed cleft in the rock surface. It was hard to tell, but it appeared the disturbance had been produced by a substantial plant being torn out of its anchorage. Could Hanworth, falling from above, have grasped that plant in a desperate attempt to arrest his fall?

No, that didn't make sense. Vertically above the disturbance was another bush, not damaged at all. Hanworth couldn't have fallen *past* the ledge I was standing on. He would have had to have fallen *from* it.

So what was he doing here? In the dark, lost, confused, perhaps terrified, and now unfortunately not available to ask, his actions defied explanation. I could only speculate he had been trying to make his way along the ledge and that one of his handholds — the torn out plant — had been less strongly fixed in place than he expected and had let him down.

I hauled on the gnarled hawthorn and returned to safer ground. It was a cautious move because if somebody, having seen the torch, was lying in wait for me up above, I'd not know they were there.

And then it hit me. The reverse would also be true.

Someone above wouldn't know there was a ledge to stand on. They'd think they were on what, at night, looked like the edge of a vertical drop. Hanworth had taken to the ledge to hide! And it had worked. Abraham and company hadn't seen him. They'd assumed he was still ahead of them, sheltering in my house.

Hanworth had gambled hugely though. Abraham had referred to a night-scope when he called on me that night in May. I don't know what kind of night-scope it was and I wondered if Hanworth knew. An image intensifier he might have got away with, but infra-red, no; he would have been glowing. (I know these things from my days as a wildlife warden.) He was taking a hell of a risk on that ledge. If he'd been seen, the videotape's bargaining power would have been lost. *Unless it was already hidden.* I'd been wrong. He hadn't hidden it after he fell, but before.

I began checking the ground around me very thoroughly, partly by hand and partly by torch.

And there, in a deep cleft in the rock hard up against the waterfall, I found what I was looking for.

13

I made my way down and into the foliage around the bathing pool. There, amidst the densest of the vegetation, I took out the couple of items I'd brought with me. As I'd hoped, they and the torch did indeed prove useful. Thereafter I took that accursed object and buried it.

The site I chose was a large rock close by the pool. A passer-by would assume the rock was an immovable extension of the ground, but this was not in reality the case. It was liftable by a few inches if you were strong enough, and it possessed an irregular underneath surface where the cassette could be stored out of sight. I selected this hiding place for three reasons. Firstly, I knew of it. Secondly, it was hard to get access to due to the surrounding vegetation. And thirdly, if anyone was watching me with fancy equipment, they'd be unable to see me unless they'd physically entered the bathing pool area, and I was sure no one had done that. It takes practice to find your way into this place in the middle of the night.

Actually, the fact that nobody had challenged me, despite the self-advertising display of the torch, was convincing evidence the moor was deserted. There was no covert surveillance by police or Abramites; Deborah hadn't tipped anybody off. I judged it safe to go over to my house. Deborah was bound to ask, so there was no avoiding it.

The sight was heartbreaking. The boards which Peter

had nailed over the windows had burnt away and the glass was shattered. Torchlight revealed an interior of familiar shapes but blackened. Debris which had fallen through from upstairs was everywhere. There were pools of water on the floor where the afternoon's rain had collected. Even after six days the smell was utterly terrible.

I didn't go inside. Merely peering through the windows was already painful beyond belief. I turned and ran, using up the adrenalin and the distress in a lung-punishing dash to the car.

I re-entered the hotel at four, by which time it was well light. I stole as noiselessly as possible into our room but that woman seems to have ultra-sensitive ears when she sleeps. Or perhaps she was awake anyway. I thought about my house and let the genuine emotion show on my face.

"Oh honey," she said and got out of bed and embraced me. "Someday we'll rebuild it, just the way it was."

I didn't reply to that because I couldn't. She undressed me and put me to bed like a child, and somehow I did manage to sleep for a couple of hours.

When I awoke on Sunday June 28th it was eight o'clock. We had breakfast and then sorted out our dispositions for the day ahead. Outside the clouds had mostly cleared. A cool west wind was blowing. The previous afternoon Deborah had bought a stack of plastic-wrapped sandwiches and a thermos flask, which latter the hotel had agreed to fill with coffee. She'd also bought a backpack for each of us. While she was sorting out the coffee, I slipped out of the hotel and used my own money — or should I say Peter's — to pay for a phone call.

Deborah got back to our room before me but didn't ask where I'd been. I reported it was quite cool outside and we'd need warm clothing at least for the first few hours.

Suitably dressed, we transferred ourselves to the hire car and set off to search for the videotape. It took all my resolve not to confess I already knew where it was, but I was still obsessed by the fear that Deborah (Genesis, chapter 35, verse 8) was a complicit participant in some treacherous Abramite deception. It seemed to me I had been so badly traumatized mentally by my recent experiences that I was unable to trust anyone except....

Except family, I was going to say, yet was that true? The way I'd met up with Peter yesterday had been cautious, certainly, but had it also been arranged subconsciously with a view to making it impossible for *him* to betray me? Did I know my own mind any more? Was I insane? At the very least I'd acquired a psychological disability. That was something else Abraham Reborn was going to answer for.

We parked the car at the same location that I had used the previous night, roughly half way between Lowhope and my house, and followed the same route to the bathing pool. We trekked openly over the moor, relying on our lack of stealth, our alertness, and the binoculars to keep us safe. Anybody we spotted in the distance was carefully scrutinized. Mostly they proved to be members of the bright-orange-cagoule brigade, doing what Deborah and I were supposedly doing, only with less consideration for the ghastly impact inappropriate coloration has on the scenery. Few of them followed routes which brought them within speaking range. Those who did come that close we made a point of talking to briefly so they'd know we were American visitors and not to be confused with George Radman and some conspiring female clan member.

The course we followed brought us to the waterfall from upstream. Peering over the edge of the drop, I pointed out the bush into which Clifford Hanworth had fallen. I showed Deborah the ledge he must have climbed down to in order to hide, and the evidence, just discernible from our vantage point in daylight, of the plant that had come away in his hand and precipitated him off the ledge. I explained my theory that he wouldn't have hidden the tape until he absolutely had to, and suggested that that would have been after I'd got him out of the bush and before I'd pulled him to the house on a blanket. In which case, we should start by concentrating our efforts amongst the vegetation below us.

We walked down the slope beside the waterfall, entered the pool area, and commenced searching.

Knowing it would be more convincing and require less acting skill on my part if Deborah found the tape, I ignored the true hiding place. Disconcertingly, so did she for quite a while. Eventually though, she pointed to the guilty rock and said: "How about under there? I can see gaps around it. And I'm not sure it hasn't been disturbed recently."

"It's possible, I suppose," I agreed.

She squatted down and felt around the base. "You

could push a cassette in here," she announced, working her hand into a gap between the rock and the ground beneath.

"Hold on," I said. "Let me see if I can lift this thing."

I did my Hercules impression and she got her hand in further, grasped the hidden cassette and drew it out.

"What do you know!" she said smiling beautifully.

I didn't smile back. This charade was beginning to make me feel disgusted with myself.

"You're just jealous because it was me that found it," she remarked.

"Yes," I agreed unenthusiastically.

"What's the matter?"

"Let's get away from here. It's not a good idea for us to hang around."

"Okay," she said. "My backpack's full of food. Better put it in yours."

I produced a plastic bag — a distinctive one with *Woolworths* printed in large letters on it — and she dropped the cassette into it. The most natural thing in the world. Then I slung my backpack to the ground and put the *Woolworths* bag with its tape inside.

My misgivings were growing by the minute. What was set to happen next, with my active connivance, was almost unforgivable. And yet I had to see it through. The option of calling the whole thing off was gone.

When we returned to the top of the waterfall I carried out a meticulous survey of the landscape through the binoculars and then suggested: "No police. No suspicious characters. And we've made good time. How about we go over to Lowhope Crag. We can be there by one. It's a good place to admire the view now the clouds have lifted. We can have our sandwiches when we get to the top."

"I know what you're up to," she said, filling me momentarily with alarm. "You want to prove you can walk the legs off me. Well, lead on, ex-shepherd man. I'll show you."

What kind of a human being are you, Radman? How can you do this?

We began the mainly up-hill slog to our revised destination. As we walked, the sun and clouds made patchwork shadows on the ground which moved across the landscape quite fast in the wind. Compared to how it must have looked in yesterday's rain, the scenery now was stunning.

We had got to within two hundred metres of the Crag when two men who'd been sitting motionless near the summit and had as a consequence been undetected by us, got to their feet. The approach to the Crag was very steep in the direction from which they were coming and the men descended the slope rapidly, with the air of people who are keeping their balance with difficulty.

Deborah spotted them immediately and said: "Are we on an official path here?"

"Why do you ask?"

"Because those men are heading straight towards us."

I looked through the binoculars. One of the men I didn't recognize. The other was Nordstrom. It wasn't unexpected. I'd called the shot and the Abramites had gone for it.

"Stand close to me," I said quietly.

"Why?" said Deborah while nonetheless obeying.

With the slightest movement of my arm I passed her the car keys. Not taking my eyes off the approaching enemy, I said: "If things turn bad, head for the car. I'll try and keep them busy and buy you some time. You see that solitary scrubby tree way over to the left? Make for that first. From there you should be able to spot a dry-stone wall. Keep it to your right. It'll lead you down to the road. Then you turn left."

"Who the hell are these two?" she asked.

"Abramites."

"I don't understand. Why aren't we running for it?"

"Not this time," I said.

We watched the men advance while nine-tenths of my brain was urging me to follow Deborah's advice and take to my heels. Considering what the Abramites had done to me on the last occasion they'd had me at their mercy, it wasn't surprising. My heart was pounding; my mouth was dry. It served me right for gambling with my life.

When the men were within speaking distance I unslung my backpack and stood there with it held in my hand. The two of them drew to a halt.

"Well, what have we here?" said the man with Nordstrom. Deep, resonant, authoritative voice, American accent.

I looked at Abraham closely, fixing his appearance in my brain better than any photograph. Six feet four, early fifties, luxuriant jet-black hair, brown eyes, clean shaven, very handsome, large bone structure (which made him look stronger than he probably was), trim figure, chest slightly too narrow for the rest of him, expensively dressed in casual clothes. There was an aura of power and authority about him: the sort of man you feel compelled to look up to, both literally and figuratively. If I hadn't been so ill-disposed towards him I might have called it charisma.

I glanced at Nordstrom. He nodded and said quietly: "Radman."

I nodded back: "Nordstrom."

Abraham eyed Deborah and asked: "Won't you introduce us?"

"This is Abraham Reborn," I informed Deborah, and then remarked to Abraham: "There's no need for you to know the lady's name."

"I insist," he said, a hard expression taking up residence on his face.

"Jane Doe," said Deborah.

"You are standing in the sight of God," Abraham stated, plainly annoyed. "You need to learn respect."

I couldn't take my eyes off him. His presence was somehow riveting. Height, shape, clothing, voice; all were impressive. But it wasn't those things which commanded the most attention; it was the face. Even when it was displaying anger it remained hauntingly beautiful. Almost angelic.

"This is wasting time," I interjected. "You're not here to socialize."

"You have the tape?" he said, getting the confrontation back on track.

I pulled the *Woolworths* plastic bag out of my backpack and unwrapped the cassette box inside. Abraham gestured for me to give it to him. I didn't want to get that close. I tossed the box onto the ground at his feet. Nordstrom conscientiously picked it up and handed it to him.

The box was opened; the contents examined. Then Abraham smiled. His handsomeness rating went off the scale. He said: "God grants his blessing to all of us this day. Even to you and your lady friend. It almost makes me want to invite you to join the chosen ones. You and Jed would make a great team."

"Jed is pretty good," I said, "but we could never work together. He attaches too much importance to religious obedience."

"More a case of you don't attach enough. Still, I guess there'd maybe be a degree of conflict anyway since three of my children in America were gathered to their people on account of you, and four others are in hospital, including one sweet, harmless lady with a busted jaw and several less teeth in her mouth than God intended for her to have."

"I'm sorry about the lady," I said, meaning also that I wasn't overwhelmingly distraught about the others.

"All in good time. When the righteous inherit the Earth, God will weigh your soul in his scales of justice. I'll leave Him to decide whether your fine deed this day cancels out the other wickednesses."

"Thank you," I said. My confidence was growing I was going to get away with it. I had got a good look at Abraham's face; I had proved Deborah was not an Abramite, not given the way they'd reacted to one another; and I was about to be allowed to walk away unharmed. Perfect.

And then Abraham spoilt it by asking a question I'd

have preferred him not to ask. "Why'd you call me up, anyhow? Kind of made it easy for me."

"You've been trying to locate me ever since I broke out of Sarai Lodge, yes?"

"Sure thing."

"And you knew I'd return to Northumberland?"

"We knew you'd try. Fact is, though, we thought the Feds had you."

"The Feds?"

"Yeh. Those reproachful and dishonourable adversaries of my soul planted one of their harlots inside Sarai Lodge, spying on us. We found her out almost from the start. It amused us to play along, letting her see what we wanted her to see. Anyhow, if we'd kicked her out they'd only have sent someone else and maybe we wouldn't have known who it was.

"She's dead now though," Abraham said, looking at me slyly. "Helping you escape was one sin too many. She was handed over to the menfolk that they might know her. Then she was gathered to her people. Not as good as the ceremony we'd planned for you, but neat. Dawn of the summer solstice."

"What was her name?" Deborah asked, an edge to her voice that I noticed but Abraham probably didn't.

He answered her question, adding; "That mean anything to you, anonymous lady?"

With difficulty I looked away from the beautiful face to glance at Deborah. She shook her head. It may have fooled Abraham but I knew her better.

"Still doesn't explain why you tipped me off," Abraham persisted.

"The point I was making before you brought the Feds into the conversation," I explained, "is that I want you off my back. I don't like having to keep looking over my shoulder wondering when you're going to come leaping out of the sewers to give me more nightmares. I've quite enough of those already. You've got what you want. Now get out of my life."

"You've got yourself a deal. You stay out of mine too, huh?"

"I only want to see you one more time, Abraham, and that's when they bury you."

He smiled. "You'll have a long wait, George. I'm going to live forever. See you around."

He and Nordstrom turned and walked smartly away in the direction of Colwick Hall. We stood there and watched them go.

When they were well out of earshot Deborah exclaimed: "Are you out of your tiny mind?"

I responded with: "If we're going to have a blazing row, this isn't the best place to do it. Let's go back to the car."

We marched to the road in deep-frozen silence. I had never seen Deborah furious before. It was an unsettling sight. It says much about our mental states that neither of us was as observant of our surroundings as we should have been, though fortunately it didn't matter; the police stayed absent.

I reflected sadly that the day wasn't as 'perfect' as I'd thought. I had quite probably wrecked a blossoming relationship, and was also confronting the new suspicion that Rodgers & Schirrel were a front organization for the

FBI. Every time you answer one question another springs up to haunt you.

She got in the left hand side of the car without thinking and slammed the door. That put me in the driver's seat. I shut my door quietly.

"Okay," she said. "Spill it."

"Why are you angry?" I asked instead of replying.

"You son of a bitch. I'll tell you why I'm angry. You know damned well why I'm angry. You had a deal with Caxton Schirrel: he gets you to Northumberland; you find the tape and pass it to me. He delivers his part. So what do you do to repay him? You hand the frigging thing to that delusional fanatic. Not only that. You knew all along those two were waiting on Lowhope Crag. You set the whole thing up. And you didn't have the guts to tell me. Oh no. You knew I'd stop you. Cax said we have to associate with low-life and scum. I never thought he meant you."

"Go on," I said dejectedly, surprised at how unhappy I felt. "I deserve every word of it. I've been a complete prat. I know I have. There's no excuse."

"Why, George? Just tell me why."

"I had to find out if you were going to betray me."

"You bastard. What have I ever done to deserve you thinking that of me? What?"

I held up my fingers and counted them off. "I trusted the police and the law courts and they lock me up like a convicted criminal. I trusted my solicitor and he tells me to plead guilty. I trusted Jed Nordstrom and it turns out all his hints about the CIA are a pack of lies. I trusted two pleasant young men who showed up at my apartment in

Boston and they kidnap me. I trusted a guy named Jared to help me escape from Melody and he hands me over to his Abramite brothers. I half-trusted an Abramite called Jacob not to hurt me and he comes within inches and seconds of gouging my eyes out with a knife. And then along you come. How do you think I'm going to react? Can you imagine what it's been like feeling for you the way I do, and all the time having this thought running round in my brain that you're only stringing me along — that you might prove to be like everyone else in my recent past? I had to find out. And until this morning I thought I was being clever doing it the way I did. Now I just feel despicable. It's not your fault, not in the tiniest respect, not in any way whatsoever. It's me. It's in my head. I know I'm being low-life and scum. I can't help it. I want to but I can't."

She didn't respond to that, so I added: "That's why I'm a prat. You're the best thing that's ever happened to me and I've blown it. I don't deserve you."

"I'll be the judge of what you deserve," she remarked coldly. And then the implication of what I'd been saying struck her. "You introduced Abraham to me because you wanted to see how we'd react to each other. Is that it? You thought *I* might be an Abramite?" she said incredulously.

"Your name's in Genesis," I stated, sounding ridiculous now even to my own ears.

"George, you idiot. Handing the tape over to Abraham was a crazy way to prove I'm not."

I deduced from the moderating tone of her voice that the worst was over. And we were still on speaking terms, which was more than I had any right to expect. I got her to give me the car keys, and set course for Newcastle.

"I need to know whose side you're on," I said after a pause to let her cool down.

"What do you mean by that?"

"The FBI?"

"No way. I'm a P.I. Poor Sandy inside Sarai Lodge was a P.I. The Abramites jumped to the wrong conclusion — like someone else I know. Cax is going to be spitting blood when he learns they've killed another member of staff."

"Okay, I accept the FBI is nothing to do with this business. It wouldn't have occurred to me they were if Abraham hadn't mentioned it. But suppose there was a conflict of interest between me and Cax. Whose side would you be on in that case?"

"There isn't a conflict. Oh, don't worry about the tape. I'll handle Cax on that one. Though god knows how."

"That's not what I was thinking of. Suppose, for the sake of argument, I hadn't given Abraham the tape. Inevitably I'd have wanted to see what was on it before handing it to Cax. Suppose it contained something that proved my innocence of the murder of Clifford Hanworth. Do you see what I'm driving at? My interests would lie in broadcasting the tape. Cax, on the other hand, only wants to use it in the interests of his client, and that probably means keeping its contents secret."

"I take your point. But this is all hypothetical. The issue doesn't arise. Not after what you've done."

"Suppose it did."

"It doesn't."

"You can't duck the question that easily. I was just using the tape as an example. There may be other things."

"Be specific, George. You're playing with words and it doesn't suit you."

"All right. Try this. Cax hasn't told me who his client is. For all I know the client is Abraham Reborn. That would make a conflict of interest, wouldn't you agree?"

"Of all the preposterous notions!" she exclaimed. And then her voice took on a gentler tone. "You really do think everyone's out to get you, don't you? You men, you act so tough. You want the world to believe that whatever gets thrown at you you can take it. But sometimes the wounds go so deep...."

"Okay, let me spell it out. Number one: betraying you is not an option. Personal commitments count for a lot in my life and it's about time you woke up to that. Number two: Abraham Reborn is absolutely not a client of Rodgers & Schirrel. Number three: if I had to choose between my job and you, until this morning I'd have chosen you. Now I'm not so sure any more. Does that set you straight?"

I took in her words for a few moments and then said: "I know saying sorry isn't enough; and I won't ask you to forgive me. But losing you would be unbearable. I'm willing to work very hard to repair the damage I've done. Will you give me that chance? Please."

She looked away and didn't answer.

"Please, Deborah. I need help. I need *your* help."

"Yeh, I guess. It's such a pity though. I've been dreaming of starting a new life with you in England. It's beautiful here and I know this is where you want to be, where you belong. Now it looks like you're going to have to start a new life with me in America. And Cax isn't going to employ you. Not now."

I dared to think I hadn't lost her. But I had yet to tell her the whole truth. Our relationship was still in the balance. I said: "You don't think I'll be able to prove my innocence?"

"The videotape was your best bet, George. I was planning for us to watch it together, and if it turned out any good to you.... But I guess we've covered the ground on that subject."

"Oh, I don't know," I said. An intense feeling of emotional release swept over me. She'd said exactly the right thing. My face broke into an uncontrollable grin. "Do you realize, if I wasn't driving I'd give you the biggest hug of your life."

"That's a step in the right direction," she remarked. Then she saw my beaming smile, and added: "What's funny?"

"Do you really think I was out of my tiny mind?"

"Well, it did kind of seem that way."

"Take a look in my backpack."

She reached over, obviously puzzled, and hooked it off the rear seats.

"I know I'm paranoid," I said, "but I'm not crazy."

She pulled out a plain white plastic bag. Inside was a black box. Inside that....

"The videotape," I said. "Abraham Reborn has gone off with a blank one. I bought it yesterday."

<h1 style="text-align:center">14</h1>

We didn't return immediately to Newcastle. I turned off and took us via Rothbury and Otterburn onto the bare moors. Not my land or Peter's but similar enough to feel familiar. There we ate our provisions, before walking for a while along the Pennine Way.

And we talked. I 'spilled' it all; how I'd bought a suitable screwdriver and a blank videocassette the previous day; how I'd found the Abramites' videotape and, using the screwdriver, had unscrewed the two cassette shells — blank and Abramite — and swapped over the tapes inside; how I'd hidden the Abramite cassette box, now containing a blank tape, for Deborah to find; and how I'd telephoned Colwick Hall and told Abraham where to wait if he wanted his property returned to him.

Deborah was still angry with me at first, and got no less angry as my confession unfolded, but she didn't storm off. I think she perceived, perhaps only vaguely at first, how much I needed her psychologically; how utterly desolate I'd be without her. It's very hard for a man like me, an archetypal self-reliant loner, to confess to such a bond with someone else. Believe me, it's very, very hard indeed. Yet I found myself thinking that if I couldn't reveal to this woman how I felt, honestly and openly, then what kind of a partner would I make for her, really? So I took her hand, went down on one knee, and told her, haltingly and with a pounding heart, what she was to me.

She cried a little then and repaid my openness by saying that no one had truly needed her since her husband had died. No one. Until me. We returned to the car very emotional and holding hands.

With ourselves sorted out it was time to start thinking of the outside world. From the first payphone we came across, Deborah rang Schirrel to inform him we had found the videotape and that she had reason to believe R & S's girl inside Sarai Lodge had been executed by the Abramites a week ago.

I declined to listen in to the call though I was offered that option. The way it seemed to me, I was going to have to relearn to trust those close to me. Deborah was the one I was most keen to succeed with, so I started with her.

Once back in Newcastle we visited a large electrical store and bought a videocassette recorder, installing it as soon as we arrived at our hotel.

And then, instead of watching the tape, we went out for a meal. The reason for imposing this unnecessary delay we didn't talk about because there was no need. We were thinking alike on the subject. If there was something on that tape that Abraham would kill for, I could be a free man in days. If not, our chances of setting up home in Northumberland were bleak. The verdict was entirely out of our hands. It was that that made us hesitate.

Not until nine p.m. did we sit down, load the cassette and steel ourselves to face the truth.

Initially there was nothing more than a vague shape on the screen. And then someone must have flicked a switch....

Let there be light! And there is light. There is also a sound: a low vibration like a large electric motor running slowly.

The camera is located high up in the centre of the wall of a room, directly facing the opposite wall but angled downwards so that the lights in the ceiling are out of view. The impression is one of whiteness: white walls, white floor.

The vague shape which could previously be barely discerned now appears to be a substantial box with four sides but no top. The sides are made of a material resembling white marble. The box is filled — to what depth it is impossible to say — with firewood. In cross-section the box is about twice as long as it is wide, and is positioned in the room such that the camera is looking along its length (as opposed to across it).

Aside from the box, the only other furnishings in view are six rectangular rugs, seemingly made of sheepskin. There are no windows. Nor are there any doors.

There is nothing to provide scale to the picture. It could be a room in a doll's house or a great hall.

After a few minutes of total inactivity there is the sound of a door opening. This entrance must be located beneath the camera, a fact confirmed almost at once when ten figures appear, coming on screen from the bottom of the picture.

The ten people are dressed in white gowns not unlike bathrobes, though with the addition of hoods which are drawn over their heads, making them unidentifiable. The gowns extend down to mid calf. Below that their ankles and feet are bare. They position themselves, five on the left and five on the right, standing alongside the box.

The dimensions of the room can now be estimated. It is about ten metres to the far wall and six or seven metres from one side to the other. The marble box is roughly the size of a single bed, albeit a high one; the surface of the firewood is at waist height.

One of the people — it is unclear which, but male — calls out: "Abraham, father of us all, guide us." The words are repeated in chorus by a mixture of male and female voices. The original speaker says a succession of other things lauding Abraham as this and that, and on each occasion his companions echo what is said, chanting in unison. After several minutes of this, the praises of Abraham have become progressively more extravagant to the point of absurdity.

The final statement is: "Abraham, supreme prophet, intimate of God, commander of angels, come amongst us. Make us as you are."

A quiet descends. The two lines of people step away from the marble box and three new arrivals enter the scene, again from beneath the camera. Two are dressed identically with those already present and, judging by what they are doing, must be men. The third is also a male, at a guess, in his late teens. He is naked and is being carried feet first and face upward by the other two. One supports him by his shoulders; the other by his knees. He struggles violently and their path is erratic as a result and they almost drop him. Then they tighten their grip and part lift, part toss him onto the bed of firewood.

It becomes clear that his ankles are bound by some kind of black cloth; and it can be concluded from the position of his arms that his wrists are tied together behind his back. A silk ribbon covers his lips, and his cheeks are blown out slightly as if there is something large in his mouth.

As soon as the two men release him he begins to twist and turn in an effort to get off the firewood. Two of the taller people on each side hasten forward and there are quickly four pairs of hands holding him firmly but not harshly in place. The naked young man's struggles are reduced to little more than twitches by this means.

The two 'porters' take up position to left and right, transforming each line of five into a line of six.

A thirteenth hooded figure now comes into the picture. He places himself at the head of the marble box so he is being viewed from behind. His body shields from sight the young man's face and neck. Clearly very tall, his being closest in the room to the camera makes him look physically overpowering. He stretches his arms out horizontally, palms down, over the naked body in front of him, and in a voice that is unmistakably Abraham Reborn's says: "My children, we are summoned here today by God." It is thus possible to identify this one participant despite the garment he is wearing.

Abraham continues to speak, extolling the virtues of God, quoting what sound like Biblical passages and mixing this praise with references to his own privileged position as the anointed father of the world and the conduit for divine knowledge.

While this monologue is being delivered, the naked

teenager on the firewood ceases to struggle, perhaps because his plight is so obviously hopeless. He does not become motionless, however, for his body is shaken by prolonged trembling. The hands holding him down do not relax their pressure.

At length, the monologue concluded, Abraham announces: "Here is my son, Isaac, the seed of my loins. Has not God commanded that I shall make of him a burnt offering?"

"It is God's will," the twelve reply in unison.

Abraham lowers his arms so they cease to be outstretched. He positions them in front of his chest, out of the camera's view. "Let us listen for the word of God," he says. "Does He command that I shall refrain from making this burnt offering?"

There is silence. No one speaks. No one hears the word of God. The young man tries once more to get off the firewood, more vigorously than ever, but the hands hold him down.

"Where is the ram, that I may substitute it for this, my son Isaac?" Abraham asks.

"There is no ram," the chorus responds.

"Then let your faces be known," Abraham commands.

One at a time, the twelve push back their hoods. This reveals that on each side are three men and three women: the men directly alongside the marble box; a woman standing behind each man. One of the men is young and blond and will die later in my kitchen.

"Where is the ram?" Abraham shouts.

"There is no ram," the twelve reply.

"Then let your flesh be known."

Again one at a time, the twelve robes are discarded. None of the participants is wearing anything underneath.

"Where is the ram?" Abraham asks for a third time, yelling now as if in desperation.

"There is no ram," comes the predictable answer.

Abraham, the only one present still completely covered by clothing, raises his arms as if to touch the ceiling. His hands are clasped together, clutching a dagger, the blade pointing downwards.

The poor kid on the firewood — 'Isaac' — breaks into a fresh paroxysm of struggling. The six male disciples hold him firmly in place, their shoulders juddering a little as the force of his protests transmits itself up their arms. Abraham waits, frozen like a statue.

Eventually, momentarily exhausted, Isaac's body briefly becomes motionless. The knife descends. There is an air of practised ease about the movement. Abraham bends forward but his head does not quite obscure the blade's point of entry, slightly below the breastbone and angled to penetrate the heart.

The victim arches his back. Darkish blood begins pulsing out of the wound, flowing down over his belly and pooling around his navel.

Abraham twists the knife. The pulsing turns brighter red. Isaac jerks stiffly in a kind of twitch which extends from shoulder to knees. The six men continue to press on him. Some now have blood on their hands.

The body relaxes. Abraham withdraws the knife. The six let go. The red pool on the victim's abdomen trickles over his sides and onto the firewood.

Abraham hands the knife to the man on his right. The

man raises it and declares: "With this knife I share the sacrifice." He plunges the dagger into the supine flesh in front of him. The weapon is passed to the next man in line. The cry and the action are repeated. The process continues until there are six stab wounds in addition to Abraham's. None of these later wounds bleeds more than slightly. The men have been mutilating a corpse.

The knife having been returned to him, Abraham says: "In sharing the sacrifice you have become Abraham and you have become Sarah."

Wisps of smoke start appearing from inside the marble box. The orange-yellow flicker of flames becomes visible. The smoke does not billow in all directions but rises cleanly towards the ceiling. This suggests the low vibration heard initially is an extractor fan.

"The sacrifice is pleasing to God," Abraham announces. "Sow then now my seed that it shall multiply as the stars of heaven and as the sand on the seashore, that we become mighty and command the gates of our enemies."

The men and women pair up and each couple selects one of the sheepskin rugs. They lie down and begin to copulate. Abraham, cloaked and motionless, watches but does not participate.

The fire is now burning brightly. The corpse appears to be trying to sit up, bending at the waist. It falls back into the flames. The flesh melts, the blood boils, entrails become visible. The six couples perform their sex acts and one by one subside into stillness.

When all are finished, Abraham calls out: "The

children of Abraham are one," and the twelve get up and resume their positions alongside the marble box. They behold the remains of what was once a human being.

"Was God present at the sowing of the seed?" Abraham asks.

"God was present," the twelve reply.

"You are blessed in the sight of Abraham."

Everyone stands still for so long they seem to be in some sort of trance. The fire continues to burn. As it does so, the surface of the woodpile collapses slowly into the marble box, taking the burnt offering with it. It is no longer a human body but blackened meat with here and there a charred bone visible.

Abruptly Abraham turns and walks off camera. At no time has his face been captured on tape. The twelve disciples put their robes back on and follow him out. The lights are switched off. The fire glows redly. The smoke rises cleanly. A skull stares through the flames at the ceiling.

*

Once the image was replaced by black-and-white noise, I fast-forwarded the tape, expecting, correctly as it turned out, that there was nothing more to see. I set the videocassette recorder to rewind.

There were beads of sweat on Deborah's forehead. She held up a trembling hand. "I thought I was going to faint," she said. "That was real, wasn't it?"

"There was no sign of any editing. And I don't believe Abraham would be bothered if Hanworth had stolen a special effects horror movie. I'm afraid that what we saw is what actually happened."

"What have we got into here, George? Low-life and scum I can handle, but ritual homicide...."

I was myself too shocked to say anything useful for a moment.

Deborah said: "Something like that was planned for you at Sarai Lodge, wasn't it?"

"I think so." And I'd thought 'sacrificing' just meant a bullet in the brain!

"Do you think they did that to Sandy?"

"Probably not. Wrong gender. Isaac was a boy."

"What did Abraham mean when he told us she was given to the menfolk so 'they might know her'?"

"I think he meant knowing carnally."

"Sweet Jesus! You couldn't give me a hug when we were driving, George. Give it to me now."

I took her in my arms and held her tightly. She was shaking all over.

"Why can't they see how evil he is?" she asked. "Why doesn't anyone stop him?"

"The religious mind," I replied. "You don't question. You don't think. Look at the original Abraham. He hears voices in his head telling him to murder his son and burn the body. If that happened today he'd be judged a dangerous schizophrenic who should be confined to a mental institution. But that's not how the story was presented to us when we were children, is it? Or how about Moses. His activities included mass murder, including of his own people, explicit genocide, using captured virgins as sex slaves, and torturing to death people who disobeyed him by throwing rocks at them. By any rational standard he was as evil as any of the nastiest dictators of the twentieth century. But religious people can't see that. Not even today in our enlightened times. Moses says he's doing God's will and that closes their minds to the reality. Abraham Reborn is the same. He claims he's doing God's will and his followers believe him. They can't see how evil he is because religious minds don't work that way."

"He's going to say *we* should be killed now, isn't he?"

"Bound to. He's been trying to kill me on and off for six weeks. Once he finds out I tricked him this morning, he's going to be after both of us."

"Is there any way he can find us? I don't want to end up like poor Sandy."

I shook my head. "He doesn't know the names we're using. Even if he did, where would he start looking? There must be hundreds of hotels and guest houses within easy reach of the moor. And then there are the caravan parks. Or we could be based further away. Or we could be staying...."

The hotel wasn't high-class enough to have a phone in every room, but there was one by the front door. I went down those stairs three at a time, slammed some money in and dialled. Waiting for a reply was agonizing.

"Hello," said Peter at last.

"This is the American you met the other day," I said, American accent and all. "Is everything all right where you are?"

"Yes. Shouldn't it be?"

"It's possible you'll be visited tonight or tomorrow by

that extremely unpleasant character I told you about. He'll be looking for me. The first time I met him he was armed, so you'll need your shotgun. Don't hesitate."

"It seems to me, Mr er.... whoever, that the situation is getting out of hand. Should I warn anyone else?"

"Richard, to be on the safe side. No one else for the moment. The guy will use the phonebook. People listed under their partner's name will take longer to find and I'll have him sorted out by then."

"Or I will, by the sound of it. Give me another call first thing tomorrow. We have to meet. I'm not happy about this."

"Neither am I, Peter. I'll be in touch."

After checking belatedly that no one had been around to overhear the conversation, I returned to Deborah and explained why I had left the room in such haste.

"But you reckon we're safe here?" she asked doubtfully.

"Till the morning."

She had put the tape back in its box and was holding it in her hand. "Cops, first thing tomorrow," she stated, waving it at me.

"Oh no. Not them."

"Well, who then?"

"I don't know, but not them. They've got closed minds where I'm concerned. Give them the tape and they'd probably lose it as inconvenient evidence."

"That's...." she stopped in mid sentence.

"Paranoid," I said on her behalf. "I know it is. Still, you've heard what they say. Just 'cause I'm paranoid doesn't mean everyone's not out to get me."

"I'm not out to get you," she said.

"You're an exception," I agreed.

At which point we decided to sleep on the problem of how to place the tape in the public domain.

Sleep was not something my brain had as its top priority that night. The graphic nature of what I'd seen on the videotape kept me awake. And I started having misgivings. Could it have been trick photography? I decided not, but would others be more cynical? And what about identifying Abraham Reborn as the knife-wielding murderer? Since he could only be recognized by his voice and voices can be faked (as any impressionist will confirm), was it likely he would be charged? The other twelve people had faces that names might be put to, but if I was Abraham I'd have got them on a plane to Brazil or wherever as soon as the tape went missing. I would also have radically redecorated the sacrificial chamber. If he'd made the right moves he'd be able to bluff and ridicule his way out of any difficulties the videotape might cause him.

As I saw it, staring into the darkness at the end of a very long day, there were four conclusions I could draw. The best one was that Deborah was truly on my side. She'd not given Schirrel even a passing mention. The second conclusion was that the settling of my score with Abraham — especially given his unpredictability — was urgent. If Peter would lend me his shotgun I'd have a crack at breaking into Colwick Hall and carrying out the execution tomorrow night. The third conclusion was not to attach too much weight to what was on the videotape. In fact I felt — perhaps unreasonably — so negative about that tape I decided to honour my agreement with Schirrel and let him have it.

My fourth conclusion was more calculated. When I passed to the authorities what I had discovered about the two people I had supposedly murdered, Clifford Hanworth and the young lad, what were the chances they'd act on it? What were the chances the information would lead to the dropping of the charges against me? My confidence in the legal system was zero, so the answer I came up with to the two questions was a defeatist one. It seemed improbable that my long-term destiny could lie in Northumberland. Or, to put it more poignantly, my future reduced to a choice between the forces of law and order in England and a firm of Bridgeport private investigators. Which of those two believed in my innocence? Which of those two had helped me when I needed help? Which of those two offered me the best prospects? There was no contest. Consequently it didn't require a genius to work out that Schirrel was someone I should court almost as much as I had courted his nicest lady employee. I needed him.

Whereupon I concluded myself to sleep.

The Day of Reckoning

June 29, 1998

15

I woke at six to find, to my great astonishment, Deborah attempting to join me in my not particularly wide bed. I knew immediately it wasn't sex she wanted; her body language was all wrong for that. She clung to me almost desperately, trembling and crying and telling me not to leave her. It transpired she'd woken up in the middle of a bad dream, one with death in it, and had taken it to be a premonition. She genuinely thought one of us was about to die.

Privately I had to admit she might be right. Killing Abraham Reborn was not going to be easy. There was a serious possibility something could go fatally wrong. But she didn't know what I was planning and I didn't tell her. Instead I asserted that dreams sometimes give expression to our fears. That's all they can do. They don't predict the future with certainty. Nothing in human life (except its end) is inevitable.

My reassurances seemed to add to her distress. Being rational was making things worse, so I changed the subject to the videotape. I said I didn't think it would be as decisive to my case as we'd thought at first. Contrariwise, she said that in order to avoid giving the impression the tape was some sort of self-serving Radman stunt, it had to be presented to the authorities in a way unconnected with me. George the pessimist; Deborah the optimist. I impressed on her the likelihood of failure; she impressed on me the chance of success.

Her dream, though, continued to haunt her. She was markedly uneasy because of it and wanted to clear out of the hotel as soon as practicable. We got dressed, intending to go down for breakfast at eight when the dining room opened, which would permit us, we calculated, to be away by nine.

There was a knock on the door at 7.12. Nobody should have been knocking at that time in the morning. I'd have been out of the window except our room was on an upstairs floor.

"Deb?" a voice called softly.

We exchanged puzzled glances. It was Caxton Schirrel. Deborah let him in. I was surprised — and so was she — that there were two other men with him: physical heavyweights. I sensed threat.

Deborah acknowledged Schirrel's companions, calling them Calvin and Al. Schirrel went to kiss her paternalistically but she drew back. "What's going on?" she asked.

I'll give Schirrel credit for plain speaking. "I need the tape," he said. "I don't want Radman refusing to hand it over."

"It's not that simple," Deborah replied. "You haven't seen what's on it."

"We had a deal," Schirrel said looking at me. "I don't care what's on it."

"Cax?" said Deborah, clearly astounded.

The two 'heavies' were blocking my exit via the door. That left the window, which happened to be wide open (this being June). I snatched up the box containing the videotape and darted towards the big outdoors.

And there I stood, me inside, the tape outside. One of the heavies advanced towards me.

"Don't be childish, Radman," said Schirrel.

"You can have the tape," I said, "but I don't like being leaned on. Call your goon off."

"Take a step back, Calvin," said Schirrel. "George is used to a lot of space."

To my relief Calvin did as he was told.

Deborah was furious again. This time it wasn't with me.

"Are you telling me," she said to Schirrel, "that you've flown here all the way from Bridgeport because you don't think I'm capable of handling things at this end on my own?"

"My confidence in your technical abilities is not the problem," Schirrel replied while continuing to look at me. "Radman is the problem. It's him I don't think you can handle."

That struck home. Deborah's lack of response told Schirrel his judgement was basically sound.

"The tape, George," he said.

"Okay," I agreed, not moving.

The situation was so unexpected I was completely unclear how to deal with it. For some reason Schirrel had become hostile to me, that was plain. But why? Whatever his motivation, it meant the deal I'd reached with him in Bridgeport, especially as regards my returning to America, was in jeopardy if not in abeyance. That was wholly bad news. I wasn't about to give up my escape route to a new life without a fight.

"Just satisfy my curiosity before I hand it over," I

said, hoping to draw Schirrel into revealing what had made him turn against me. "You intend to use this tape to get something for your client. A 'gentleman' you called him in Bridgeport. It has to be something this gentleman wants from the Abramites. Yet you don't want to see the kind of video this is. So blackmail isn't on your agenda. That leaves what? A swap?"

"That's a confidential matter."

The client had to be after one of three things: information, money, or a person. At least, they were the only possibilities to occur to me in the heat of the moment. I gambled on number three. "You want to swap somebody. You want someone out of their clutches. Am I correct?"

"I'm running out of patience."

Deborah said swiftly: "R & S are being retained by a client to get his son away from Colwick Hall."

"That is privileged information," said Schirrel, taking his turn to be furious. "You're in breach of your contract revealing it."

"Yeh? So fire me."

"I just have, as of now."

Oh well done, Radman. Brilliant! As if things weren't bad enough already, now I'd got Deborah the sack into the bargain. Being round-about wasn't my style. Why don't I stick with being direct? It could hardly make matters worse.

"We've got a misunderstanding here, Mr Schirrel," I said. "We had a deal. We still have as far as I'm concerned. There was no need to involve a couple of goons."

"Insurance," said Schirrel shrugging.

I brought the tape back inside the window. "I concede this is a property you have a right to. Can I make a point before you take it away?"

"If you must," said Schirrel, switching from furious to bored.

"Deborah," I said, "is the son of your client on this video?"

"No, he's not."

"Good. So the client has no direct interest in viewing this tasteless home movie. He won't mind if you swap it. And neither do I. I've already explained to Deborah I don't think this tape will get me off the murder charges. In the light of that, I've got a proposition or two to put to you. If you'll hear me out?"

"Frankly," Schirrel remarked, "I don't believe you have much to offer."

"Oh for Christ's sake," Deborah shouted. "Stop treating George like he's the enemy."

"Say your piece, Radman," said Schirrel, shifting his bored demeanour into neutral. "I'm listening."

"I recall in Bridgeport you talked proudly about getting justice for your personnel, including Clifford Hanworth. And Sandy. Was that all bullshit? If you do a deal with Abraham, will that include agreeing to walk away and forget him?"

"No way."

"Let's say, mentioning no felonies, that I undertake to exact payment for you. You'd get what you want risk-free and with minimal delay. In return I'd want a new identity in the U.S. courtesy of Rodgers & Schirrel."

"We'd have to talk about that in private, George."

"Okay. I think we understand each other. And there's this tape-for-kid swap. My guess is Clifford Hanworth was supposed to find the boy and get him out of Colwick Hall and pass him to Deborah. Only I'll bet no Abramite would ever leave voluntarily. That means you were planning to abduct him. Rodgers & Schirrel contemplating a felony, and not even in the United States. Very naughty. But you don't have to go to that extreme now. A swap makes better sense all round. I'm surprised, though, if you seriously think you can pull it off with just you and a couple of goons."

"Boss," said Calvin, "if he calls me a goon one more time...."

"It's a compliment, Calvin," I explained, making a mental note not to push my luck with him. "I don't look at you and think of ballerinas."

And then speaking to Schirrel, I continued: "I'll bet you're all unarmed. With airport security and the gun laws over here working against you, you have to be. Yet Abraham packs a forty-five. What happens to your swap if he shows up waving that in your face? Count me in and I know where I can lay my hands on a shotgun. And then again, can you fix a location for the swap without the help of someone with local knowledge?"

"Hold it a second. I buy the line you're selling me, except for one thing. You're mighty keen to be in on this. Why?"

"Because if you and your two.... If you and Calvin and Al take the tape and leave me behind it's obvious that's the last I'll ever see of you. You've decided not to honour

our agreement. I don't know why, but whatever your reason I've got to convince you you're wrong. That's what I'm trying to do. I can be useful to you; maybe provide you with some decisive help. And I'll tell you straight why doing that is so important to me. It's because you represent my best hope of salvaging something worthwhile from the wreck of my former life. I want our agreement reinstated. And since it's not in my nature to beg or ask for favours, I'm setting out what's on offer in return.

"Frankly," I said, mimicking Schirrel's use of that word earlier, "I think you're getting a bargain."

"You know, George, when I met you in Bridgeport I thought you were a tad short on brain power. I was wrong. You're smarter than you look. You've captured my attention. What else is in this bargain I'm getting?"

"Setting up the swap; who's the best person to do that? Does Abraham know your voice? I guarantee he'll recognize mine. Has he any idea who Caxton Schirrel is? There's no problem like that with George Radman. Abraham will want to talk to me because he believes I've got the tape. I don't have to persuade him. With you he'd be thinking to himself, who is this guy, a hustler or what?

"So I can arrange the deal, vouch for where it takes place, supply a firearm, and increase your manpower by thirty-three per cent. How am I doing?"

Schirrel looked at Deborah in a what-do-you-think way.

"Don't ask me, Cax," she said. "I don't work for you any more. I got fired."

"Something else for you, Mr Schirrel," I added in her

defence. "Deborah could have told me any time since we left Bridgeport all she knows about your client, and she told me nothing until just now. And I didn't embarrass her by asking. Here!" I tossed the cassette to Calvin, who wasn't paying attention, fumbled it and let it fall to the floor. He picked it up looking disgusted.

"Tell me, George," said Schirrel. "The way I had it figured, you intended to keep the tape for yourself. I can't believe I could have been wrong about that."

There it was: the reason for his hostility out in the open at last. For once he'd been *too* clever.

I shrugged and said: "Keeping the tape was an option I was bearing in mind, not an intention. You were looking at me from the point of view of a criminal psychologist so you were bound to be off-centre. You see, I'm not a criminal."

"Touché," he said. "Fine. I'll go for it. You help me to achieve a successful swap of the tape and I'll stand by my guarantee of a position with R & S in Bridgeport whenever you want it."

"What about Deborah?"

Schirrel gave me a look which said: "Do I have to do this?" I held his gaze.

"I apologize, Mrs Czerny," he said. "I was out of line. If you want to be reinstated I'll reinstate you."

"I'm not sure," she said. "This morning has been kind of a surprise. Let's get the exchange done. Then will be the time to review our respective positions."

"Right. The hard part first. The happy-families stuff can wait till later. Are you confident you can negotiate an agreement, George?"

"From our end easily. The trouble is that Abraham thinks he's only one step down from God. His decisions can be irrational."

"He's rational enough. You're confusing irrationality with criminality. Do you have his number?"

"Yes. I rang it only yesterday."

I told Schirrel what to push-button on his mobile phone and then he passed the contraption to me. First time I'd ever held one.

"Who do you want to swap?" I asked.

He hesitated. Confidentiality and all that. "A kid named Aaron Bernheim."

I waited for someone to answer at the other end. When I heard a hello I announced I was Walt Westlebury. (Not calling myself George Radman had become practically instinctive.) At first the message didn't get through and I was treated to a sequence of monosyllabic remarks like those I'd encountered when I rang Sarai Lodge. Plainly it was some sort of official policy to discourage frivolous enquiries.

Persistence was eventually rewarded and Abraham came to the phone. He didn't give me a chance to speak. The deluge of Bible-based invective lasted uninterrupted for a good two minutes. I was, amongst many forgettable things, a pestilence, a defiler, a worshipper of Baal, a six-headed beast, and the spawn of maggots. On and on. I have to admit it was the most imaginative abuse I'd ever heard.

"Abraham," I said when he seemed to have exhausted his vocabulary of insults, "do you want this tape back or don't you?"

"Have you seen what's on it, you loathsome affront to creation?"

"What's on it is no concern of mine. You can have the accursed thing just as soon as I can get to Colwick Hall. But there's a price."

"You dare to demand money! Oh, I shall make your name to stink amongst the peoples of the Earth. The spittle of the Great Serpent shall be accorded more respect than...."

"Not money!" I shouted above the renewed torrent. "I want you to release Aaron Bernheim into the care of a friend of mine. That's all."

Abraham was silent for a moment. I'd taken him by surprise. "What's Aaron to you?" he asked, sounding devious.

"My friend here helped me when I was in America. I'm returning the favour."

"Let me think," he said. A pause ensued lasting several minutes, so long I asked a couple of times if he was still there, to no effect. And then: "Eight a.m. Front gates to Colwick Hall. Don't be late or Aaron will be my next Isaac."

The line went dead.

The time was 7.21. Abraham must have thought I was phoning from close by, not forty miles down the road.

"We've got to be at Colwick Hall by eight or Aaron Bernheim dies," I told my audience.

"Great negotiation," said Calvin.

I started making for the door. Calvin blocked my path and said: "We don't need you unless Mr Schirrel approves."

"Do any of you know where Colwick Hall actually is?" I asked.

"Deborah must," said Calvin.

"George and I are one item," Deborah stated firmly.

"And I'd better take the wheel," I added. "I'm used to driving on the left. None of you are."

Schirrel nodded his agreement. The five of us headed out of the hotel at a run.

Schirrel's car being larger than the one Deborah and I had hired, we set off in his. Traffic into Newcastle was beginning to pick up, but in the outward direction we had the road almost to ourselves. Furthermore, the weather was favourable: dry, cool, with a light westerly wind and only scattered clouds. God must have been on our side.

Despite some complaints from Schirrel I stuck to the speed limit as we made our way out of the city. The reason for that was that there was someone behind us. They'd pulled out from the kerb as we left the hotel car park and had followed us ever since. I didn't comment but I watched them, hoping they'd turn off, and telling myself I was being paranoid.

They obliged eventually as we reached open countryside. A strange thing happened, though. Another car had come up fast from behind, overtaken them but not me, and then slowed down to my speed. In consequence, after being followed out of Newcastle by one car, we were now being followed by another.

"Are Calvin and Al the only people you brought with you from Bridgeport?" I asked Schirrel, who was sitting beside me.

He didn't answer. Instead he pulled his sun-visor

down and used the vanity mirror to look out of the rear window. "Abramites?" he asked.

I said: "I don't see how they could have found the hotel. In any case, the passenger's been using what looks like a mobile phone or a radio. If he's an Abramite reporting in, he'll have been told where we're going. So why follow us?"

"That leaves cops," said Schirrel, voicing the same conclusion I'd come to.

"It's possible. A couple of days ago I was stopped in Newcastle by a constable. I told him I was Geoff Czerny and the hotel I was staying in. Perhaps he wasn't fooled as much as I thought."

"No. He didn't arrest you. Therefore you fooled him. But let's think it through. Say he files a report of a possible suspect — a low priority one. The cops assigned the task of finding George Radman pick up the report next day — no hurry — and check it out. Geoff Czerny and Deborah Czerny, U.S. citizens, staying where they said they were. All looks kosher. It shouldn't have added up to a problem. There must be something else."

"I rang my cousin from the hotel last night, using a false name," I suggested.

"Maybe it's that," said Schirrel without conviction. "I guess we could speculate endlessly. More important right now, can you lose these guys?"

"I could try, but no guarantees."

"In that case we'll play it cool. We don't want to force their hand. The way I see it, if they know it's you, George, they're holding fire because they want to find out what you're up to. Alternatively their enquiries may be at an early enough stage they're still only suspicious. We can live with those two possibilities for the moment."

"I told you we should have left him behind," said Calvin. "If we're to be at the hall by eight we don't even have time to fetch his shotgun. And *I'd* have no trouble ditching these cops if I was driving."

"It so happens you're not," I said over my shoulder, "unless you want to try swapping places at seventy miles an hour."

We travelled on in an uncomfortable silence. I suspect we were all wondering what difference a police presence would make to the tape-for-kid swap. The situation was becoming extremely complicated.

A full five minutes passed without anyone saying anything. Then Schirrel announced he'd 'got it'. He explained: "I bet there's an entry on a file somewhere recording a Mrs Deborah Czerny visited George Radman when he was in jail. Add that to the police patrolman's report and alarm bells start ringing. Say they tied the two bits of information together yesterday evening. Because you might just be a legit U.S. citizen, they don't want to move against you until they're sure. Hence the surveillance operation. They should be dusting your hotel room for fingerprints right about now while you're safely out of the way. Once they confirm a match, the cop car behind becomes a homing beacon, fixing your position as they close the net around you."

"How much time do you think I've got?" I asked.

"I can't say. It depends on equipment and methodology. I'm not familiar with how police departments do these things in England."

The conversation lapsed again. Schirrel's metaphor of a closing net redirected my thoughts. I stopped worrying about the forthcoming swap in favour of contemplating the prospect of arrest. And not just my own. Deborah could hardly escape prosecution for knowingly assisting me. Schirrel too was likely to be at least highly embarrassed. I wondered how effective his lawyer partner, Ms Rodgers, would be if she had to practise her skills on the British side of the Atlantic.

Once more it was Schirrel who broke the silence, this time asking me to describe the entrance to Colwick Hall and the landscape round about. It wasn't an area I'd frequented much but it was surprising what I could find in my memory once I made the effort.

To get to the hall we would turn off the main highway onto a well-maintained private road belonging to the Colwick estate. That ran for a couple of miles over undulating moorland, the land surface being sufficiently uneven to restrict visibility in all directions — in some places quite badly, down to a hundred metres or less. We'd then come to the main gate, which was set in a dilapidated wall, and where I recommended we insist the swap takes place. Could someone hide behind the wall? Not unless they were lying down; even crouching a person's head would show. How far from the gate to the hall? Hard to recall but no more than half a mile along a gravel driveway. Hall visible from the gate? Definitely yes, the ground being fairly level inside the perimeter wall. Trees? None. Any other roads leading to the hall? No: one way in; same way out.

Schirrel did his deep thought act for a few minutes

and then gave us our orders, for all the world like an officer in the army commanding a patrol about to go into action. I approved. It inspired confidence. And a necessary commodity that was, given his main concern that Abraham might be armed and we weren't. I questioned whether we oughtn't to be as worried about our police tail, but he asserted confidently they wouldn't bother us. That seemed a rash prediction, though I didn't say so.

It was as well I kept my opinion to myself, for when we turned off the main road and onto the Colwick estate, the police didn't follow. They merely pulled into the verge and stopped. Obvious really. The turning I'd taken was a dead-end, which meant they couldn't pursue us along it without blowing their cover — cover they may have thought was still intact because I'd made no attempt to lose them. The sensible course from their point of view was to wait until I returned to the main road and then simply resume their tailing operation. I didn't doubt Schirrel had worked this out in advance. As I've remarked before, he was one clever man.

In due course we reached the top of a small ridge and Colwick Hall came into sight half a mile away, standing magnificent and solitary, a stately home with a lawn in front of it and otherwise surrounded by moorland. I applied the brakes as we coasted down a gentle incline, bringing the car to a halt, as per Schirrel's instructions, five metres short of the gate in the wall guarding the entrance to the Abramites' lair.

As I got out of the car, the gravity of our situation came home to me. We were about to confront a psychopath, certainly capable of murder, and probably carrying a gun. Someone who wanted at least me dead. Suddenly I knew how a condemned man must feel as he takes his final walk to the gallows. Deborah had been asleep when she'd had her bad dream. Lucky Deborah. I was having the same dream now. Only I was wide awake and living it.

16

How I managed to saunter calmly up to the gate in the wall I'll never know. Schirrel, Al and Deborah followed me. Calvin stayed with the car, turning it around. The time was 8.12.

Inside the wall was a garden shed adapted for use as a gatehouse. As we approached, a short, chubby man came out, looking at his watch and clutching a two-way radio.

"You're right to turn your car around. You can't go no further. Private property," he informed us.

"We're expected," I said.

"Yeh? And who might you be?"

I decided there was no need for names. I said: "I'm here to deliver a tape and collect a young man."

That made sense to the chap. He pushed a button on his radio and said into it: "You there, Mr Reborn? Geezer's just arrived but he isn't alone. There's three other blokes and a lady with him." He listened for a reply, then passed the radio to me.

"That you, Radman?" I heard Abraham ask.

"Yes."

"You're late."

"Your clocks are fast."

"I told you to come alone."

"No you didn't. Anyhow, as there are eighty of you and only five of us, you've no cause to object."

"I do object. But since your friends are here, you can all drive up to the house. Put the guard back on the line."

"I'm not coming to the house. None of us are. You bring Aaron Bernheim to the gate."

"That ain't what I've got in mind. I want to view that tape before anyone is swapped. You ain't conning me again."

"So take a walk out here and discuss it. I'm not coming to the house."

"Man, I'll see you burn in hell for this. Give me a few minutes."

By the sound of it, Abraham had slipped his radio into a pocket. I kept hold of the guard's.

"Is he coming?" asked Schirrel.

"Don't know," I said shrugging.

"Are you an Abramite?" I said to the guard.

"Do me a favour," he said. "I'm a sentry, mate. Here to stop people invading Mr Reborn's privacy. I'll worry about the wrath of God when I'm dead."

A tense five minutes passed.

Eventually a black limousine emerged from around one side of Colwick Hall and cruised towards us.

Calvin reversed our own car nearer to the gate. Its doors were still open.

"You'd better get in, Deb," said Schirrel.

Deborah looked at me. I didn't tell her yes and I didn't tell her no. It was her decision. She came to my side and held my hand.

The guard seemed to sense the fear of violence that had started to grip my party. A worried frown came over his face and he retreated to his gatehouse.

The approaching limousine turned broadside on to us as it neared the gate. There were three people inside. The driver was Jed Nordstrom, and he stayed put. The two passengers got out: Abraham and a teenage boy.

Leaving the boy by the limousine, Abraham walked up to the gatehouse. "Take the day off," he said to the guard.

When the man, too surprised to obey at once, failed to react, Abraham added firmly: "Go home."

The guard hauled out a moped from behind his shed, donned a crash helmet, opened the gate and pootled away.

The eight people left behind watched him depart. Each of us knew why he'd been dismissed. Abraham didn't want him to be a witness. But a witness to what?

"Well, what have we here?" said Abraham, regarding Deborah. "The nameless lady. Only you ain't so nameless, Mrs Czerny."

How the hell had he found out who she was?

He gestured towards the limousine. "That's Aaron," he said.

I glanced at Schirrel, who nodded.

Abraham looked at him hard, drawing conclusions. "Where's the tape?"

Schirrel passed it to me.

Abraham said: "Now, like I told you, I want to view the tape before we do the exchange."

I shook my head.

"Aaron," Abraham called out over his shoulder, "are you willing to be gathered to your people for your brothers and sisters?"

"Yes, Abraham," Aaron replied.

"Show them," Abraham commanded.

Nordstrom reached across to the glove compartment and took out a revolver. He passed it to the boy. We watched the young man cock it and put it to his head.

In one way this was the nightmare the members of my party had been dreading: that the Abramites would produce firearms. Yet in another way it wasn't. We'd assumed they'd want to shoot us, not one of their own. Schirrel's impressive powers of anticipation had been confounded by Abraham's unpredictability.

"I ain't bluffing," said Abraham. "Give me the tape."

I shook my head again. If I complied without being certain of securing Aaron in return, the game was over, and we'd lost.

I wasn't the one who blinked first. Nor was Abraham.

Schirrel said: "Hold it. Maybe we can work this out. How about if you swap Aaron for me. Aaron stays here. You and I go into the hall and check out the tape. Once you're satisfied it's genuine, I walk out."

"That's a mighty fine suggestion, friend," said Abraham, grinning. It was as if the proposal was one he'd been expecting. Something was very wrong somewhere. "Not you, though," he continued, addressing Schirrel. "I don't know you, and maybe I don't want to; leastways, not this side of the Day of Judgement. I'll take him," he said, pointing to me.

I quashed that idea right away. "Not a chance," I said. "Not after what you wanted to do to me in Sarai Lodge."

"I'm more important than he is," said Schirrel.

"Maybe you're right. And maybe it wouldn't be such a smart idea to take George, here. He's a real dangerous man. But I still ain't taking you," he said to Schirrel.

"What about the dame? I figure George will behave himself better if it's the lady who comes with me. After all, him and Mrs Czerny are pretty pally. Must be, as they shared a room in a motel in Bewel after he got out of Sarai Lodge. Yeh," Abraham added, speaking to me, "we traced you to that licentious place. Reservation in the name of D Czerny. I hope you enjoyed your fornication."

"You either take my friend," I said referring to Schirrel, "or Aaron can blow his brains out. It doesn't matter much to me which. Either way, Mrs Czerny stays here."

"How about it, Deb?" said Schirrel. "For me. As a friend?"

"I'll go," said Deborah.

"*No*," I said, horrified.

I've no skill at negotiating and this confrontation had gone totally out of my control. The problem was that while on Abraham's side it was all up to him, on our side we seemed to have a committee.

Schirrel moved to stand in front of me. I resigned.

"She goes on one condition," Schirrel said. "She keeps in radio contact with us at all times. Radman's got the handset the guard was using. I'm betting you've got yours in the car."

Abraham grinned yet again and the same horrible feeling swept over me. We were doing what he wanted us to do. Schirrel was so sure of his own intellectual superiority and so certain Abraham was just another rational criminal it had made him over-confident.

"It's not in the car. It's in my pocket," Abraham said. "I wanted to be able to call up reinforcements from the house if you tried pulling anything fancy. But I can see you're playing this straight as an arrow. You'll be able to face God with clean hearts, my friends. Not like Radman back there. That visitation from the everlasting realms of hell will suffer mightily before the flames consume his tainted flesh."

Abraham handed his radio to Deborah.

She looked at me, anxiety all over my face. "See you in a little while," she said, and it was like my heart was breaking. She wasn't my property. I had no right to command her. What could I do?

Abraham saw and understood. "She hollers, you come running," he said to me, and smiled his mesmerizingly beautiful smile.

Aaron uncocked the gun and returned it to the glove compartment. Abraham signalled and Aaron came through the gate and over to our side. Schirrel gestured for me to give him the videotape, which I reluctantly handed over, and he passed it to Abraham. Deborah got in the black limousine along with Abraham. Nordstrom got the car moving and his party set off for Colwick Hall.

"Relax, George," said Schirrel. "It's working out fine."

"Like hell it is. If she doesn't come out of there, Abraham isn't the only one I'm going to kill."

"Jesus, Radman, cool it! That guy's got no reason to harm Deborah. I suggest we all sit in the car."

Al and I got in the back, with Aaron between us. Schirrel sat up front next to Calvin.

"When she rejoins us," Schirrel said to me, "we'll drive a way and let you out. You take to the moor. The cops will follow us back to Newcastle. That'll put everyone in the clear. Once the heat's off, call me on my cell phone and we can settle our next moves."

He was so damned confident he was right, and I knew, without being able to put it into words why, that he was wrong. I screwed round in my seat to look back at the hall. The black limousine was no longer in view.

Over the two-way radio we heard doors slam, a 'this way ma'am', and then the background noise changed from outdoors to indoors.

"You there, Radman?" Abraham asked suddenly over the radio.

"Yes."

"By the gate?" he asked speaking slowly and clearly.

"Where else?"

"Aaron still with you?"

Schirrel and I exchanged glances. "Of course," I said.

"And your *three* friends?"

"Yes. We're waiting in the guard's hut."

"That's fine. I'd hate for you to leave without Mrs Czerny. Really would."

I switched the radio to receive-only and laid it quietly on the shelf behind my seat.

"Al," said Schirrel, "take a run up the road to the top of the rise. See if there's anybody coming our way."

Schirrel looked at me and his eyes conveyed the word he couldn't get his voice to utter. Sorry. Abraham had been using the radio to pass a message to someone else, telling them who was with me and where we were. Schirrel had understood that as well as I had. We'd just been set up.

"Turn the car round, Calvin," I said. "We've got to go and get her out of there."

Calvin, ever dutiful, looked to Schirrel for confirmation.

"Take Aaron," Schirrel ordered Calvin. "Get him to the road any way you can."

"On foot?" Calvin asked.

"George and I need the car."

Calvin nodded.

Al, by now on the road near the top of the ridge, unexpectedly turned, waved and began running towards us. Calvin swore and said urgently: "Doors closed. Now!"

A car — not the police car that had followed us earlier — came into sight, doing around forty. They must have been waiting somewhere along the main road — waiting for Abraham to order them in. What the two Abramites inside should have done is drive up to us slowly. We'd have had to consider the possibility they were harmless tourists or visitors to the hall, and by the time we were sure they weren't it would have been too late. But these characters weren't into subtlety. They ran Al down. He jumped to one side at the last instant but the right wing of the car caught his hip and flung him to the ground.

Calvin screamed the tyres. Schirrel fastened his seatbelt. He was the only one with that much presence of mind. I braced myself. Aaron sat and stared.

The enemy braked to a halt, turning to their right so as to block the road at an angle of about forty-five degrees. The passenger began to get out. I caught sight of a large machine-pistol.

Not wanting to hit the opposition head on, Calvin swung a little to the right immediately before impact. The man with the machine-pistol was just not quite fast enough. The collision crushed him between his partly open door and the doorframe as he was about to pull the trigger. He burst open like a tomato hit with a hammer. It's what happens when the hammer is one and a half tonnes of metal. Red gunk splattered everywhere.

We came to a crashing halt against the enemy vehicle, obstructing our left-hand doors. Calvin and I, on the right, got out fast. The enemy driver was probably armed like his newly-deceased colleague and needed to be dealt with.

Calvin, being twenty years younger than me and undoubtedly combat-trained, was ahead of me. He went round the front of our car. I went round the back. The driver saw Calvin first and took a shot at him. Not with a machine-pistol fortunately; just a boring old semi-automatic handgun. Calvin disappeared from sight, hit or hiding; I couldn't tell which.

The gunman turned as I came up behind him. I kicked his door hard, thumping it into him and knocking him backwards. It bought me enough time to lock a hand round the wrist holding the gun. With my other arm I aimed a blow at his face but he blocked that and we grappled. The gun fired once, harmlessly.

We toppled over. While there was only one gun between us, I couldn't allow him to pull apart. We rolled on the ground.

Somehow we managed to get to our knees and then to our feet, wrestling the whole time. He smashed me several times into his car. Unlike the Abramite I had fought in Boston this one was strong. That was when it occurred to me I might not win this fight.

But I needn't have worried. As we flailed at each other's throats with our free hands I allowed him to force me down onto the boot. A perfect position. Schirrel came up behind him and clubbed him on the back of his head with the butt of the machine-pistol. Almost comically he went cross-eyed, and then slumped onto me, just so much dead weight.

I threw him off, taking possession of his gun as I did so. Without exchanging words, Schirrel and I raced round to our own car. Aaron had gone. Tough. I got to the car first and so was able to take command of the driver's seat. Schirrel sat behind me. The engine had stalled with the impact but it started again readily. I reversed away from the enemy vehicle and turned the car to face towards the hall.

Coming over the two-way radio now was a sound like bedlam: not individual voices; a collective noise as if many people were talking excitedly at once. Shouting to be heard. And then someone screamed. I didn't think it was Deborah but it must have been.

"You hear that, Radman," said Abraham, audible over the din. "She's going to burn instead of you. She's going to die for your wickedness."

I switched on the windscreen wipers to clear the late Abramite's gore off, but they only smeared it into a greasy red film. There was no time to seek out the windscreen washer button. I set the wiper control to its torrential downpour setting and floored the accelerator.

I heard Schirrel mutter something and, thinking I was being spoken to, asked him to repeat what he'd said.

"I should have foreseen," he responded dully.

"Foreseen what?"

"Destroying you must be as important to Reborn as getting the tape back. He had those guns waiting out there all along to make certain you didn't get away. He wants everything: the tape, Aaron Bernheim, you. And I've given him Deborah. What have I done! Dear god...."

Over the radio more screams could be heard. A lot of women, a few men. There was a quite different sound in the background. A new one.

We had passed through the open gate and were half way to the hall when we overtook Aaron loping towards the building.

"I want that kid in the back," I said to Schirrel. "Seatbelt on. And that goes for you too."

I overtook the boy and did an emergency stop. Schirrel got out and grabbed hold of Aaron before he could react.

Aaron struggled. We didn't have the time for that. Schirrel threw him bodily onto the back seat.

"George," I heard Deborah cry over the radio. She coughed and gasped for breath.

"What's going on in there, Aaron?" I asked.

"I don't know. The disbanding ceremony."

"What's that mean?"

"I don't know. Abraham said we have to journey to new pastures."

I fastened my own seatbelt and accelerated towards the hall. Aaron resisted being belted up so Schirrel hit him hard. All that talk about the client coming first had been crap. When it came to it, Caxton Schirrel was a human being after all.

The driveway obligingly runs straight to the main double-door entrance. The doors were shut. I wasn't about to knock. I was doing around sixty when I hit the solitary step in front of the doors. The car's front wheels went airborne. And then, immediately, came the impact. The ancient solid oak doors might have been unmoved but the hinges weren't up to the impact. The upper ones partly held; the lower ones didn't. Neither did the locks.

The car careered into a large, high-ceilinged reception area. Chandeliers, marble staircase, the lot.

Perhaps Deborah heard the crash, for she suddenly shouted: "By the door," — coughing — "by the window." And then she cried out in pain. The screaming of other people continued. The background noise was something I could now identify. It was fire.

Schirrel dragged Aaron out of the car.

"I love you, George," I heard Deborah cry. She wouldn't have said that unless she thought it was all over. Time, I cursed. This is all taking too long. I was almost frantic.

The three of us, me with the handgun, Schirrel with the machine-pistol, and Aaron with a half-hearted protest against Schirrel's hold on him, advanced into the building. Aaron appeared to be in two minds about joining his friends now he'd heard them over the radio. Disbanding probably wasn't supposed to be this painful.

The smell of smoke reached my nostrils. Don't lose your grip now, Radman. Not now.

I turned to Aaron and slapped him across the face. "Where will they be?" I demanded.

"In the temple."

"Show me."

He stopped protesting and led us deeper into the building. As we advanced the smoke got thicker and more pungent. And the screaming, previously only heard over the radio, became audible.

There was the sound of automatic gunfire.

Aaron led us along a corridor. We weren't coughing yet though breathing was becoming harder.

On our left we came to a large double-door. It didn't need Aaron to tell us we'd arrived. Smoke was seeping out round the door frame. I tried to open it but it was locked. Probably barricaded on the inside too.

"We need another way in," I said.

"There's Abraham's vestry," Aaron said, indicating the next door, further down the corridor.

As he spoke, the vestry door opened. Abraham appeared. He saw me. I pushed Aaron away, raised my gun and fired. Abraham flung himself back inside the vestry. The door slammed. I heard it lock.

"Disbanding everyone but himself," I said to Aaron.

Schirrel ordered Aaron to get out of the building and wait for him outside. He aimed the machine-pistol at the vestry door lock and fired several rounds.

I ran to the door and kicked it open. I had to crouch to see the vestry was empty. Its upper half was obscured by black smoke and reeked of plastic and rubber and burnt flesh. On the floor was the accursed videotape. There were no flames.

Two other things I took in at a glance. Abraham had escaped out of the window; and there was a gown like the ones worn at human sacrifices draped over a chair. I put the garment on, pulled up the hood and went through into the temple.

Eighty people were dying in hell in there. The heat was intense; the smoke so thick visibility was well below a metre. I couldn't see. I couldn't breathe. I screamed for Deborah. The roar of the fire, the moans and cries of the so-called chosen ones drowned any response.

Almost at once I trod on someone and pitched over. It was a fortunate accident for it revealed that next to the floor was a layer, perhaps six inches high, where the air stank but was cool and breathable. From down at this level I could see flames. They seemed to be all around but distant. The walls were clearly alight.

"By the door, by the window," Deborah had said. The windows were to my right. If she wasn't there it would be hopeless. Pieces of ceiling were raining down in showers of sparks. Once the timbers up there — ancient and probably none too sound in any case — were weakened enough, the contents of the floor above would come crashing through. I reckoned I had seconds rather than minutes.

As I crawled crocodile-like towards the windows, I had to avoid several corpses, or near corpses. Some had bullet wounds. One was a baby.

There was a chair ahead of me, a simple wooden-framed affair, tipped onto its back. Someone was tied to it. I recognized the clothes. And the radio. I seized the nearest leg and began working my way backwards towards the door, dragging the chair and its human burden with me.

Some of the ceiling gave way. A large object hit the floor towards the centre of the room with a tremendous crash. A wall of flame surged outwards, rising into the smoke.

The heat was seriously penetrating the gown I was wearing, especially as it was riding up in consequence of my wriggling feet first towards the vestry.

Schirrel shouted out: "Radman!"

"Here," I yelled.

The next thing I knew I was drenched in cold water. Schirrel had filled a bucket from somewhere. Then he grabbed my ankles and pulled me out, and I in turn brought with me the chair to which Deborah was tied.

The vestry was no place to pause. The smoke was nearly as thick as in the temple, the heat almost palpable. The ceiling must have been very close to flashing over.

Dragging the chair between us we got it into the corridor. There was a 'whoomph' from the room we had just left. A sheet of flame surged over our heads. Schirrel hastily pulled the door closed.

Still we couldn't rest. Coughing and retching, I helped Schirrel carry the chair and its precious cargo into the open air, down the step and onto the lawn. Aaron was there, staring white-faced at the building.

An explosion boomed out.

"What the hell was that?" said Schirrel as he struggled to undo the ropes tying Deborah to the chair.

"The collection in the basement," Aaron answered. "There's guns, dynamite, flamethrowers, napalm, hand grenades. Mostly smuggled in from Ireland. It was in case we had to stand a siege."

I looked at Deborah. It only took one glance to register it had all been a waste of time. She was unrecognizable. Her clothes were smouldering. There was a bullet wound below her left collar bone. She wasn't breathing.

Before this appalling personal catastrophe had time to properly register in my mind, an unexpected sound caught my ears and I looked up. Abraham's black limousine had emerged from the side of the hall and was scrunching along the gravel driveway, heading for the gate half a mile away.

I was momentarily stunned. I'd put my gun down in the vestry before donning the gown. It was still there. The same fate I presume had befallen Schirrel's machine-pistol. It was an understandable error for us to have made. We'd had more immediate things on our minds.

In a way I'd have welcomed it if Abraham had pulled out a firearm and blazed away at us. But he didn't. He slowed, smiled his handsome smile at me, and then turned his head regally to face the road.

I snarled and ran towards him. He accelerated away, leaving me staring impotently up his exhaust pipe. He couldn't have made his point better if he'd said it with words: you forced me to liquidate my cult, Radman; it's your fault; I want you to suffer for it, either on Earth or in hell; I hate you.

I watched him receding into the distance. He carefully drove round the car Calvin had crashed into. If that car was still serviceable....

I began sprinting towards it. A horn sounded behind me, approaching rapidly. I glanced over my shoulder. Another car skidded to a halt inches from my feet. The driver was half out of his door. It was Jed Nordstrom.

"You want Abraham?" he said. "Get in."

The only thing which could stop me coming apart at the seams was action. Keep moving. Don't think. Especially don't think about Deborah. Going into shock can wait. Grief can wait. You've got a job to do, Radman. Do it.

There was nothing left to me worth hanging onto other than vengeance. I got in the car and we took off, spraying gravel behind us.

17

We almost fell at the first hurdle. The unmarked police car which had followed us from Newcastle appeared over the brow of the hill. They must have seen the rising column of smoke and were coming to investigate. To them, Nordstrom and I would have looked like suspicious characters fleeing the scene. They flashed their headlights and tried to block our path.

"Amateurs," Nordstrom growled. He turned our own headlights onto main beam, slammed his hand on the horn, and continued to accelerate.

The police driver, staring a head-on collision in the face, lost his nerve and attempted to get out of our way. We clipped his tail for him, buckling our bonnet and leaving him with some impressive dents. He wasn't disposed to pursue us. There was a burning mansion in front of him which rated a higher priority.

We passed Al and Calvin and the Abramite who'd been knocked out by Schirrel. Calvin was the only one obviously wounded (by a bullet). The three of them were together at the side of the road, like wounded enemy soldiers who've stumbled into the same dug-out and decided to call a private armistice.

Nordstrom didn't pay any attention to them. We crested the incline doing sixty. Abraham was too far ahead to be seen.

"Do I call you Jed or Bryce?" I asked to break the silence.

"Parents called me Bryce. 'Jed' can go to hell."

We screamed round a bend in the road and caught a glimpse of Abraham about a mile in front of us.

Nordstrom continued: "He said we were going to disband. I didn't realize what that was. And when I did, it was too late to save them. Those poor stupid people." Bryce Nordstrom was nearly in tears.

Our quarry came into view again as we approached the main road. He turned south. Thirty seconds later so did we.

"I saved your life once," Nordstrom said, regaining his composure. "That night in your bedroom when Abraham was fixing to sacrifice you. That was me who talked him out of it."

"I know."

"You want to save *my* life?"

"I'm no good at saving lives," I said dully. "Not even those I love. What I do is kill people."

Abraham knew we were after him. If our own speed was anything to judge by he was hitting at least a hundred and twenty miles an hour.

Several minutes passed as the landscape flashed by.

Nordstrom said: "I was going after that maniac personally. But now you're here I figure I can leave him to you. That way I won't have to risk a murder rap."

"I wouldn't want it any other way," I said.

A police car passed us, doubtless heading for Colwick Hall, headlights blazing, siren blaring. The driver took no notice of us despite our speed. He had more important matters to attend to than a couple of motorists staging a race on a public highway.

Because of a gentle bend in the road where it cut through a shallow hill, we temporarily lost sight of our quarry. When the view ahead was clear again he'd disappeared.

"Over there!" I yelled, pointing to a barely discernible track.

Nordstrom's reactions were superb. He swung the car almost on two wheels across the carriageway. A speeding fire engine heading hall-wards passed the track as Nordstrom brought the car to a halt.

"Are you sure he went up here?" Nordstrom asked.

"I'm sure. This is the only turning which would have enabled him to get out of sight."

"I don't reckon it leads anywhere."

"It doesn't. The track peters out about three miles further on. There's no way a car could go beyond that."

Nordstrom got out. I slid across into the driving seat.

"I've got to make some calls," he said. "Where's the nearest payphone?"

"Half a mile down the road from here. It's outside an inn."

"Promise me you'll get him."

"He's a dead man. Even if I have to pursue him to the ends of the Earth."

"Good enough. Do me a favour. You never saw me. I don't exist."

"Okay."

"One other thing before you take off. The gun Aaron held to his head earlier on today is still in Abraham's car. Six-chambered revolver."

"Oh great! Spare shells?"

"No. Six is it. That make a difference?"

He saw the expression on my face and shrugged. "Fool question. So long, Radman. Good hunting."

He slammed the car door and I watched him for a moment walking dejectedly towards the main road. Just one more of Abraham's victims. Another tough man who was going to have to live with some deep wounds. And I'd never know whether I was right to suspect Bryce Nordstrom was more than just another Abramite.

I let out the clutch and set off after the devil incarnate.

*

My huge disadvantage, as I saw it, was simple. I had no firearm. That meant I could only get within reach of Abraham if he didn't see me coming. To counter that, my great advantage was that I knew the lie of the land. The track I was cautiously trundling Nordstrom's car up was the one which led to my house. I knew every outcrop, every dip in the ground, every place you could launch an ambush from, everywhere you could hide.

Balancing the disadvantage against the advantage, I reckoned I came out on the losing side. Especially as, despite my various encounters with Abraham, his mental processes were a mystery. I didn't know my enemy. I couldn't predict what he'd do. His degree of mechanization (one black limousine, confined to the track), the armament at his disposal (one loaded revolver), and his approximate location (up ahead but as yet out of sight) were all useful pieces of information, but what I really needed was to get inside his mind.

Why, for example, had he turned off the main road? The logical thing would have been to make for Newcastle where anyone chasing him could be lost in the city centre traffic. Perhaps he was too low on fuel for that? No, George, you're making calculations. Abraham didn't do that. He was aware he was being pursued and it was bugging him. When he sees the track — which he must have been familiar with, having gone up it more than once in the course of ruining my life — he acts instinctively; if he can get far enough away from the main road to be out of sight, the people on his tail would go rushing by, putting him in the clear.

Right! But he'd be unsure if his subterfuge had succeeded. He couldn't merely turn round and drive back to the road. He'd have to get out beforehand and take a look on foot.

I stopped the car, switched off the engine, and leaned my head out of the window. There was no sound I could attribute to another vehicle nearby, either moving or stationary. Nor could I see anyone.

As I surveyed the landscape, I realized Abraham wouldn't attempt a reconnaissance here anyway. He wouldn't appreciate the possibilities of the terrain. No, he'd go for the obvious place, the one which even a novice would spot. It was a bend about a mile and a half ahead, flanked on one side by a rock outcrop which would hide his limousine and provide a vantage point for observing any pursuit. If he had positioned himself there I could take to the hills and come up behind him.

I considered the manoeuvre and rejected it. Suppose he caught sight of me? He could get in his car and drive back to the main road while I was cunningly stalking someone who was no longer present. Come to think of it, he'd be able to do that even if he hadn't caught sight of me. The conclusion was that to keep him bottled up I had to stay on the track, and that meant remaining in Nordstrom's car, since otherwise I'd have no protection at all against being gunned down.

I restarted the engine and resumed lumbering towards my house. I was soon travelling along the edge of the familiar V-shaped valley with the stream gurgling along the bottom.

As I came within sight of the rock outcrop where Abraham should have been lying in wait, I floored the accelerator on the principle that the faster I was moving the harder I'd be to hit. Tensed to duck behind the dashboard I rounded the bend.

There was no sign of him or his limousine. To say I was taken aback would be an understatement. If proof was needed that Abraham's mind was a mystery to me, this was it. Where the hell was he?

I went through the stop, look and listen routine again, and learnt exactly as much as the previous time; that is, nothing positive. There was no option but to press on, since Abraham had to still be ahead of me. Somewhere!

I saw his limousine at last, at the very end of the track about twenty metres from my burnt-out house. No sign of the driver. It presented me with an unmissable opportunity. That limousine was his passport to freedom; put it out of action and Abraham's chances of escaping would drop like a stone. I accelerated towards it.

As my speed picked up he showed himself, standing

against the end wall of the house by the latrine. I saw him raise his gun. There was nothing I could do about that so I ignored him.

He fired a moment before the cars collided. The bullet smashed a side window but not me.

I'd aimed for a point behind his right front wheel and scored a bulls-eye. The forty mile an hour impact locked the two cars together in a tangle of twisted metal. Write off one means of escape.

My house being on the left of the track, I now had the limousine as well as Nordstrom's car between Abraham and me. I fell out of my open door to take advantage of that fact. It wasn't a fraction of a second too soon. He fired a second shot and it seemed to come so close I fancied I felt it passing above my head.

There was a pause for thought on both sides. For my part, I quickly realized that any delay was to his advantage, not mine. So I got on with it. I came out from behind the cars and ran for the opposite end wall of my house, and Blue Beauty's empty garage. I must have covered the twenty metres in no more than three seconds. It was a very long three seconds. He fired a third bullet and missed again.

I didn't enter the garage but sprinted round the back and climbed into the living room through the rear window. It was blackened and gloomy inside and smelt of burnt wood. On the floor was a fair amount of broken glass, some pieces with weapon potential. There were also some charred timbers, and it was the best of those which I settled on for use in defence. I listened.

Sometimes I can be a little slow. I still hadn't got the

hang of how irrational he was. Consequently his next move took me completely by surprise. I heard a starter motor turning over.

Creeping to the front window I saw he was endeavouring, by pumping the accelerator and bouncing himself around in the limousine, to rock the two cars apart. I watched him advance spasmodically a metre further up the track. The tactic plainly wasn't working. He desisted after a minute or so and got out via the passenger's door, the driver's door being blocked by Nordstrom's car.

He went round the side furthest from me and studied the interlocked metal. He crouched and studied some more. Then he began walking towards the latrine. Nothing furtive about it or hurried or aggressive. He glanced at the house and saw me, but the gun in his hand stayed pointing downwards.

Think, George. Get inside his mind. Okay, why would he head for the latrine? Not to use it, that's for sure!

I pulled back into the hallway and took off the white sacrificial gown I'd been wearing since my failed rescue of Deborah. This I hooked onto the charred timber I'd picked up. Whatever he was up to, I wanted him to have a false target to fire at.

I heard him moving about in the tool-shed behind the latrine. The tool-shed was where I kept my larger tools. He made an amount of noise, dropping things on the ground with a thud, and then emerged into the open carrying a crowbar. I thrust the gown through the open window on its timber and shouted: "Hey!"

He spun round, gun raised. Unfortunately he saw through the ruse in time to avoid wasting a bullet.

"You abomination from the pit!" he yelled and charged at me.

I dropped the timber and frantically withdrew into the hallway. He fired through the window. The bullet splintered the remains of the doorframe about level with my chest.

I stepped back further out of sight, badly shaken. I estimated he'd missed me by two inches.

He didn't pursue me into the house. Presently I heard him scrunching metal with my crowbar.

So that was what he was up to! He wanted to get his limousine back in commission and drive away. Suppose he succeeded in separating the two cars. How could I stop him escaping? Somehow I had to find or fashion a weapon with a range long enough to counter his revolver. Seeking inspiration I went through into the kitchen. There were sharp and pointed objects in here — the cutlery had survived, for instance — but it was all close range stuff, not things which could have an effect at twenty metres. The only objects which I could theorize a use for were the hotplates from the stove: two circular lumps of solid iron, ten inches in diameter. They'd be reliably bulletproof. I picked one up and felt the weight of it. No good. It was far too heavy to wear as armour plating under my clothes.

Abraham was back in the limousine again, revving the engine. I watched, powerless to get close enough to interfere. My heart sank as the two cars pulled apart. Could I risk charging him as he drove past? Could he steer and shoot at the same time? Yes, I was feeling that desperate. Failure was staring me in the face.

He turned the limousine to point down the track and I almost laughed with relief. There was no way it was going anywhere. The right front wheel was angled askew.

He got out, apparently in a furious temper, glared at the wheel, then at the house, then at the sky, and shook his fist. I was unsure whether it was God or me he wanted to punch. Perhaps it was both of us, in which case I was in good company.

He went over to Nordstrom's car. That had a flat tyre — the left front one — plus a smashed-in left front wing, and a bonnet which was buckled far worse than when Bryce had clipped the police car.

Undeterred he got in and started the engine. That worked satisfactorily, but when he tried to reverse the car, presumably with a view to turning it round, it seemed reluctant to budge.

Once more he was compelled to carry out a visual inspection. Something must have been obstructing the free movement of the left front wheel, for he took up the crowbar and began levering it inside the wheel arch. It involved a lot of effort; I could hear his grunts and gasps clearly. And an occasional curse.

Then abruptly he returned to the driver's seat, turned the car round without difficulty, and started off for the main road. For a few awful seconds I thought he was going to get away.

However, he must have realized getting Nordstrom's car back in commission was not enough; he had to replace the flat tyre. I watched as he got out the spare wheel and set about fixing the problem. He was clearly obsessed with escaping by car. Never mind that if (or when) he reached the highway he'd be driving the most conspicuous motorized transport in England.

Changing the wheel would take him a few minutes. I was still clutching one of the hotplates from the stove, and it gave me an idea.

Carrying the hotplate I ran out of the back door and up the hill behind the house. Either he didn't see me or else by the time he did I was too far away for effective shooting. I didn't have time to look over my shoulder to find out which.

Once out of his sight, I altered course and headed for the road. Soon I passed a couple of hill-walkers making for Lowhope Crag, adorned with all the regulation gear. It was early yet for the hills to be alive with the tramp of hiking boots, but I wasn't unduly surprised. There are always a few early risers. Quite what they made of me, wild-eyed, running like a sprinter on steroids, clothes still damp from Schirrel's bucket of water at Colwick Hall, hair styled like a second world war G.I., and clutching a metal disk to my chest, I can't imagine. They certainly stared.

It took five minutes for me to reach the rock outcrop where I'd expected to encounter Abraham on my way up the track earlier on. Once he'd changed the wheel he was going to be driving past this spot. Believing me to have fled, he'd be off-guard. The gun wouldn't be instantly accessible. My hotplate, in contrast, was.

Waiting is the worst thing in a situation like this; standing like a statue doing nothing, the worries building up. Is the enemy creeping up on me on foot this very minute? Has he abandoned wheel changing in favour of tramping away over the moor? Have I guessed his next move wrongly yet again? The seconds ticked by.

For once, my pessimism proved groundless. I could hear the car approaching. I was tensed and ready. He passed my location doing about twenty. I stepped out and hurled the metal plate directly at him.

Two unanticipated things happened. Firstly, being entirely unskilled at throwing heavy iron disks, I misjudged my aim. A lot of the force of my throw was lost through an unintended impact with the doorframe. Secondly, in an unwise reflex, Abraham tried to avoid the projectile by turning the car leftwards, away from me.

The hotplate knocked him sideways or he ducked — one of the two — and the car went out of control. It left the track, which was barely wider than the car, and began accelerating diagonally down into the valley and towards the stream at the bottom.

Attempting to return to the track, Abraham turned the steering wheel to the right. The result was spectacular. The car tipped onto its side, its back end rose into the air, and with majestic slowness it rolled onto its roof. That mostly held up, permitting the rotation to continue, bringing the car upright again; and then onto its side once more as it finally hit the stream.

Nothing moved. I lay down, just the top half of my head showing, looking into the valley.

As the minutes passed with no sign of life I started to feel easier in my mind. If he was dead — perhaps pinned under the water and drowned — that was my mission accomplished. If he was alive, then when the police showed up as they eventually would, he'd be taken away to spend the rest of his life in a maximum security hospital for the criminally insane. I could settle for that. In the meantime all I had to do was stay put, though it did strike me as ridiculous that I might be single-handedly, and unarmed, pinning down a gun-toting madman.

Possibly it struck him as ridiculous too. At length he clambered out of the car via the rear window, which had disintegrated. The hotplate appeared to have caught him on the side of his head, for there was a broad streak of blood from his right ear down to his collar.

He looked in my direction, possibly seeing me, possibly not. Either way he chose to keep clear of my location. Perhaps the crash had knocked the stuffing out of him. Perhaps he had some other reason. I don't know. As I've remarked before, his mind was a mystery.

He had clearly decided, rather than making for the main road, to try to escape across the moor on foot — which is what he should have done all along once I'd rammed his limousine. To avoid me he kept to the floor of the valley, squelching his way towards the bathing pool. The ground down there is boggy and slippery and compelled him to move slowly.

I paralleled him for a time, keeping just out of his sight on the track. As confident as I could be — not much! — that he wouldn't change course, I decided to get ahead of him. When I arrived at the house, I found the limousine still had its ignition key in place. I got in, started it up and tried to move it forward in first gear. It responded as far as power was concerned, but it steered like a drunken three-legged sheep. Even so there were possibilities.

Leaving the engine running, I went to see where Abraham had got to. He was a couple of hundred metres away and no longer on the valley floor. He'd realized he had to climb out of it to get round the bathing pool and so was angling up the valley slope towards me. From the way he kept looking round I concluded he didn't know where I was. Satisfied, I returned to the limousine and got it moving.

The bent wheel was trying to take a chunk out of the ground every few metres. Fighting the steering wheel's attempts to turn in my hands, I brought the car very slowly to the edge of the valley.

I caught sight of Abraham when he was mainly below me but a little off to one side. He froze. I precipitated the limousine into the valley, aiming it straight at him.

He couldn't resist that. He raised the gun and fired. I ducked down as he did so. It was a good shot, smashing a hole in the windscreen.

The car gained speed and decided to veer to the left. I struggled, while staying below window level, to keep it pointing downhill. Not being strapped in, I didn't want the car to roll over.

I finally lost control completely seconds before reaching the stream. The limousine plunged into the water, heading for the bathing pool and immediately struck an immovable rock. Not so much an emergency stop as an instantaneous one. I was hurled beneath the dashboard into the front seat leg bins, striking various bits of projecting hardware en route.

The driver's door had opened itself and I wriggled out through the aperture and into the stream. Raising my head gingerly from behind the bonnet I could see Abraham, uninjured, turn his back and resume trudging towards the bathing pool. Not the outcome I'd intended but not a complete failure. He'd used up another bullet.

I waited until he was about thirty metres distant and then set off at a run up the far side of the valley. I was confident he wouldn't fire at me. His one remaining bullet was functioning as a last-ditch deterrent: the only thing keeping me away from him. And deterrents only work if they're *not* used.

Abraham was not a particularly fit man. I was able to get out of the valley, up the far side of the hill, and to the top of the waterfall well ahead of him. And that was despite having done my back an injury in the limousine. It was hurting like hell.

I stood there prominently, observing his laboured approach, daring him to open fire. When I judged him too close for comfort I backed off.

He passed the top of the waterfall and began the hike to Lowhope. I crossed to his side of the stream and followed. About a hundred metres separated us. He kept looking round at me. I made sure he knew I was there. And always would be there.

After a quarter of a mile he turned and yelled an obscenity. And then he began marching aggressively straight for me. I matched his speed, retreating towards the bathing pool. He broke into a trot. So did I.

I could outpace him easily despite the pain in my back. When I reached the top of the waterfall, he was still coming on. I ran down beside the bushes, heading for my house.

As I reached Blue Beauty's garage I saw he had stopped and was regarding me. I took a few steps in his direction. It was as plain a statement of what I'd do if he turned his back as I could convey without speech. If he wanted to escape he had to kill me first, otherwise I'd be right behind him, wherever he went.

He resumed jogging towards me. I darted across the front of the house, grabbing in passing the gown I'd dropped before dodging bullet number four. After that I hastened to the rear of the property, passing the tool-shed and the kitchen, and climbed through the window into the living room.

This time, instead of a charred timber, I picked up a piece of broken glass. I gripped it through the gown to avoid lacerating myself.

The interior of my house was a very dangerous place to be. I'd learnt that lesson from the fourth bullet. There were too many openings I could be attacked through — two windows and a door at the front, and the same at the back. It was impossible to guard them all. I had come inside to acquire a weapon, but I'd lose more than I'd gained unless I got out again quickly.

But I couldn't just walk into the open; I had to know where Abraham was first.

I listened intently. Abraham was keeping silent. I was about to congratulate him for getting something right at last when he shouted out: "Radman!"

Front of the house, to the left of the window, possibly beside the garage. I peered out of the back window. As expected it was clear.

I was about to jump into the open when Abraham

came swiftly into sight. I threw myself back inside, rushed across the room and exited to the outside through the front window. Then I transferred myself to the corner of the garage. Theoretically at least, that was a safer place to be as it gave me only two directions to defend; namely, the two corners he could come round to bring me into view.

"Radman," he called out from somewhere round the back, "this is totally dumb. You want to die, I'll oblige you. Otherwise I ain't got the time for this. Why don't you quit bugging me?"

It was hard to be sure but I got the impression he was moving as he spoke, heading towards the tool-shed. I risked abandoning the corner I was currently guarding, in favour of a sneak glance round the back end of the garage.

I saw him passing the tool-shed, facing away from me. Feeling comparatively safe for a few moments I attempted to get onto the garage roof, which was made entirely of corrugated iron and had survived the fire. Knowing Abraham was still down the far end of the house, I judged I had enough time.

I part jumped, part hauled myself up, kicking my legs about and making a hell of a lot more noise than I'd intended. The pain in my back, which I'd been successfully managing to suppress, became agonizing. It was a muscle problem, I was fairly sure. Something had torn and I'd just made it very much worse. I lay on the roof, hurting so much I felt sick, and realizing with horror that the damage was so severe it rendered me incapable of movement. I think I may even have fainted briefly.

I heard Abraham muttering. He was no longer by the latrine. He was very close.

"Damn you, Radman, you vile consort of darkness," he shouted. "Come here and face me, you coward."

His shouting had fixed his position for me. I raised my head and caught sight of his luxuriant black hair. He was just out of my reach, creeping towards me alongside the garage wall. Nearer and nearer.

And then he was directly below. I rolled off the roof. He detected me at the last instant and swung round, raising the gun. With one hand I grabbed for him, and with the other I stabbed at his neck with the shard of glass.

The gun fired, hitting me low in the abdomen. A fraction of a second later we were in physical contact. He toppled over as my weight hit him.

We struck the ground together, with him on his side, and me face down mostly on top of him.

And then I had him. The people Abraham had wanted me to be gathered to, the Radmans of twenty generations and more, demanded nothing less. I sliced his throat with the glass shard. The first wound was fairly superficial. The second one wasn't. I severed his windpipe. He gurgled, unable to speak. He tried turning, perhaps in a reflex reaction, and the glass went deeper, cutting a major blood vessel. He writhed, pushed upwards and rolled me off him so I was facing the sky. Somehow he got to his feet, neck bleeding copiously, and staggered a few paces. Then he fell to his knees, put his hands together as if in prayer, and pitched forward. I watched him dispassionately for the long couple of minutes it took him to die.

Vengeance is mine, sayeth George Radman. Vengeance is mine.

But there was no joy in the victory. His last bullet had struck my pelvis. The damage was impossible to assess, but I knew it was bad. I did what I could for the wound, which was almost nothing because the pain in my back made the slightest movement excruciating. Bleeding wasn't severe, but neither could I cause what flow there was to abate.

I gave up the struggle. What was the point? Deborah was dead; my house was burnt out; the police were determined to prosecute me for two murders I didn't commit, and doubtless now for a third which I did. The future promised to be one long, unending torment. Stuff it.

As growing weakness and shock overtook me I looked for the last time at the sky above me. I'd always wanted that to be the last thing I ever saw. Perhaps Deborah was up there somewhere waiting for me.

Staring at a glorious blue expanse flecked with clouds, I felt surprisingly at peace. Apart from my years at university and some of the time when I'd been earning my living as an ecologist, I had spent all my life in this land. I was born here, I grew up here, and now I was going to die outside the very house where my life began. Full circle. No regrets. I'd enjoyed nearly all that wonderful existence.

I watched calmly as the sky darkened and everything drifted away.

Paradise Regained

July 1998

18

I was aware my existence was continuing in some form or other; a warm, pleasant sensation enveloped me like bathing in a sea of bliss. As someone who doesn't believe in life after death — other than as a comforting fantasy — I'd have been seriously worried, except that worry was the last thing on my mind. I just hung in there and enjoyed it.

Nor was I completely alone in this ante-room to heaven. There were meaningless voices which I knew belonged to friends, nearby but beyond my sphere of being. There were movements and lights and sounds. I experienced these things without response. I was disembodied. A ghost. It was lovely.

I woke with shattering suddenness. The bliss was replaced by a mild discomfort in the region of my hip. I no longer felt disembodied; you can't be disembodied and have a hip. I had other parts too. For instance, something was attached to my arm. There was a mystery here that needed solving but why rush things. I waited for a long time and nothing happened. I heard a couple of voices whispering indistinctly. When they'd stopped for a while I opened my eyes.

Hospital room, bright lights, tube taped to my forearm, Peter sitting in a chair reading a newspaper, no one else in sight. I must be a private patient, I thought, and wondered immediately who was paying. It certainly wasn't me.

"Hello, Peter," I said.

He jumped, but the wide-eyed astonishment was swiftly replaced by a beaming grin. He leapt to his feet and said: "About time. Don't move. I'll fetch the nurse."

He hastened out of the room.

I didn't feel comfortable, so I changed position slightly in the bed. Apart from causing some shooting pains around my hip, the move didn't produce any untoward consequences.

I was about to tidy up the sheet covering me when the promised nurse entered. There was something wrong somewhere. What kind of hospital was this? This carer for the sick looked a lot worse than I felt. One side of her face was bandaged and the other side was an odd colour. She had almost no hair, as if she'd been to a barber with a grudge. And she couldn't even be bothered to wear a proper uniform; the thing she had on most nearly resembled a hospital gown.

I stared at her; she stared at me. A frown appeared in amongst the bandages, and she took a couple of steps forward.

"Hello," I said politely.

"Hi George," she responded in a horrible rasping wheeze.

That shook me because only one person had ever greeted me like that, and she was dead. I decided this woman must be a patient but, whoever she was, her impersonation of Deborah was rubbish and in extremely poor taste.

"Trust me to be visiting the bathroom when you come to," she said gruffly.

That shook me even more. She'd got the accent. And the fine figure. And now I was looking more closely, the eyes as well. In fact if you removed the bandages, added some hair and ignored the asthmatic harshness of the voice....

"Deborah?" I said, very doubtfully.

She sat down by the bed and took my hand. "I knew you wouldn't let me down," she said. "Some of the folk here didn't believe you were going to make it. But I knew."

"I thought you were dead," I said, and choked.

"Me? Nah. Takes more than a head case like Abraham Reborn to put me out of business; especially when I have my own private one-man seventh cavalry riding to the rescue. And," she added after a pause, "an ex-boss who hangs around to carry out CPR."

I almost cringed. "I thought you were dead," I repeated pathetically.

"Yes, well, we both came close."

Her final words to me over the radio after I'd smashed my way into Colwick Hall came floating into my mind. "I love you too, Deb," I whispered.

She leaned forward and kissed me, and then decided to be more demonstrative. She knelt on the bed, lifting one leg over so she was astride me.

It was a pity she didn't get any further.

"For goodness sake, what *are* you doing?" a woman's voice said loudly.

Deborah reversed direction as if she'd been stung. Peter had returned with a proper nurse.

"You'll have his drip out," the nurse scolded.

"That wasn't the part she was after," Peter ventured. "Did I ever tell you about Tupper, my prize ram?"

"We'd better continue this conversation later," I proposed as the nurse treated me to a few routine ministrations. I decided it was good to be back.

*

Before the rest of the world began intruding, Deborah and Peter had about half an hour to bring me up to date.

Naturally my first concern was Deborah's health. She'd sustained first degree burns on various parts of her body which had hurt like hell but were clearing up gradually, and worse burns on her head and neck. It was possible she'd need a skin graft or two. The bullet wound — Abraham had opened fire randomly on his chosen ones when some of them had had the effrontery to try and escape the blaze — had damaged the apex of her left lung but had otherwise done surprisingly little harm. The smoke, though, was a different matter; it was that that had nearly killed her. Her entire respiratory system was still inflamed. Nevertheless, so long as she avoided chest infections for a while yet, the prognosis was good.

As for me, they told me I'd been saved by a couple of hill-walkers who'd come upon me promptly and administered first aid. Shortly afterwards, a helicopter had conveyed me to hospital to be patched up. The trouble was I'd lost so much blood my kidneys rapidly failed. I'd been in intensive care, in a coma and on dialysis while the medical profession fought to prevent my other organs from following the example set by my kidneys. Their success was assured when my kidneys revived. After that, all anyone could do was wait for me to regain consciousness and pray that I had sustained no brain damage. I was pleased to confirm that my mental faculties were all intact. Everything considered, Deborah's word 'close' seemed about right.

Outside the protective bounds of the hospital, Planet Earth had been appalled by the fire at Colwick Hall, and a conflagration shortly after in the South African branch. In Brazil, the 'Jacob' there had preferred not to appal people, had left his firelighters unlit, and had proclaimed himself the new Abraham. Sarai Lodge's Jacob had faced a different dilemma. He'd not been given time to burn the place down. Someone — I suspect it may have been Nordstrom — had triggered a major police operation and the lodge had been stormed. The Abramites had resisted, the police had been repelled, and a siege had ensued which had only just ended. There had been major casualties on both sides.

That was about all the ground we had time to cover before a uniformed police officer arrived, handcuffed me to the bed, and took up station in the corner of the room — just in case I'd forgotten I was a prisoner on remand awaiting trial for murder. Even more incredible, the man was armed, supposedly to deter any renewed attempts to liberate me. Who did they think I was? The head of the Northumberland wing of the mafia?

Later that day the policeman on guard was joined by a detective. He wanted to conduct an interview, under caution, about my escape from the prison van, and about recent events at Colwick Hall. I was very brief. I told him that for as long as it remained the case that he and his colleagues accused me of two murders I did not commit, I would not cooperate with him in any way. Thereafter I said not a word. He gave up very quickly. His fellow officers must have warned him not to waste his time if I had an attack of the Big Silence.

That left one more item of news I didn't really want to hear. A surgeon spoke to me privately, explaining that Abraham's last bullet had done a lot of damage to my pelvic bones. My hip joint was never likely in future to be free of pain, I would need a lot of physiotherapy, and a hip replacement would probably be necessary within a few years. I thanked the doctor for the information. What else can you say to someone who tells you you'll never walk properly again?

After that, things began to look up. Ms Rodgers breezed into my room next morning, informing me she was my lawyer, wasn't she? — absolutely, yes — and introducing Richard House, the famous publicity agent. Sign here, please, Mr Radman. And what for, I wanted to know. Because there are currently thirty journalists camped outside this hospital, any one of whom would sell their spouse for a photograph of yours truly, or their soul for an exclusive interview. That's what for. I signed.

The next time I saw Richard House he brought me a copy of the nation's best-selling tabloid and showed me the front page headline.

George Radman Rescued Me
From Satanic Inferno

Below was a picture of Deborah, bandages and all. The story was marked: 'Exclusive.'

The following day the finest broadsheet fought back with:

Alleged Murderer George Radman
Risked Life In Attempt To Bring
Mad Minister To Justice

House informed me I was being well paid. And that was despite my not saying anything to anybody yet. The wonders of the mass media!

That was Richard House doing his job. Ms Rodgers also did hers. In a private conversation from which the police were excluded she made clear that House was being paid by R & S to make it as difficult as possible for the police to proceed with their case against me. R & S were also paying for my hospital treatment. The reason for their generosity was not gratitude (though they *were* grateful) but because they wanted in return my silence regarding the identity of Aaron Bernheim. He had made a full statement to the police and, since he had committed no crimes and was legally a juvenile, the boy had subsequently been returned to his parents in America. Strings were being pulled at a very high level to keep his name secret, Aaron's father being an influential and powerful man with a lot of self-interest to protect. If I cooperated, R & S, on Mr Bernheim's behalf, would guarantee me the best lawyers and, if necessary, as many appeals as it took to get me free. It was nice to have friends, even if their motives were selfish. I gave my word no one would learn of Aaron Bernheim from me.

[*Note added by author Harry Senthill: Mr Radman names the boy here because Aaron Bernheim himself put his involvement into the public domain a few years ago in the course of a Senate hearing on cults and their methods. Ironically, 'Aaron' was his original given name. Being a name from the Old Testament, he had no need to change it when he joined the Abramites.*]

Perhaps Mr Bernheim had more clout than I realized, or perhaps he had nothing to do with the next development in my life. I doubt if I'll ever know. What happened was that Detective Superintendent Adcock paid a remarkable visit to my hospital room. Peter and Ms Rodgers chanced to be present at the time.

"You can clear off," Adcock said to my guardian constable of the hour. "And take the cuffs with you."

When the constable had gone, Adcock rudely told Peter and Ms Rodgers to bugger off as well as he wanted a word with me in private.

"Ms Rodgers is my lawyer," I said, "and Peter is family. They stay."

Adcock glared and said: "Suit yourself. I've got some questions to ask you. And don't get lockjaw this time. Now. When Colwick Hall burnt down, you were seen fleeing in a car being driven by someone else. We need to talk to him. Who was he?"

"I've no idea."

"Really? Well, I suspect it was the same man, someone with an American accent, who phoned in and tipped us off that Abraham Reborn was gunning for you and where we should send an ambulance just in case.

That's how we found you and got you to hospital while you were still alive. He helped save your life, that man. Are you going to insist on telling me you don't know who he was?"

"I can't imagine."

"Cooperative as ever! You're aware the other people who helped save you were a couple of first-aiding hill-walkers?"

I nodded.

"According to them, they first saw you when you ran past them clutching some sort of discus. They say you appeared deranged."

"It's my land," I interrupted. "I can appear deranged on it if I want to."

"Don't get funny with me, Radman. These two same walkers, shortly afterwards, observed you attempting to run Abraham Reborn down with a car. To my mind that demonstrates evidence of murderous intent."

"I was trying to get him to empty his revolver so I could make a citizen's arrest," I explained. "That was the sole object of the exercise."

"Well, you succeeded in the end, didn't you?"

I caught Ms Rodgers shake her head slightly out of the corner of my eye. It was quite unnecessary.

"Did I?" I said.

The legal position was simple. If I'd cut Abraham's throat knowing the gun had been emptied, the action might be judged to be retribution, and that was murder. If I hadn't known the gun was empty, the action would be judged to be reasonable, and that was self-defence.

"You must have counted the shots," said Adcock.

"You've obviously never been under fire, superintendent. One doesn't keep a count in that situation. One is too busy ducking, believe me."

"No I don't believe you. But be that as it may, even excluding what you did to Abraham Reborn, I've got you on assault and battery, malicious wounding, false imprisonment, two murders, attempting to pervert the course of justice, occasioning actual bodily harm to a police officer in the execution of his duty, escaping lawful custody, and withholding evidence. And do you know the joke, Radman? You're not going to be prosecuted for any of it. I have been advised that in view of statements made by Deborah Czerny, Caxton Schirrel and two of his employees, and the two surviving Abramites from Colwick Hall, one of whom is a young man whose name I have been ordered not to disclose, plus all the media attention that that swine Richard House has stirred up, there's no realistic prospect of obtaining a conviction. That sticks in my throat."

"I don't see why it should. I didn't commit those two murders. Honestly."

"And I'm the Queen of Sheba. No, don't say anything. I haven't finished. From now on I'll be watching you. You put a toe-nail over the line and I'll be down on you. Hard. Clear?"

"You needn't trouble yourself. I'm not a criminal. It was only when you and the Abramites left me no choice that I got unorthodox. I was a victim from the start."

"One hell of a victim! Arrogant bastards like you make me sick. Now if you don't mind I'll get out of here before I vomit."

330

"Just one moment, superintendent," said Peter in such a friendly fashion that Adcock paused on his way to the door. "I'll be sending you a map of the Radman estate in the next day or two so you know where it is." And then his voice hardened. "Because if I ever catch you on my land I shall take the greatest pleasure in ejecting you by the scruff of your neck."

Adcock muttered: "Bloody Radmans," and stormed out.

"Obnoxious, mean-spirited little man," said Peter to no one in particular as the door slammed. Then he added for Ms Rodger's benefit: "I let him off very lightly, actually. If this had been a hundred and fifty years ago, I'd have shot him dead for talking to one of my kin like that. We Radmans used to make awful enemies."

"So what's changed?" said Ms Rodgers.

I smiled sweetly at her. Some people say the nicest things.

*

With the charges dropped I felt able to make a helpful statement to the authorities. I conscientiously denied all knowledge of Aaron Bernheim's and Bryce Nordstrom's names. I'd given my word in both cases and that bound me as a matter of honour. (Nordstrom is a pseudonym.)

Nobody believed my account of what I had seen on the videotape, and as no videotapes of human sacrifices had survived the fires at Colwick Hall and in South Africa, and the 'Jacobs' in Brazil and at Sarai Lodge must have sensibly destroyed any videotapes they may have had, my report of the matter was judged to be a gaudy lie. In addition, Bernheim senior put pressure on Deborah and me (via R & S) to go quiet on that aspect of the affair. So I complied, as did she. The fact is I didn't want fame — or should that be notoriety? — and I wasn't short of money. Selling that part of my story was a matter of indifference to me. It was an indifference which quickly came to apply to the whole ghastly business. Let the world believe what it likes. And the media, being the sensation-seeking, fickle bunch they are, soon lost interest in me anyway. I considered that a blessing.

There were two unresolved police issues to be addressed. I dealt with the first by apologizing both privately and publicly to the officer I'd punched while I was in custody. We agreed a modest payment in damages and the matter was closed. Peter dealt with the second. Unlike me, he is a very outgoing man and has contacts in the sort of social circles that go with being the owner of extensive land holdings; it gives him a fair amount of influence in local affairs. Towards the end of 1999, Superintendent Adcock was advised by his superiors to get a transfer to somewhere else in Britain or to take early retirement. He chose the latter and was heard from no more.

Deborah and I were married by then — April 15th, 1999 to be precise. Deborah's 'the less said the better' daughter was fetched from California by her brother and brought over for the wedding. Unknown to Deborah and me, Peter had a word with her at the reception, explaining that with all the lambs running about he needed a sheep warden — there's no such job but she didn't know that

— and the position was hers if she wanted it. He pitched it as a six-month working holiday (*not* vacation!). She took the bait, Northumberland cast its spell on her and she never returned to America. In the end she fell in love with a tree surgeon from Newcastle and they produced two grandchildren that Deborah adored.

My house on the moor we rebuilt (I like the solitude sometimes) and we also bought a large house in Alnwick (Deborah liked her home comforts). Colwick Hall was left as a ruin: a stark monument to the evil side of religion. Deborah never went back there, and I never have and never will. The ghost of the Mad Minister casts a long enough shadow as it is without our revisiting its source.

I've had to get used to walking with a permanent limp, and Deborah had to get used to never again being quite as good looking as she was when I met her. But when you've 'come close' those sorts of things lose their significance. We were alive, we were together, and we were in love. That's what really mattered. That and our freedom to roam unmolested in the place where I belong — and Deborah came to belong too: the wild, desolate, beautiful Scotsmans Moor, Northumberland.

Our little bit of paradise lost — and paradise regained.

ACKNOWLEDGEMENT

For an insight into what it is like to be charged with a serious crime you didn't commit, I am indebted to Noel Fellowes and his autobiography *Killing Time* (2nd edition, Lion Publishing, 1996). For anyone brought up on television detectives and their ultimate rectitude and infallibility, reading what really happens comes as a disturbing shock.

(I hasten to add here that Detective Superintendent Adcock bears no resemblance to any police officer I have encountered or come to know about.)